Deadly

Circumstances

Ordinary people changed by extraordinary circumstances

By

Dorothy Ruthven

Copyright©

Dorothy Ruthven 2015

All rights reserved

Deadly Circumstances is a work of fiction inspired by actual events.

Forward

I chose the name *Deadly Circumstances,* because who we are and the outcomes of the events of our lives are largely controlled by our circumstances. Our circumstances surround us and move us to take action in one direction or another. We all have choices, but our circumstances are the driving force behind those choices. Our circumstances in large part determine what we become and what we do with our lives, whether we are good people or not. Our circumstances expose us to the good and evil in the world and influence us to develop our good selves or to let our evil selves take over. In truth, most of us constantly engage in the struggle between good and evil at some level.

This story is fiction. As is true of any written work, some of the characters in this story are derived from actual people whom I have met or heard about, as are some of the circumstances. Most of the people and events are simple generalizations or composites of basic personality types and events that, although they come from my imagination, could be true.

MISSING HEART

Her heart is missing from her life.

Is he dead or did he leave?

She moves from anger into fear,

and all that's left is for her to grieve.

And when the truth is finally told,

it is her soul that's ripped away

from all that she had once believed,

and there is nothing left to say.

She can't trust him, she doubts herself.

She sees no way to carry on.

She doesn't even want to live

now that her heart and soul are gone

DR

Dedication

This book is dedicated to my friend, Tracy.

Prologue

Anna leaned back against the chaise lounge and took in the clear blue sky reflected in the crystal water of one of the resort's swimming pools. Sipping her Margarita, she felt totally languid, which was strange considering that she was hiding under a false identity in an attempt to escape a warrant for her arrest. Even stranger was how relaxed she felt, since she was a fairly obsessive person with a strong helping of anxiety and depression mixed in. Reflecting on her situation, she smiled a half smile with barely upturned lips. This feeling was delicious and she was going to enjoy every minute of it, even if it only lasted a few days or a few weeks. The guilt that accompanied her emotions was outweighed at this moment by a feeling of freedom. Do the ends justify the means? She wasn't sure. But somehow she knew that she would eventually be apprehended. At this moment, however, the end result felt worth whatever punishment she faced.

Glancing around the pool deck, Anna noted the beautiful bodies that had come to the resort for sun and fun in a tropical atmosphere. She knew that she was here due to the extraordinary circumstances that had ruled her life, and she wondered about the people around her. Were any of them on the run from the law? Had any of them ever faced the critical decisions she had made during her life? As she looked around, she saw lots of boobs in bikinis, and lots of great butts in swim trunks. This resort was a surfer's paradise and that showed in the clientele. She, however, appeared plain in comparison. She was not young and beautiful. No, she wasn't even striking to look at, although she had a great figure and was very fit. She was ordinary, and that was a good thing in her situation. The only person who seemed to notice her was her companion, Gray, as he strode across the deck toward her. Gray, too, was ordinary: not too tall, not too good looking, but attractive and well built. He enjoyed being ordinary. That's why he called himself *Gray* instead of *Grayson*, his given name. That name, he said, belonged to a British banker. They made an excellent ordinary couple.

She had to wonder…would she be in this situation if it weren't for Gray, for her desire to be with him, for his encouragement to free herself from the destructive circumstances in which she was caught? She really hadn't known him that long. Six months, maybe. But they fit together so well, he with his chortling chuckle and she with her boisterous belly laugh. They spent hours hiking, biking, taking long walks, planting a garden and talking. Talking about everything and anything. He was so undemanding and easy to spend time with. And he clearly was crazy about her, despite her unavailability. He was the one who had encouraged her to take the situation in hand and escape before the circumstances in which she was embroiled caught up with her. And now, here they were, acting as if they were on a long-awaited vacation to a tropical isle. One with no extradition to the U.S.

She thought back to when she moved to Taos, New Mexico, almost 15 years before, and how she had come to meet Gray. Taos, a thriving artists' colony and year-round tourist mecca, lies at the base of the beautiful mountains of northern New Mexico. An avid weaver, Anna came to Taos to take weaving classes from some of the better-known weavers in the country. She was a semi-wealthy woman, married to an absentee husband, and enjoyed the artistic and social life she cultivated in Taos and the surrounding communities.

Fourteen years later her circumstances had drastically changed. She and Gray met in the souvenir shop on the plaza in Taos where she was working for just above minimum wage. Gray was friends with the owner of the shop and had come in to look at some remodeling work he had been asked to do. As the owner of a successful remodeling company, Gray lived in an ancient adobé home on several acres of lovely high desert land with views of Taos Mountain on the outskirts of town. Anna, too, had at one time enjoyed living in a lovely home, more contemporary than Gray's, but with a style that welcomed her large collection of native and South American art and antiquities, as well as several large looms on which she wove authentic native rug patterns with yarn she had learned to dye herself by boiling plants and bugs she found on the high desert and in the mountains.

When she met Gray, Anna was barely scraping by in a rented studio apartment a short walk from the plaza in a seedy, low-income neighborhood. Her only view was of the peeling stucco and the gas and electric meters on the apartment next door. When Gray walked into the souvenir shop for the first time, there was an instant connection between them; however, it was two days before either of them got up the courage to speak, and several days after that before she had the nerve to ask him out to lunch. She was, after all, a married woman.

Chapter One: 28 Years Earlier

Anna stepped carefully down from the ladder and put the lid back on the paint can. She was bone tired, but she wanted to finish painting before one-year old Bradley woke from his nap. Her new home was tiny: a living room/dining room/kitchen all in one small space, and two small bedrooms with a bathroom between. In truth, the cottage was little more than a converted chicken coop with plumbing. The good thing was that Anna was almost able to furnish the space with just the bedroom furniture she took from her childhood home. The rest of her needs she scavenged at flea markets and garage sales. She took great pleasure in restoring an old piece of furniture that had been forsaken by its former owner. She would sand, stain, and polish the piece until it gleamed like new. In some subconscious way, she related to those abandoned pieces.

Anna had survived living with her abusive father and then living with an abusive husband. Her father had never been much of a factor in her life, but when her mother died and left Anna a savings account that she had secretly put aside for Anna's education, Anna's father was apoplectic with anger. Anna could still remember his reaction when the banker came to their house that night.

*****

"Your mother set up an account for you at the bank," the banker told Anna solemnly. "Over the years, she saved up quite a bit of money. Her intention was that you should use it to pay for college once you graduate from high school."

"She did what?" Anna's father shouted angrily. "She had no right to do that! That money was mine. I'm the one who worked the whole time we were married. All she ever did was spend every last dime I made. Any money she had was mine!"

I'm afraid that's not how it works," the banker calmly replied. "The way she set up the account, only Anna has access to the money, and your wife very clearly specified that the money was to be used for Anna's schooling."

With that, Anna's father rose and stomped from the room.

Things between Anna and him had always been strained, but from that moment on, there was no way that Anna could please him, no matter how hard she might try. In her mother's absence, Anna became a passable cook and began taking an interest in the garden, even learning to put up preserves and can tomatoes. Most of all, though, Anna treasured the new sense of independence that came with being in charge of things at home, despite the unpleasant atmosphere between her and her father.

When Anna thought of her father, she pictured him asleep in his recliner chair, the newspaper spread across his chest and large belly, quietly rustling as it moved with the rise and fall of his breathing while he slept soundly through whatever sporting event was on the television set. A beer and a pack of cigarettes were fixtures on the table beside his chair, although they often remained untouched while he slept the evening away. Anna saw from an early age that her parents were not happy being married to each other. Anna's mother would walk by her father's chair and mumble unintelligible words to him as he slept. She never smiled when he was home, but always seemed to be on edge. At night, Anna could hear them arguing through the thin walls of the old house.

*****

Anna settled into a slightly wobbly chair and took stock of her blessings. Besides Bradley, Anna's younger sister, Clare, was a bright spot in her life. Clare seemed unscathed by growing up in the same house as Anna. While Anna was outspoken and independent, Clare quietly kept to herself. It didn't take long for Anna to realize that Clare's reclusive personality was a result of her trying to escape the unhappiness in their home. Following her mother's death, Anna took care of Clare as more than a sister. She did her best to make Clare feel loved and appreciated, carefully taping Clare's art work to the refrigerator, talking to Clare about her interests and friends, helping with her school work, and including Clare in outings with

Anna's own friends whenever she could. Anna was determined that Clare would spend her final years at home in circumstances more pleasant than the ones in which Anna had grown up. Now Anna was finally on her own, and glad of it.

Anna's thoughts were interrupted when she heard Bradley calling her from his crib. She hurried in to get him from his nap. She needed to change his diaper and get him fed. When she saw him standing in the crib and holding his arms out to be picked up, she noticed once again how much he looked like his father.

She and Jack had married following her high school graduation. Looking back, she knew that her main reason for getting married was to escape her father and the constant unhappiness at home. Jack's reasons for getting married weren't much better, and once Bradley was born, their relationship fell apart quickly. Anna's father employed Jack at the hardware store, despite her father's continuing animosity toward Anna. Jack was an unhappy man, however, and his verbal abuse escalated to physical abuse. He finally walked out on Anna and Bradley, claiming that Bradley wasn't even his son. Anna was stunned and watched silently as Jack quickly moved into the local dating scene of their small Midwestern town and was regarded as the town's current bachelor-in-demand. No one had witnessed his verbal abuse, nor had they seen the handprint on her face the day he left.

Devastated and lonely, she moved back to her childhood home with Bradley, but the situation was bleak. Her father seemed to blame her for the breakup of her marriage and had little to do with her or her son. He seemed quite happy to continue employing Jack at the hardware store and having Jack assist him with chores around the house from time to time. Jack was like a son to him, and many evenings they would sit in the office at the store and share a beer, telling stories of their former days of glory. They were bonded by their unhappiness and perceived unfairness of life.

One night, when Anna failed to have dinner ready exactly on time, her father threw his plate on the floor and screamed, " Get out of this house and take your bastard son with you!" Then he ranted,

"You're a whore and you're the daughter of a whore. Your mother stole money from me to give to you. Sluts don't need an education. That was my money and you owe me. She had no right to do that! Do you understand?"

Anna did understand. She understood that she needed to get Bradley out of there as soon as possible. She had nowhere to go and had grown afraid that her father might resort to physical violence against her or Bradley. He had begun to drink more both at work and at home, and she realized that he was quickly losing control. She was determined to escape the situation, but she didn't know how, so she remained in the shadows as much as possible and tried not to antagonize her father in any way. Making sure Bradley didn't cry once her father came home, Anna retreated to their bedroom once she cleaned up from dinner and only came out when she had to. She didn't know how long she could continue to live like that.

Anna's nerves were frayed, she began to lose weight, and she felt anxious all the time. She had nightmares about being unable to take care of her son, and she was plagued by fears about Bradley's safety. Finally, she went to the family physician, who prescribed anti-anxiety medication for her. He had been her mother's doctor also, so he was familiar with the family history of depression and anxiety. He had a long talk with Anna about the way her mother's life had ended and cautioned Anna about allowing herself to go down the same road. Anna was glad to have the medication available if she needed it, but she was determined not to take it unless things were unendurable. Surely she could handle her problems with hard work and tenacity.

She had little money left and lived as frugally as possible. Finally, she found a part-time job doing filing at the local insurance agency. Clare agreed to watch Bradley after school while Anna was at work, and their relationship took on a new aspect of respect and love. Although Clare was still in high school, she was wise and unassuming. She was an observer, and she had watched as Anna's life had been swept away from her original dreams. She and Anna talked for long hours into the night, and Clare became Anna's best and only friend. But Anna was hurting and depressed. She felt as if she were becoming her mother: staying in the house unless absolutely necessary, abandoning the few friends she had left. She lived only to survive and raise her son. Perhaps that was how her mother had felt at the end of her life. But she had given up and Anna swore that she would never do that. She held onto the hope that someday she would be able to move out of her father's house and live on her own with Bradley. That thought alone kept her motivated to keep living.

Anna took on her part-time job responsibilities as if they were a life raft in the stormy sea that had become her life. She dedicated herself to learning the insurance business. She was smart and observant, impressing her boss with suggestions to help the agency run more smoothly. As other employees left or retired, Anna moved into positions of more responsibility with greater pay. She enjoyed feeling valued and respected for the first time in her adult life, and she looked forward to going to work every day. Finally, she was promoted to Office Manager and her salary was enough to allow her to move to her own place. Her boss, knowing everything about everyone in their small town, was familiar with Anna's situation and offered to let her and Bradley rent a small guesthouse on one of her properties. Anna felt hopeful for the first time in a long time.

After moving into the small space, the first thing Anna did was scrub the house from top to bottom, she made curtains from some fabric she found at a garage sale, and, by the end of the first week, the little house was cozy and comfortable. Even Bradley, who was on the verge of walking, seemed more happy and relaxed in his new home. He would crawl all around, pulling himself up on a chair or a table, and chatter away as Anna cooked or cleaned after work. His favorite game was peek-a-boo, and he would ask Anna to "pay boo" for hours on end. She loved hearing him laugh and watching his amazement as he discovered new things around him.

Chapter Two: Anna Meets Charlie

Anna was a good mother to Bradley, taking him to the park on her days off, reading to him each night before bed, and showering him with the love that she had never felt growing up. Bradley was a happy, well-loved, rambunctious toddler. Anna was still content in her little rental house, and over the years she had turned it into a pretty cottage worthy of a fairy tale. She had a cozy home, a beautiful four-year old son, and a rewarding job. She was startled to realize that she felt a twinge of jealousy toward her sister. Clare had graduated from high school and was busy with community college and a blossoming social life. She was a talented artist and enjoyed taking art classes along with the more practical business curriculum she had chosen. Along with her artistic side, she had also developed a pleasing personality and found herself turning down dates in order to have enough time to study.

Anna's father had no hesitation about paying for Clare's schooling. Looking back, Anna realized that Clare had always been her father's favorite and Clare had not suffered the emotional abuse that Anna had. Anna didn't understand why her father felt this way toward her, but she knew that she was more like her mother than Clare. Perhaps her father had been taking out his resentment toward her mother on Anna. Despite the profound influence this behavior had on Anna's life, she was not resentful of Clare. *This is all on him,* she thought.

While Clare still took care of Bradley from time to time, Anna saw her less often, and they seldom had time to sit down and talk as they used to. So Anna was pleased when Clare asked if she could bring her new boyfriend, Rick, over to meet Anna. Anna set a lovely table and cooked one of her specialty dishes for the occasion. She put fresh flowers from her garden in several containers around the room and made sure that everything was perfect. Just before Clare came, Anna looked around and wished that she had gone to all that trouble for a boyfriend of her own!

Conversation flowed easily among the three of them over dinner and coffee, and Anna felt that she had made a new friend in Rick. During the course of the evening, Anna learned that Rick came from a large family. He was the youngest of five children. He was working hard, as had his older siblings, to escape the farmer's life that might have been his inheritance. This set off a warning bell for Anna, as she thought back to Jack and his reluctance to follow in his farmer father's footsteps.

Anna was particularly interested in hearing about Rick's older brother, Charlie. To hear Rick tell it, Charlie seemed like a character out of one of the romance novels Anna had read. He was four years older than Anna, tall, handsome, had a great job, made lots of money…and he was single! Dating someone like that seemed beyond hope to Anna, but the idea was planted in her mind and a few days later she mentioned her thoughts to Clare, who became very excited at the idea of being a matchmaker for her sister. The problem was that Charlie worked out of town for weeks at a time in the oil fields in Oklahoma, so the prospect of getting the two of them together appeared daunting.

A month after meeting Rick, however, Anna received a call from Clare.

"Charlie's coming back to town for three days and is interested in meeting you, Anna."

Instantly, Anna's stomach was in her throat and she could hardly breathe because her heart was pounding. "Oh, Clare, I haven't dated in years. I'm not sure I even dated ever! Surely Jack doesn't count as 'dating'!"

"You're not dating Charlie, either," Clare retorted. "You're just going to meet him and see how it goes. Are you at least willing to do that?"

"I guess so," Anna haltingly replied. "What harm could it do?"

When her doorbell rang the following Saturday night, Anna took a deep breath and walked deliberately to the door. When she pulled it open, her breath caught, but she recovered quickly and invited Charlie inside. He was even taller than she had imagined, with broad shoulders and a slim waist and hips. His hair was a rich brown and he was tanned and muscular. She was overwhelmed by what a beautiful man he was.

As she moved away from the door, she almost tripped over Bradley, who was clinging to her leg and hiding behind her skirt. Charlie laughed—not a deriding laugh, but one of easy humor at the situation. He knelt down to be at the boy's eye level and reached out to shake Bradley's hand. That was all it took to win Bradley over. From that time until Anna put Bradley to bed, Bradley never left Charlie's side. He showed Charlie all of his favorite toys. Anna had fixed a light supper for the three of them, and the evening flew by as they chatted about their families, their jobs, and the things they enjoyed doing, in between Bradley's insistence that Charlie see his room or meet his favorite stuffed animal.

Anna and Charlie shared a love for reading, traveling, hiking and almost everything outdoors. Anna learned that Charlie had also married young and was the father of a 10-year old daughter, Christine. Because of the demands of his job, as well as Charlie's ex-wife's controlling nature, Charlie saw little of his daughter, although he phoned her faithfully on the first of every month. His ex's agreement to this arrangement was primarily so that she could "remind" Charlie to send the child support check that she awaited impatiently each month. Charlie's personality was quiet and agreeable, and he even seemed to enjoy talking to and playing with Bradley. As Anna closed the door behind Charlie at the end of the evening, she felt wishful for a relationship for the first time in several years.

Chapter Three: Charlie's Decision

Charlie walked away from Anna's house wondering what he had just begun. He liked Anna, and he was crazy about Bradley. This, he saw, was the opportunity to be the father that he wasn't allowed to be with his own daughter. Being a good father was important to him. His own father, while a stern taskmaster and harsh disciplinarian, had loved Charlie in his own way, and Charlie missed him terribly when he was killed in a farming accident just before Charlie's 18th birthday.

Charlie's mother, Grace, struggled to maintain the farm, but none of her children had farming as a vision for their futures. She became extremely manipulative in order to get her way after Charlie's father died, using tears or anger as best suited her to keep her children in line to follow the farming path. But they resisted, and finally she gave up, selling the farm and retiring into town, where she was able to buy a small home on a pleasant street not far from Charlie's sister's home. The adjustment to town was difficult for her, and she made her children's lives miserable as she constantly called with dire health crises, needing help with the smallest chores around the house, and asking for rides even though she was perfectly capable of driving herself.

As her children grew and had families of their own, Grace became a passionate grandmother and spent hours babysitting, cooking, and inserting herself into the growing families' lives in whatever ways she could. Often, her children wished she were less involved; but, once again, she played on their sympathies as the lonely widow or pouted when she didn't get her way and managed to maintain her place at the center of their families. Charlie, because he was gone so much for his work and had no wife or children at home, was less troubled by her interference in his life; but he knew that, should he begin a relationship with Anna—or any woman, for that matter—his mother would be right in the middle, giving advice and wanting to know every detail about everything. Even so, he cared for his mother and wanted her to be secure.

As a young boy, Charlie found out early that doing what you're told isn't always necessary. He became a procrastinator in school and in doing his chores at home. More often than not, one of the younger children would be asked to do Charlie's work just so that it would get done, so he quickly learned that the best way to get to do what he wanted was to put off doing what he was supposed to do. As he grew, this passive approach to responsibilities became his normal mode of operation. He barely made it though high school and was overwhelmed when he felt the pressure to get a job and begin earning his own living. Through a family friend, he was offered an entry-level job with a company that produced natural gas in Oklahoma. It would be taxing, physical work, and Charlie accepted the offer with trepidation. When he left home to begin that first job, he quickly learned that his passivity was not going to get him anywhere. He resented his boss' orders and instructions and initially slacked off from completing the tasks he was given. But, unlike at home, there were no younger siblings to come to the rescue. Before long, Charlie was given an ultimatum: either do the work or find work elsewhere.

Not wanting to go home having been fired, Charlie began applying himself to each job he was given and quickly moved up the ranks from general roustabout to production supervisor. He was bright and available, with no real responsibilities to keep him away from his duties in the field, even for extended periods of time. He was on his way to becoming one of a few experts in the field of fracking, natural gas production by fracturing the rock bed below the surface of the ground. This process, which was the fodder for contentious debate among the citizens where it was being done, released volumes of natural gas (that would otherwise be inaccessible) by breaking the rock that held the gas underground. Charlie was in on the rise of this process and enjoyed being sought after for his expertise. Most surprising of all was Charlie's realization that it felt good to complete a project on time and to do quality work. As his skills and knowledge increased, so did his pay. He soon graduated from a respectable hourly wage to a salaried position and found himself making more money than he could spend, despite the monthly child support payments he owed.

For the first time in his life, Charlie was able to indulge himself. He began buying grown-up toys. Despite the fact that he drove a company-owned truck, he bought a personal truck that was tricked out with every gadget and electronic feature available. He also bought two different motorcycles. He bought nothing but the best, whether it was clothing, fishing gear, or presents for his nieces and nephews. The more money he made, the more money he spent. He was generous with his family, and took unique pleasure in helping his mother out financially. It made him feel powerful to know that he could do more for her than she could do for him or for herself—a major role reversal from his younger days.

Because of all this, Charlie was hesitant to start a relationship with Anna. It would be easier to just maintain things the way they were. Much less complicated. He enjoyed sex and had no trouble finding women to sleep with when he was out of town. On the other hand, he found himself thinking about Anna much of the time, especially when he was out in the field and feeling lonely. He had been calling her whenever he was in town and they had enjoyed going to restaurants and movies, hiking, riding bicycles, and attending concerts in the town square. Anna had even expressed an interest in learning to ride her own motorcycle!

His feelings for her were growing, and he could tell that she felt the same. Charlie was good with Bradley and they laughed often when they were together. He also offered her the prospect of financial security that she had never enjoyed previously in her life. He was sure that the fact that he was out of town for days and even weeks at a time was a problem they could overcome. And so, after 18 months of dating, Charlie asked Anna to marry him and she joyfully said, "Yes!"

They were married by a judge at the County Clerk's office on a chilly September day with Clare and Rick as their witnesses. The judge's clerk held Bradley in her arms during the ceremony, and they all smiled afterward as the clerk took pictures of the new family on the courthouse steps. Charlie's mother claimed a migraine and Anna's father never responded to their invitation to attend, so the happy couple and their siblings celebrated by going to the local steakhouse for the wedding feast without any other fanfare. There wasn't time for a honeymoon, because Charlie had to leave for Oklahoma in two days. Just one month later, they were back in the County Clerk's office filing the papers for Charlie to adopt Bradley. Charlie looked forward to spending the rest of his life with his new little family. He had no idea that his contentment was not going to last.

Chapter Four: Married Life

Charlie was still away from home most of the time; but each time he did come home, Anna felt as if she were living the honeymoon they never had. He would come bursting through the door, smelling of the gas fields and fresh air. She loved that smell, because it meant that her husband was back where he belonged once more. He would hug Anna in a bone-crushing embrace and then he would grab Bradley, who would be standing by expectantly, and toss him up in the air and swing him around and around. Bradley would giggle and laugh until Anna made them stop for fear that Bradley would throw up. He always brought little gifts, too—a scarf or a bracelet for Anna and a small toy or book for Bradley.

But what surprised Anna most about Charlie's homecomings was the lovemaking. Jack had been her first and only lover. He had been selfish and fast, not caring particularly if Anna was satisfied or not. In fact, he often left her on the verge of orgasm, jumping out of bed to have a cigarette or to head for the store. Anna's frustration with sex had grown to the point that she became an unwilling partner, and Jack, feeling her rejection, seldom approached her. Charlie, it seemed, couldn't get enough of her, and Anna relished the way he made her feel beautiful and cherished. They could make love for hours, and Charlie always made sure that she was as satisfied as he. She loved his long, muscular body and the way he made her feel petite and fragile. After several months, she even felt confident enough to be the assertive partner, and that turned Charlie on even more.

Before they were married, Anna and Charlie had talked about finances and what Anna wanted to do about her job. As grateful as she was to her boss at the insurance agency for renting her the cottage, she and Charlie bought a larger home and moved in just before being wed. Money was no longer an issue for her, so she quit her job to become a full-time stay-at-home mother to Bradley. She and Charlie bought a brindled boxer puppy and named her Dixie. With Charlie gone to Oklahoma, Anna filled her days caring for Bradley, house training Dixie, and decorating her new home.

After a few months, however, she began to feel an emptiness in her life. As much as she loved Bradley, he alone was not enough to make her feel fulfilled. She had a few friends; but, unlike her mother, she was not inclined to do volunteer work or play bridge with a bunch of gossiping women. She tried several hobbies, and rediscovered her love for knitting. Her mother had taught her well, and she began to knit beautiful blankets, baby booties, sweaters, caps and scarves. After a time, she had so many articles of knitwear that she didn't know what to do with them all, so she decided to buy a table at a local craft fair to see if they would sell. Not only did she sell out on the first day, but she also received orders for more. She was amazed and went in search of new patterns and exotic yarns.

Eventually, she came up with the idea of opening a yarn shop. She had read books about a town in which the yarn shop was the center of several women's lives. They would get together most afternoons and talk while they knit, sharing their problems and their stories and becoming great friends. This sounded so appealing to her that she talked it over with Charlie and he agreed that a yarn shop would be good for her, giving her opportunities to form new friendships and to expand her expertise as a knitter.

"Besides," he told her, "you need to have a life of your own, since I'm gone so much!"

So she opened *Anna's Yarn Boutique* in the fall of the year. She advertised special classes to help people learn to make Christmas gifts for family and friends, and she explored sources the world over to supply her shop with the most lovely, exotic yarns she could buy. She also carried an assortment of beautiful, handcrafted buttons and other items to accessorize the articles that her customers knit.

She opened the shop when Bradley started kindergarten and, after school, he would hang out in the back room and play or nap until closing time. Dixie would walk around, charming the customers and keeping Anna company during slow times.

Her yarn shop dream was quickly a success. She became acquainted with many of her customers, and the back-room knitting sessions she had envisioned soon became a reality. Anna shared her customers' life experiences vicariously as she helped them knit blankets and sweaters for their grandchildren, Baptismal gowns for new babies, and afghans that would be given as wedding presents. She and her yarn shop soon became a fixture in the lives of many women in the town.

In fact, Anna found herself feeling irritated that she had to spend less time at the shop when Charlie came home from the field. At work she was a successful businesswoman, but when he was home, Charlie expected her to be there for him and cater to his needs rather than her own. The luster was beginning to wear off their relationship in Anna's eyes.

Managing the business gave Anna a new sense of purpose and independence, and the boutique became one of the mainstay businesses in town. As it grew, Anna needed to find more help. After inquiring around town and asking the ladies who met regularly in the back room, Anna learned about a young woman in need of a job. Stacey was a single mother who had dropped out of high school to have a baby the year before. From what Anna was told, Stacey was very bright but was finding life as a single mother difficult. *Well,* Anna thought, *I certainly know what she's dealing with. I'll give her a call.*

When Stacey came into the boutique for her interview, Anna liked her immediately. Stacey was nervous, but Anna could see something in her that she liked. Anna showed Stacey around the shop and noticed that she fingered the fine yarns in appreciation and wasn't afraid to ask questions about some of the items that were unfamiliar. She had taken basic accounting in high school prior to dropping out, but she had never worked in retail before. She was living with her parents, who were willing to watch her baby if she could find a job. Anna sensed that Stacey would be an asset to her growing business and would easily learn to interact with the customers. After talking for a bit, Anna discovered that Stacey had been taught to knit by her grandmother, so she knew at least the fundamentals of the art. This, Anna believed, was an unexpected bonus.

Then, just after Bradley's sixth birthday, Anna discovered that she was pregnant. She was excited to be having Charlie's child and felt that this might be the boost their marriage needed. She was also hopeful that a younger brother or sister would be good for Bradley. Charlie seemed elated and talked of how he would take Bradley's new sibling along on their fishing expeditions and trips to the playground. But, as time went on, Anna began to have mixed feelings. She loved her life, running the boutique and caring for Bradley when he wasn't in school. Having a new baby would surely change all that. But Charlie said he had always wanted to be a father to his own child and he could hardly wait. What Charlie seemed not to understand was that all of the child rearing responsibilities would fall on Anna. Charlie would come home every few weeks and be the "good guy" who took the children for ice cream or on camping trips. Anna knew that she would be the one who would manage the day-to-day catastrophes and discipline. Two children were surely going to be more than double the work of one!

Anna handled pregnancy well and was not troubled by morning sickness, swollen ankles, or any of the other problems her pregnant acquaintances suffered. In fact, she loved being pregnant and was quietly thrilled as she knit baby clothes and planned the decorations for the nursery. She was careful to prepare Bradley to be a big brother, impressing on him what an important role he would play in their expanding family. She felt as if she were living a dream life with very few problems or worries. This was definitely the best time of her life.

Once Anna became pregnant, she kept the shop running as always but began turning more and more of the responsibilities over to Stacey. By the time she went into labor, Anna was pretty much through with *Anna's Yarn Boutique*. She wasn't sure if she wanted to continue running the shop or not. She felt torn between being the kind of mother she knew her children needed and being the independent woman that owning her own business had made her. Despite her misgivings, she eventually sold the boutique to Stacey, whose parents co-signed for a loan so that she could purchase the business from Anna. The shop wasn't worth much, but Anna put the money in a special "rainy day" account. She felt good, knowing that she had a nest egg of her own that hadn't come from Charlie's salary.

Charlie was in Oklahoma when David was born and didn't get home to meet his new son until David was three weeks old. Clare was there with Anna for the birth and came over often to help with Bradley in the weeks after Anna brought David home. Unlike Bradley, David was a fussy baby, crying for hours on end with Anna unable to quiet him down or appease him with milk or cuddling. By the time Charlie came home, however, Anna had managed to establish somewhat of a routine with caring for both David and Bradley, as well as the dog, so Charlie's impression was that things were going smoothly and he didn't quite understand Anna's fatigue or short temper.

One day, Anna was fixing dinner and Charlie was in his easy chair reading the paper. Bradley was playing with his building blocks on the floor next to Charlie's chair, Dixie was sleeping in her corner, and David was lying on a blanket on the floor, almost asleep. All of a sudden, Bradley tripped and fell, crashing down on one of his blocks, causing a bruise on his forehead. He began to scream, so Anna rushed from the kitchen to comfort him and assess the damage. Bradley's crying startled David and he began to cry also. Dixie, hearing the commotion, began to bark, and Anna realized that the spaghetti pot was boiling over in the kitchen. Anna looked to Charlie to help out, but Charlie just sat there and continued to read the paper. A picture of her father sleeping in his recliner flashed in Anna's mind.

She turned on Charlie and shouted, "Get off your lazy rear end and pick up your son!"

Charlie seemed startled, as if he hadn't even heard the commotion or realized what was going on. Anna, still angry, marched back into the kitchen to turn off the stove and get an ice pack for Bradley's head. She didn't speak to Charlie again until after dinner. Charlie apologized that night, saying that he was used to tuning out the shouting and clatter of the gas rigs. Once again, Anna felt like she was doing the whole marriage thing on her own.

The good times when Charlie was home overshadowed the bad, however, and during the few times when Charlie was available and the boys were not in school, the family loved traveling. They went to Lake Michigan and the boys played for hours on the beach, collecting pretty rocks and throwing sticks into the water for Dixie to chase. One summer, they took a trip to the southwest, where the boys got to see the snow-capped peaks of the Rocky Mountains and smell the sweet pine forests. They dipped their toes in the icy mountain streams and shrieked with joy at the tingling cold. They drove all the way to California and saw the giant redwood trees, but the boys were too young to appreciate the ancient mystery of those dark forests. They saw the ocean for the first time, and laughed as they ran back to shore ahead of the tiny waves that kept rolling onto the sand. They camped in the woods close to home, and Charlie taught his sons to fish and, when they were older, to hunt small game and birds. When Charlie was home, they were a family again, and Anna's life felt complete. Charlie still wasn't much help around the house and had to be reminded several times before he would remember to pick up his dirty socks or finish even the smallest chore, but Anna was glad to have him home and she tried hard to overlook his faults.

Chapter Five: The Boys

As the boys grew, Anna was definitely the go-to parent in Charlie's absence. Bradley was active in sports, playing both soccer and basketball, so it was up to Anna to make sure that he got to practice and had someone there to cheer him on during his games. He was a steady, if not stellar, student and seemed to be liked by his teachers. He had many friends from the neighborhood and his sports teams, and he kept busy going on outings with their families, since Anna could seldom chaperone because of David. When Bradley graduated from high school, Charlie helped him get a job with a company that Charlie had worked with in the gas fields. Bradley would start at the bottom, just as Charlie had, but the job held great promise if Bradley worked hard and showed himself to be committed. Bradley did just that, and within a few years he was making a good wage and finally proposed to his high school sweetheart, Julie. They moved into a small home on a large lot near a lake and, although it was not fancy, they seemed happy and were doing well. Anna was thrilled at Bradley's success and looked forward to having grandchildren before too long.

David, on the other hand, was a handful. He disliked school and did as little as he could to get by without being held back. As a young child he seemed to understand just how much he could get away with before getting into serious trouble with his teachers. He disliked sports, claiming that they were a waste of time and energy, but he loved riding his bicycle. Even more, he loved taking his bike apart, modifying it in some way that was a mystery to Anna, and putting it back together again. As he grew older, his love of the mechanical changed from bicycles to automobiles and it seemed that he had finally found his niche when he enrolled in the high school auto mechanics class. For once in his life, David was the exceptional student and his teacher raved about his ability to understand and fix problems with engines. Anna sighed in relief, thinking that, at last, David might have come across something that would serve him well as an adult. After graduation, however, David refused Charlie's offer to help him get a job in the gas industry just as he had done for Bradley. Instead, David drifted from one minimum wage job to another, working at fast food restaurants and gas stations.

When he landed his first job at a gas station, Anna was excited to think that, at last, David would have the opportunity to use his skills and knowledge as a mechanic. She went to see him at work one day, and was disheartened to find him working behind the counter in the convenience store section of the station, rather than working on cars in the bay of the auto repair shop out back.

David had fixed Anna's basement into a makeshift apartment for himself, although he still had to go upstairs to use the bathroom or kitchen. But Anna hoped that David would develop a sense of independence since there was an outside entrance and he could come and go as he pleased. David dated a number of young women and eventually asked a friend from high school named Valerie to marry him. Anna was taken aback.

How does David think he's going to support a family when he isn't even making enough money to pay for a place of his own? Anna thought. *Valerie seems bossy and crude. She just looks sloppy, sounds uneducated, and doesn't hesitate to tell David what he should and should not do right in front of me. Valerie is clearly going to be the head of this family. But David is an adult and there's little I can do or say to discourage him. I give up. I'm just wasting my words. I just hope they don't get pregnant!*

Chapter Six: The Surprise

Anna went to Oklahoma for a surprise weekend with Charlie to celebrate their twenty-third anniversary. She had made arrangements with one of his co-workers to take Charlie out to dinner and, while he was gone, she arrived and waited for him in his apartment. Charlie's apartment was typical of a small town. Located above the local drug store, it had a living room with a sofa and a television, a small table and two chairs, and a functional bedroom with a bed, nightstand, and dresser. The closet was tiny, as was the bathroom, but there was heat and running water. Charlie was out in the field most of the time anyway, so he hardly needed luxurious accommodations when he was in town for the night.

While she waited for Charlie to arrive, Anna checked out the apartment. To her surprise, the place was immaculate. There were no dirty socks on the floor—not even under the bed—and there was no dust on the furniture. The refrigerator, although almost empty, was clean and held no spoiled food. She finally decided that Charlie's co-worker had told him she was coming, because Charlie had obviously cleaned up for her. Even more thoughtful, he had left room for her clothes in the closet, had emptied out a dresser drawer, and had even left space in the bathroom medicine chest for her cosmetics. She was so anxious to see Charlie again that it never occurred to her that this was not typical behavior for him. When he finally came in from dinner, he had obviously been drinking and she could smell cigarette smoke and perfume on his clothes. It didn't take her long to put two and two together. Charlie had almost certainly been out with a woman, not the co-worker with whom she had conspired.

When she confronted him about seeing someone else, he denied it vehemently, took her in his arms, and whispered, "You're being silly, Sweetheart. Surely you know there's no one else but you."

He made love to her that night as passionately as ever, and Anna decided that she had let her imagination run away with her. She put her suspicions in the back of her mind for the time being.

Chapter Seven: New Mexico

The next time Charlie had a week off, he and Anna took a trip to New Mexico. They were intrigued when they heard that this was as close to leaving the country as one could get without actually traveling beyond the borders of the U.S. This saying turned out to be true, and the beauty of the state, as well as the unusual culture enchanted Anna. As they drove south on I-25, she marveled at the wild plains where cattle and sheep grazed between Raton and Las Vegas, the forested Sangré de Cristo Mountains in the north, the art galleries and wonderful restaurants of Santa Fe, the bustling city of Albuquerque, and the jagged peaks of the Organ Mountains outside of Las Cruces. The miles of white sand that stretched north from the road to Alamogordo awed her, and they walked the ancient pathways that led through a forest of stalagmites and stalactites in Carlsbad Caverns. She was struck with the full impact of the mixed Native American and Spanish cultures and their influence on the art, the food, the architecture, and the atmosphere of the state.

Charlie was ready to leave New Mexico when Anna spoke up about one more visit she wanted to make. "I want to go to Gallup, Charlie", she stated firmly.

"But Gallup is a long way from here. Besides, it's the wrong direction to go when we're ready to head for home."

"I don't care," she replied. "I've heard about the native weaving and jewelry-making artists, and I really want to see them!"

"If you insist," Charlie relented. "But that needs to be our last stop. We need to be heading home!"

So they ended their time in New Mexico with a trip to Gallup, where Anna fell in love with the beautiful Navajo rugs on display in the shops. She enjoyed looking at the beautiful jewelry as it was being made, but she was totally fascinated by the use of elementary colors to create intricate patterns from the most basic wool yarn, and she left the state vowing to learn more about weaving and, perhaps, give it a try herself.

"See, Charlie? It was worth driving all those extra miles. That was the best part of our entire trip!" Anna raved.

Once home again, she researched doggedly and discovered a weaving shop within driving distance of her home. When she visited the store, she discovered that the weaving was entirely different from that which she had seen in New Mexico. It was designed on a computer and done by a machine. She was disappointed, and even more determined to learn to weave in the style and manner of the Navajo artisans she had seen on her trip. Eventually she bought her first loom and began weaving small pieces, giving place mats and table runners to all the members of her family. When she finally attempted her first rug, it took her much longer than she anticipated. But she stuck with it, going back to fix each mistake before moving on to the next row, and she was quite pleased with the end result. Anna was hooked on weaving, and little did she know what an important role it would play in her future.

Chapter Eight: Changes

Anna began to feel that she needed a change. She had put down her beloved Dixie months before. The loss of her first pet hit her hard, and she grieved outwardly. Her heart ached each time she came in the door and Dixie was not there to greet her. She felt very alone. Bradley was happily settled with a growing family of his own, and David had moved from her basement into a squalid apartment, but he was holding down a job and his wife was also working. They seemed to be surviving on their own.

Charlie had quit his job in Oklahoma and a company from India recruited him heavily to come work there. "That means months, rather than weeks, apart," Anna moaned. "The amount of money you would be making is obscene, but not worth taking you half way across the world."

"This will set us up for the rest of our lives," Charlie insisted. "And I'm anxious to take on this new challenge."

It seemed to Anna that Charlie's work personality was energetic and enthused, while his home personality was quiet and almost unresponsive at times.

"All right," Anna relented. "I agree that the India job is a good move for you, but I need a new start, too. I've been looking online and found that there's a famous weaving school in El Rito, a tiny town in northern New Mexico. I could live in Taos and commute to El Rito for classes and develop my weaving skills while you work in India." Then she added, hopefully, "I could still visit you from time to time, and you would come home for extended visits also, so how bad could it be?"

After much Internet research and mountains of emails with a real estate agent she had never met, Anna agreed to purchase a home in Taos. It was what she called pueblo modern style, with simple lines and sharp corners. The home had plenty of windows and was on a full acre of ground. By then, Anna had rescued a lovely German shepherd that she named Bella. Bella would be able to run the property, chasing rabbits and lizards to her heart's content. Anna also had acquired a cat that she named Simba, because he was the tawny color of a lion and skulked around, always on the prowl. Simba loved being outside, and he would do well hunting field mice and birds in the wilds of her property. The kitchen of the new home was equipped for having huge parties. Anna doubted that, with Charlie gone, she would be hosting dinner parties, but she loved the tile countertops and copper sink. The best part for Anna was the room that the real estate agent called a "bonus" room. It was large enough for her loom, with plenty of natural light and built in storage for her yarns and dyeing equipment. It even had its own sink and would be perfect for her new passion. And so, before Charlie took off for India, Anna moved into their new home with a promise from Charlie that he would be back in three months for a lengthy visit.

Anna's life in Taos developed slowly. She met her new neighbors, an older retired couple named Helen and Lee. Helen was a retired counselor, and Lee had taught high school in Colorado for many years. They had grown up in New Mexico and couldn't wait to return once they were no longer working. They were good neighbors, friendly but not overbearing or nosey. They had an adorable Yorkie named Maddy, who loved to bark at Bella when she was out in the yard. Anna was quick to inform Helen and Lee of her situation with Charlie gone, in case she needed help or there was an emergency. As time went on, the three of them became good friends, watering each others plants when someone went out of town, letting their dogs in or out if needed, and visiting over the fence that separated their properties whenever they were outside at the same time.

Feeling a need to explore the area, Anna loaded Bella into her car and set out for Angel Fire. She took a circuitous route through Red River, which was quiet at this time of year but would be bustling with skiers once the winter snow came. The road wound through the mountains and, finally, Anna drove the winding road down the steep hill that led into Angel Fire. The town was nestled in a meadow-spotted valley surrounded by mountains on all sides. It appeared deserted as she approached, but she knew that it, like Red River, would be filled with skiers come winter. As she drove toward the village, she kept to the north and spotted her destination.

Angel Fire was noted not only as a mecca for skiers, but also for the amazing Viet Nam Memorial that rested atop a hill on the north end of the valley. When Anna reached the site, she parked and wandered through the gardens, reading the various plaques and inspecting the giant helicopter that dominated the entrance. Inside, she watched a film that showed images of the war and the soldiers who fought so far away from home. The film was brutally honest, and she witnessed pure grief as one man in the audience began weeping and had to leave the theater. She could only imagine his story and what he might have endured during the conflict. She took time to page through some of the hundreds of letters and biographies of soldiers who went to Viet Nam, most of them younger than her own sons. Finally, she sat in the open-air chapel that overlooked the valley and the village of Angel Fire. She was struck by the irony of the moment...that such a lovely setting could hold memories of so much grief and violence. She sat there for a long time, thinking about the young soldiers she had seen in the film. She wasn't sure if she was actually praying, but she was hoping with all her might that they were at rest somewhere and that their families were at peace with their loss.

After stopping in town to purchase a hamburger for herself and just a meat patty for Bella, she drove back up the mountain toward home. She was still feeling emotional from her time at the memorial, so she stopped at a picnic area and let Bella out to run. Bella ran quickly into the trees, having caught the scent of some forest creature, but she came back obediently when Anna called. Anna marveled at how beautiful she was. She ran with such grace and power! And when she returned to Anna, tail wagging and coat shining in the sun, Anna's heart was full of love for this amazing animal. Stretching her own legs released the tension that Anna was feeling, and she and Bella played fetch for quite some time before Anna called her back to the car and they continued toward Taos.

Anna planted a large vegetable garden, which flourished despite the short growing season in the mountainous Taos climate. She also began attending classes in El Rito and quickly made friends with other weavers in the area. She spent hours working at her loom and roaming the local fields and forests in search of materials for dyeing the wool for her rugs. She enjoyed Taos and the local art scene, spending time walking from one studio to another, admiring the variety of artistic styles on display. She met some of the local artists and shop owners, and began to slowly establish herself in the community.

But she was lonely, and Charlie was thousands of miles away. In addition to an occasional phone call, their only communication was by email, and, when Charlie was out in the field, it could be weeks between messages. She kept in touch with Bradley and enjoyed receiving pictures of his three boys. David, however, seldom called or emailed, and she was never sure what was going on in his life. After two months in Taos, Anna flew back to her hometown to visit her family. She saw Clare, who was still going to school, only now she was at the University pursuing an advanced degree in fine art and selling her paintings at several galleries in the city. Anna could sense Clare's excitement as she spoke of opening her own gallery as soon as she graduated, and she was making plans for doing just that with one of her professors. Anna couldn't help but wonder if Clare's attraction to this particular professor went beyond a business partnership, since Clare and Rick had broken up many months before. She figured it was none of her business and said nothing.

Bradley and Julie welcomed Anna into their home and put her up in one of their bedrooms, made available by having the three boys sleep together on the living room floor during her stay. The boys thought this was great fun ... camping right in the house where it wasn't cold or scary. Anna found the bunk bed narrow and uncomfortable, but she enjoyed being around the children, attending their sporting events, and listening to them squabble like normal, healthy kids. Bradley and Julie had saved money to buy a larger house, but were unable to sell the one in which they were living because of its remote location and the downturn in the economy. So Anna came up with what she thought was a great idea. Why didn't she and Charlie buy Bradley's present home. That way, when they came back to visit, they would have a place to stay without having to impose on anyone. Charlie agreed with the plan, and, before Anna left, the paperwork was signed and the little house was theirs. This would make her visits so much more pleasant.

David and Valerie invited Anna over to their cramped apartment, which was made even smaller by two large dogs. The conversation at dinner was difficult and seemed primarily to center on which kind of beer David and Valerie preferred. Anna was astounded at their familiarity with what seemed to her to be every kind of beer ever manufactured. Once the topic of beer was exhausted, they began speaking with encyclopedic knowledge of various flavors of hard liquor, especially vodka. Anna could hardly believe her ears and contributed nothing to the conversation. She just sat there stunned and nodded her head when they spoke in her direction. As she was getting ready to leave, David came up to her with a silly grin on his face and said, "We're pregnant!" He added that they could use some money to help pay doctor bills and buy baby equipment. Anna took out her wallet and handed David several hundred dollars that she had with her for traveling money. David had "borrowed" money from Anna before, and she knew that he also had been getting money from Charlie, although neither of them had told her about that. There was little chance that David would ever pay them back, but she rationalized that it was good that she and Charlie were in a position to help out, especially with a baby on the way. She couldn't imagine David and Valerie as parents. They were appallingly immature themselves. Anna left their apartment, saying a quiet prayer for the welfare of this unborn child and feeling depressed and anxious to get back home to Taos.

Chapter Nine: Homecoming

Shortly after Anna's return to Taos, Charlie sent word that he was coming to Taos for two weeks. Excitement took over Anna's life. She scrubbed every surface in their home, making sure that there was not a speck of dust or grime anywhere. She washed Bella's bed and eliminated every cat hair she could find. Charlie had asthma and was allergic to cats, so she made sure that Simba would be confined to the guest room or kept outside during Charlie's visit. She planned special meals and shopped carefully at the local growers' markets to get the freshest ingredients. She even bought several new outfits, which was unusual for Anna who very seldom shopped for clothes. At last she would once again have a husband at home. By now, she reasoned, her friends and neighbors must think that Charlie was a figment of her imagination. She planned outings to show him the area and have him meet her friends. She also made a list of things she hoped he might do around the house. She hoped that these much-needed chores would help him feel that the home was his as well as hers. Her anticipation grew with each day that passed.

At last the day of Charlie's arrival came, and Anna drove to Albuquerque to pick him up. Getting to Albuquerque from Taos took some time. First Anna drove from Taos' 7,000-foot elevation down a steep, winding road along the Rio Grande River to the town of Española. The scenery was beautiful, but the road was dangerous and had to be driven with caution. On the way down, there were many side roads and turn offs for wineries and antique shops, as well as a few restaurants. She drove through the quaint villages of Velarde and Rinconada with their fruit stands displaying colorful ristras made of red chilé. She continued down through the deep canyon carved by the river, which flowed many feet below her on her right. She marveled at the engineering in place on the steep sides of the canyon where an elaborate fence had been erected to keep the granite rocks and boulders from crashing down onto the vehicles traveling on the road. She stopped at a turn off in the Embudo

Valley to stretch her legs. Looking back up the canyon, she could see the granite-rimmed mesa, punctuated with sandstone cliffs and outcrops, rising above the river. As she took in the view, Anna was awed by the rugged beauty of the land that she now called home.

Once she reached the flat land of the Rio Grande River Valley, she merged onto the highway and drove to Santa Fe. Luckily for Anna, there was a by-pass around the ancient city that cut a significant amount of time from her trip. Having finally gotten around Santa Fe, she merged onto I-25 and drove the rest of the way to Albuquerque, still following the general course of the Rio Grande and passing through the Santo Domingo, San Felipe, Santa Ana and Sandia Indian Reservations along the way.

She had descended almost 2,000 feet in elevation, but she looked up to see the Sandia Mountains presiding over the valley. She saw the skeletal blue towers standing tall on the foothills and remembered that Sandia Crest, which rose to over 10,000 feet, was accessible by an aerial tram that afforded breathtaking views of the entire valley and high desert plains to the west. Albuquerque, the largest city in New Mexico, rambled along the Rio Grande River, taking up the valley and rising onto the high desert in the west, then spreading up the foothills of the Sandia Mountains on the east. Surrounded by Native American pueblos and reservation land, Albuquerque and its surrounding communities have a unique culture that attracts visitors from all over the world. Anna had to drive the interstate all the way through the city to reach the airport on the south side.

The road to the airport greeted her with giant Native American pots surrounded by lovely indigenous plants in the medians. She parked in the multi-level parking garage and walked to the terminal. Once inside, she was impressed by the interior of the building. On one wall was a gigantic painting of the Sandia Mountains that seemed to glow from a sunset. There were also displays of beautiful Native American pottery, kachina dolls and jewelry, along with other artifacts. The pillars and beams were whitewashed and carved in the local style, and the shops carried a wide variety of local artwork, as well as the expected tourist junk.

She stationed herself near the security gate and waited with the other expectant families for the arriving passengers to come through the revolving door.

When she saw Charlie, she could hardly catch her breath. She felt like a giddy teenager being courted by the town hunk, only this time the hunk was hers! They held hands as they walked through the terminal, stopped to retrieve his bag, and crossed over to the parking garage.

Chapter Ten: Charlie's Return

As he folded himself into the front seat of her truck, Charlie's blue eyes were shining. He was glad to be back in the U.S. and especially glad to be back with Anna. He had found India a difficult place to live and work. He took a deep breath of the clean, high desert air and sighed. His lungs had suffered while he was in Mumbai because of the inescapable pollution.

"I hope that two weeks in the mountains will help my breathing," he told Anna. "And I'm glad to see you, of course."

Anna bristled at his comment. "Am I always in second place? I thought you were coming home to see me, not to get a health treatment!"

"Now Anna, you've always been here for me, taking care of business in the States while I'm overseas. You manage the house and pay the bills, albeit with the generous amount of money I send you every month. You're the constant in my life, which seems to be ruled by the need to be neither here nor there for any length of time. My company is generous beyond imagination when it comes to financial matters, but my bosses are demanding and unreasonable in their expectations. I feel like a small boat being buffeted about in a stormy sea. The move to India was my idea, though, and I will admit that."

Just as Charlie expected, Anna turned to him and said, "I told you so. Why don't you quit and come home?"

Charlie's thoughts turned negative. "I can't be happy in Taos either. The house is yours. I wasn't involved in choosing or buying it. It suits your needs, not mine. You have a busy and meaningful life in New Mexico, but I don't."

In the stony silence that followed his admission, Charlie thought, *I don't plan to return to Taos, even for another visit. As unhappy as I am with my job in India, I'm not willing to go through changing jobs and moving again.*

Their time together was pleasant on the surface, but Anna had to stifle her desire to continue their previous conversation. She didn't want to spend their brief time together arguing, but she could sense a change in Charlie. He willingly went with her to all the places she had planned and was pleasant and charming as he met her new neighbors and friends. He enjoyed playing with Bella and watching her run after the ball he threw, and he agreed with Anna that having a watchdog was a good precaution. They even explored the area around a large lake a few hours' drive from Taos and Anna decided it would be the perfect location to retire. At Anna's insistence, they purchased a large parcel of land. Charlie listened as Anna talked of the house they would build and the possibility of raising sheep and alpaca so that Anna would have a source for making her own wool. Anna's dreams now focused on a future when Charlie would be home and they would finally live together permanently, but Charlie knew that was Anna's dream, not his.

Charlie just went along with Anna and her talk about the future. He didn't have the desire to protest her plans, but his heart was not in it, either. Anna found his lack of enthusiasm frustrating.

"I don't understand you, Charlie. We're finally together for once, and you're acting like it's an imposition to meet my friends or go anywhere to see the area. What's the matter with you?"

"I'm just tired and want to rest and relax while I'm here," Charlie lied.

So Anna reluctantly canceled the rest of her plans and they did little during the last part of his visit. Their lovemaking was tepid and seemed to be more out of expectation than passion. As Anna drove out of Albuquerque after dropping Charlie off to catch his flight, she realized that she felt depressed for the first time in many months. None of this had turned out as she had hoped. Charlie did not seem to be a part of her life any more. In fact, Charlie hadn't done even one chore on the list she had given him. Anna began to wonder if Charlie would ever consider Taos to be his home.

Chapter Eleven: Warning Signs

Anna returned to Taos and fought her depression to get back into the life and routine she had established before Charlie's return home. She decided that she needed a project, so she began cleaning out closets and drawers, filling trash bags with items to be donated to charity. When she got to Charlie's dresser, however, she was puzzled. When she moved in, Charlie had left a complete wardrobe at home in the States, taking only his work clothes and a few nicer items with him to India. He reasoned that he would have little free time and would be almost constantly on the job out in the field. But when Anna opened his dresser drawers, she found that they were almost empty. She went to his closet and found the same thing. Charlie had taken almost all of his clothes with him back to India. She had noticed that he brought a great deal of luggage with him for a two-week stay, and when he left he seemed to have to wrestle the bags onto the luggage cart. The entire situation was a mystery to her, and she made a mental note to ask Charlie about it the next time she emailed him.

As Anna recounted the events of Charlie's visit in her mind, she felt a stirring of anxiety. They hadn't fought or even argued while Charlie was there. But then, Charlie never fought and seldom argued. His nature was to be passive and to let others have their way, giving in to their demands without argument. In the beginning, he seemed to enjoy the things they had done together and had interacted genuinely with her new friends. He had been attentive to her and seemed glad to be home. But as his stay continued, his attitude seemed to change. Perhaps he was just exhausted as he claimed. Traveling to and from India would, in itself, sap a person's energy. And perhaps he had discovered that he needed more non-work clothing for his life in India. There was surely nothing alarming about that. She realized that he had actually said little about his life in Mumbai, but mostly spoke of his co-workers and events that had taken place out in the field. She forced herself to take a deep breath and calm down. She told herself that she was overreacting.

When she replied to Charlie's next email a few days later, she forgot to ask him about the clothes. Charlie informed her that his mother had decided to move. She was too old to deal with the brutal midwestern winters and was going to Tennessee to be near Charlie's brother, Rick, who would help her locate a house and move. Charlie had agreed to purchase the house for her there, but Anna would need to make the house payments from Taos. Anna was now responsible for making the payments on the house in Taos, the truck she drove, the house they had purchased from Bradley, the property in New Mexico, and now Charlie's mother's home in Tennessee. Additionally, they were still sending Charlie's mother money for living expenses each month. Their finances seemed to have become quite complicated. Charlie sent Anna plenty of money every month to cover all those expenses and more, so money wasn't a problem, but she wondered if she needed to set up a system to help her keep everything straight. At least he was finished making child support payments for Christine. They bought things on time rather than paying cash, because a large portion of Charlie's immense salary was going into a retirement account. This account was under the auspices of the Indian government and overseen by his company. Charlie's plan was to put the bulk of his salary aside for retirement so that they would have no financial worries for the rest of their lives, but the money would not be accessible to them. The company would release it when Charlie retired.

Chapter Twelve: Anna in India

Several months went by, and Anna's life seemed to return to normal. She continued her classes in El Rito and had several of her weavings on display at a small gallery in Taos. The owner of the gallery was a successful artist who took great pleasure in encouraging upcoming artists from the El Rito school and elsewhere. When her first piece sold, Anna was elated. It was a small rug, but it sold for several hundred dollars to a tourist from New York. At last she felt vindicated for the move to Taos, the time and money spent on wool and looms, the countless trips to and from El Rito, and, in truth, her entire life style. Her self-esteem was bolstered immediately, and she felt that she had accomplished something noteworthy. She sent emails to everyone telling of her success. She was elated. She heard back from Clare, who sounded excited and encouraging. Clare promised that, once she opened her own gallery, she would exhibit Anna's work there. Bradley responded with his congratulations, as did Charlie's brother, Rick, with whom Anna had become well acquainted due to the business of closing the purchase of their mother's house in Tennessee. She heard from David, who suggested that, since she was so successful, perhaps she could send him more money. But she didn't hear from Charlie, and that was a huge disappointment. She knew he was back in the field; it seemed to her that he was always out in the field when she needed him.

Anna took several short trips to various weaving shows and presentations. She visited the monthly rug auction Crownpoint, where she purchased a wonderful Navajo *Two Gray Hills* rug at an exorbitant price. It was so beautiful that she ignored the cost and was elated when she hung it in her home. While driving home from the reservation, she stopped in Gallup, where she purchased several lovely pieces of Native American jewelry. She may not have been much of a clothes shopper, but she did appreciate the handcrafted turquoise and silver pieces that were everywhere in New Mexico. In Albuquerque, she attended a workshop at the Indian Pueblo Cultural Center, where a famous Shumakalowa weaver discussed native

Navajo weaving styles. Her weaving expertise was expanding, and she was becoming fairly well known in her own small circle of weavers.

Communication with Charlie was not going as well as her weaving career, however. His emails were becoming more infrequent and brief. She felt the lack of connection keenly and began to worry over the stability of their marriage. She hardly knew him any more. She finally decided that the only way to remedy the situation was to go to India herself. The company would pay for her ticket, as they had paid for Charlie's flat in Mumbai, all the furnishings, and even a car and driver. They may have been overly demanding of Charlie's time, but they were more than generous in other ways. She made her reservations, planning to stay for a month. She reasoned that, as long as she was going that far, she would stay long enough to make the trip worthwhile. Having emailed Charlie about her plans, she waited anxiously for over a week before hearing from him. He said he was glad she was coming, would send his driver to meet her at the airport in Mumbai, and would try to arrange his schedule to be in the city during most of her stay. The tone of his email was reassuring, and, once again, she wondered if she had overreacted by being so concerned about their relationship.

Anna's trip did not start well. Helen and Lee offered to drive her to the airport in Albuquerque, but Anna didn't want to cause them any inconvenience. Instead, she wrestled her large suitcase and over-stuffed backpack into the commuter van that would take her to Santa Fe. There, she once again fought her luggage onto the *Railrunner*, the commuter train that would take her to Albuquerque. Finally, she transferred her bag and backpack onto a city bus that took her to the airport, where she gladly turned her suitcase over to a porter but kept her backpack with her as carryon for the plane. From Albuquerque she flew to Atlanta, where she barely made her connection to India. She was exhausted, and she hadn't even begun the 20-hour flight to Mumbai.

Once she was on the plane to India, however, conditions improved. Charlie's company had paid for a business class ticket, so she found herself in a comfortable seat with more legroom than she had expected. The flight attendant was quite solicitous and offered a pillow and blanket, along with the glass of wine that Anna had ordered. After a second glass of wine, a light meal, a sleeping pill, and a few more paragraphs of the book she was reading, Anna slept for most of the trip.

She was awakened when she sensed the plane slowing down and beginning its descent into Mumbai. She looked out the window and saw the city approaching beneath her. She couldn't believe the size of the city. It was massive and she wondered how she would ever find her way around such a large metropolis. But something seemed amiss. Finally she realized that there was a putrid smell permeating the air. When she asked the flight attendant about it, she was told, "Oh, that's nothing to worry about. It's just the smell of India!" Anna could hardly believe that the smell of the city was entering the plane's ventilation system at this altitude, and she wondered: *If it's that bad up here, how bad will it smell when I'm on the ground in Mumbai?*

She didn't have long to wait to find out. When she entered the airport terminal after clearing customs, she was once again struck by the smell. But even more overwhelming was the heat and the noise and crush of people. The airport was so crowded that she could hardly get her bearings, because she was being pushed and carried along by the throng. And even inside the building, she could hear the noise of traffic, honking and shouting coming from outside. After retrieving her suitcase, she looked around for her ride. Charlie had said that his driver, Rajeesh, would be there to meet her, because Charlie would be tied up in a meeting when she arrived. Searching the crowd of drivers holding name signs, she finally saw a young man waving a placard with her name on it. Relieved, she started making her way toward him, and he seemed to recognize her and came running over to help with her bag and backpack. She followed him without speaking, not knowing how much English he spoke, until they reached a black Honda, into which he put her luggage. Thankfully, she sank into the back seat, took a deep breath, and realized that maybe deep breathing was not a good idea in Mumbai.

Rajeesh introduced himself in highly accented but excellent English. He sounded familiar, and Anna realized that she had heard that same accent many times on the telephone when making calls to various service representatives regarding questions about American products.

Rajeesh explained, "I am 23 years old and have worked for the company since I am 16. I have worked hard to reach driver status. I admire Mr. Charlie and am pleased to have Mrs. Charlie in my vehicle."

Anna found him pleasant and charming, which turned out to be good, since Rajeesh was going to be her guide and almost constant companion while in India.

As they drove through the city toward Charlie's flat, Anna was amazed at the sights, sounds, and smell of her surroundings. The pollution in the air was frightening. She was almost afraid to breathe. Anna had never seen anything like it, especially in the pure air of the northern New Mexico mountains. Anna had become somewhat acclimated to the smell, but she next noticed the noise. With so many people rushing around, there was the rumble of cars and scooters, shouting and horns blaring at a volume to which she wasn't accustomed. Everyone seemed to be on their way somewhere—on foot, bicycle, motor scooter, and car. She saw entire families piled onto a single scooter, the young children barely hanging on as they chugged down the street to their destination. The heat was suffocating. Having come from the dry, high-desert air of Taos, the humidity made it hard to breathe and made the heat that much more uncomfortable. All of this was mind-boggling, and Anna felt her anxiety rising. She finally closed her eyes and just let Rajeesh drive without conversation or looking out the window.

When she finally arrived at the location of Charlie's flat, she was surprised to see a modern-looking high-rise apartment building. On the way there, she had seen many modern buildings, but she had also seen many other structures that were not so appealing, so she didn't know what to expect. Mixed in with the newer construction were shops and stalls that had been standing for many years, along with hovels in which people lived while eking out an existence that she could only visualize in her imagination. Like New Mexico, poverty seemed to live right next door to wealth, but here the poverty seemed extreme beyond comprehension.

When he pulled up to the front of the building, Rajeesh proudly announced, "Mr. Charlie live on 29th floor. No worries. There is an elevator!"

Glad to hear this news, Anna followed Rajeesh into the building, which appeared to be still under construction inside. There were workers in the polished marble lobby finishing up detail work, putting up trim, and busily moving back and forth carrying buckets and ladders. Avoiding a collision, Anna and Rajeesh moved through the construction zone to the elevator, piled Anna's luggage inside, and began the ascent. The elevator moved slowly, and Anna began to feel nervous about the strange grinding noises she heard coming from overhead as they crawled upward.

Finally, the doors opened and Anna entered a hallway, paved in marble, with one ornate doorway to her right. It would seem that Charlie's flat was the only one on the entire floor! When Rajeesh opened the door and ushered her into the flat, Anna just stood in astonishment. The room looked like something out of the tales of the Arabian nights. Everything was marble, glossy and gleaming. All of that stone made the flat feel cool compared to the blistering heat outside, and Anna was relieved to think that she could escape the heat up here.

The furnishings were practical and well made, but they seemed plain and simple compared to the elaborate construction of the space. She sat in an upholstered chair and found it to be quite comfortable. In addition to the chair, the main room held a large sectional, side tables, a coffee table, lamps, and a large television in a cabinet. There was no artwork on the walls and nothing to personalize the space, but she knew that Charlie spent very little time here, so that was understandable. All of the wooden furniture was made from what Rajeesh described as "local wood", although Anna didn't know exactly what that meant. She had never seen pictures of forests in India. There was a long table with eight chairs, and overhead was an elaborate chandelier of brass and crystal. Clearly, the designer had thought that this flat would host amazing dinner parties, because the kitchen was well equipped with professional-grade modern appliances. The bathroom gleamed in European luxury, and Anna looked askance at the bidet. Following the marble-dominated floor into the bedroom, Anna found a king-sized bed furnished with sheets, but no blanket or spread. She supposed that, in India, one didn't really need a blanket with the heat and humidity. There were also a dresser with a mirror, a side chair, and two bedside tables with lamps. The room looked as if it had been sparsely furnished from a Sears catalog. Again, there was nothing personal in the room and no decorations. A second bathroom was located off the master bedroom, along with a sizeable closet in which Anna could see Charlie's clothes that he had brought from Taos. A second bedroom was similar to the first, although smaller, and held a queen sized bed and other basic bedroom furnishings. There were no linens on this bed, and the bare mattress was littered with paperwork, a laptop computer, and several cell phone chargers. It seemed that Charlie was using this as office storage.

Anna thanked Rajeesh for picking her up at the airport and Rajeesh refused her offer of a tip, saying, "The company pays for my driving. I am well compensated. No tip is necessary."

He then told her how to reach him on his personal cell phone or by calling the gas company's office. He was at her service, day or night, he said. Then he politely excused himself and Anna was alone for the first time in what seemed like many days. She could still hear the sounds from the street even twenty-nine stories up, but they were muffled because of the distance and closed windows. She approached the living room window with caution, not being used to such a high building, and carefully looked out. She could see Mumbai Bay, the water looking blue and clean, compared to the filth she had seen in the city as they drove in. The sun was just beginning to set, and the sky glowed bright orange from the pollution in the air, she supposed. She had seen similar colors in the sunsets in Taos when there were forest fires in the area. She suddenly realized how tired she was and headed for the bedroom to unpack, take a shower, and change into fresh clothes in anticipation of seeing Charlie for the first time in months.

She had finished showering and was combing her hair when she sensed something moving beside her. Turning, she gasped when she saw a huge lizard on the wall about ten inches from her head. She dropped her comb and dashed out of the bathroom, panting from fright rather than exertion. She wondered what other wildlife might inhabit the flat. Putting on her robe, Anna walked carefully through the spacious rooms, checking the walls and ceilings for more lizards.

When she saw none, she went to the kitchen and began opening cupboard doors. The first door she opened revealed an unpleasant scene. There were dozens of cockroaches gathered in the cupboard. They seemed undisturbed by her presence and continued about the business of scuttling here and there in search of crumbs. She slammed the door shut and held it closed, as if she thought the roaches could open the door if she weren't pushing against it. Finally, she came to her senses and walked gingerly back to the bedroom to dress. Anna wondered how these insects and reptiles managed to get into a flat on the 29th floor of a building that wasn't even completed yet. Even more, though, she wondered if she would be able to sleep in this place, knowing that unseen creatures were lurking in the dark.

When Charlie came through the door, Anna was sitting on the couch reading a book with her feet tucked underneath her. She felt lovely in the soft glow of the reading lamp with the lights of the city as a backdrop behind her. Charlie walked over, pulled her up from the couch and greeted her with a hard kiss. Anna melted inside, and suddenly all the past hurt was forgotten. His kiss told her that he had missed her more than she thought, and she vowed to make the most of this time they had together. When Charlie left Taos, Anna was sure he would never return. She hoped that her visit would make him change his mind.

Charlie led Anna to the bedroom, and they made love as if there had never been a breech in their relationship. Anna was sure that everything was going to turn out all right after all. Later, they returned to the living room and began to talk.

They sat on the couch and exchanged small talk. Their conversation felt awkward after having been apart for so long, but Anna was determined to put Charlie at ease and restore their relationship to the level it had once been. She began to talk about how much she missed him and how much she was looking forward to Charlie's retiring some day so they could be together again.

She was just beginning to say something when a lizard suddenly fell from the ceiling and plopped onto the coffee table in front of her. Anna screamed, jumped up from the couch, and ran quickly into the next room. Charlie just laughed.

"They're everywhere," he told her, as she peeked around the corner. "You can't get away from them. Besides, the locals say that, if you touch a lizard, you will get a new set of clothes. Wouldn't you like a new wardrobe?"

Charlie's eyes were sparkling with humor, but Anna didn't find the situation amusing at all. "What about all the roaches in the kitchen? I suppose you can't get rid of them either. Do you just think of all these creatures as house pets?"

Charlie laughed aloud then, and Anna's heart softened a bit. "You get used to them after a while," he said. "I never use the kitchen anyway, so the cockroaches don't bother me. I don't even know why they're there, because there is very little food around."

"I guess I'll have to try not to let them bother me either. I think I could actually get used to the lizards, but they are so big and ugly compared to the ones back home. The cockroaches are another matter altogether. They're dirty and disgusting. Can't we call an exterminator or something?" She pleaded.

"I'll see what I can do; but, honestly, lizards and roaches are just part of living in India. If you're going to be visiting me here, you're going to have to get used to them. After all, they were here long before we were," Charlie reasoned.

Anna just nodded, and, with a doubtful look on her face, she took Charlie's hand and led him to the door. She was more than ready to leave the flat and explore the neighborhood.

They went to a nearby restaurant, walking the few blocks from the apartment building. As they walked by, Anna couldn't believe the conditions in which some people were living. There were entire families occupying a small hovel made of cardboard, wood scraps, and corrugated metal. They were cooking over fires right in the middle of the Nave Mumbai (new Mumbai) part of the city in which Charlie lived. Even the new, modern building where Charlie had his flat housed workers living in the unfinished portion of the building. She moved closer to Charlie, not so much because of fear, but more because all of this was so unfamiliar to her.

When they reached the restaurant, a lovely sari-clad woman smiled warmly at Charlie and called him by name. She escorted them to a table by the window and took their order from Charlie, bringing their wine almost immediately afterward. This was obviously a place Charlie frequented. Anna looked at the menu and realized that, even though it was printed partially in English, she had a lot of learning to do when it came to Indian food. She decided that learning to cook this cuisine was one of the goals she would reach while she was there. The food was excellent. Anna enjoyed the spicy saffron chicken and the rice was seasoned just right. She felt relaxed from the wine and happy to be with Charlie once more. Her expectations for her time in India were high.

She came down to reality the next day, however, when Charlie arose early and began packing his field bag. He explained that he would be gone for five days, but that she should call Rajeesh and have him take her wherever she wanted to go. He cautioned her about exploring on her own, especially after dark, but said that during the day she should be fine as long as she stayed in the Nave Mumbai section of the city. He left her with an abrupt kiss on the cheek, which seemed to Anna to erase all of her warm feeling from their lovemaking the night before. She was once again alone, in a strange city, in a foreign land, knowing no one. And Charlie was gone...again.

After showering and having a light breakfast of yogurt and an egg that she found in Charlie's refrigerator, she decided that she would go ahead without Charlie and make the most of her time in India. So she set out on foot to explore the area adjacent to the apartment building. In addition to the restaurant where they had eaten the night before, she found many other places to dine. Some were more like the fast food places one would find in the U.S., with vendors quickly preparing food that could be carried off and eaten while walking or taken to one's home or place of work. She guessed that Charlie dined this way often, as she had seen little evidence that he cooked in the elaborate kitchen of the flat. She also saw a myriad of shops selling everything from cloth and curiosities to meat and produce. The meat was mostly various forms of chicken and some of the produce looked questionable to Anna. This was the part of Mumbai where many foreigners came to live, work, or visit, so most of the signage was in English. Some were also in Spanish or French, and she was able to make out enough words to figure out what the signs were advertising.

She enjoyed identifying all the different nationalities she saw and guessing why each person might be in Nave Mumbai. She noticed businessmen, and tourists who were clearly from the U.S. or Europe, as well as Indian nationals. She took note of their clothing and accents. It was a game she used to help her pass the time. She noticed one Indian woman, dressed in sophisticated clothing, who seemed to be staring at her, but the woman wheeled around and walked into an office building and Anna quickly forgot her.

At one point she turned a corner and saw an elephant being led down the street. The beast was painted with bright colors and decorated with cloth and paper flowers. She could see tourists come up to the man who owned the animal and speak to him, handing him money, after which they would reach out and touch the elephant, patting the tough hide tentatively. Anna doubted that the elephant could even feel their touch. After a brief time, the man continued down the street in search of someone else to pay him for the privilege of petting his elephant.

Anna began to feel hungry, so she went back to the restaurant where she and Charlie had eaten the night before. The same smiling woman greeted her as "Mrs. Charlie" and seated her at a pleasant table toward the back of the room. In the back, she was farther away from the noisy street and a ceiling fan made a slight dent in the heat of the day. She asked the woman to choose a dish for her, and, when it came, she was enchanted with the amazing aroma and taste of the food. She struck up a conversation with the woman, whose name was Alaka, which, the woman told her, meant girl with beautiful hair. Alaka was the owner of the establishment and spoke excellent English, again with that familiar accent. Anna asked her several questions about Indian cooking ingredients, and she seemed more than eager to share her knowledge. Finally, Anna asked if Alaka would consider teaching Anna to cook in the East Indian style and was given an enthusiastic "Yes!" and a big hug. Anna understood most Indian people to be somewhat shy, so the hug surprised her. After only a second's hesitation, however, Anna hugged her back and thanked her for her willingness to share her skills.

Anna left the restaurant feeling that she had accomplished something worthwhile and, her feet hurting from the hard pavement and heat, she headed back to the flat. She passed several more interesting shops on her way and decided that passing the time while Charlie was in the field would not be so hard after all. When she got back to the apartment building, however, she was dismayed to find an "Out of Order" sign on the elevator. She would have to walk the twenty-nine flights of stairs to reach their flat. She ran back out onto the sidewalk and purchased a small meal from one of the street vendors so she wouldn't have to go back out (and up and down all those stairs) to get dinner. Tomorrow she would definitely have to find some groceries and stock the flat's kitchen. By the time she climbed the stairs, taking her shoes off at the eighteenth floor, she was sweating and exhausted. She took another shower, put on her pajamas, ate her little meal, and fell into a deep and dreamless sleep. Her first day on her own in Mumbai was behind her.

The next four days went quickly as Anna began her cooking classes, found an outdoor market where local farmers came into town to sell their produce and other food, and she bought several decorative craft items made by Indian artisans to personalize the flat. She especially loved one tapestry that she purchased from a stall in an open-air market down a side street near the apartment building. It was large enough to hang on the large, open space of the living room wall and was an intricate pattern of lovely colors, both bright and subtle. There were tiny gold threads woven into the pattern that would sparkle when the sun shone through the window or the lights were on in the evening. She also purchased several gifts to take home to her friends and family. These were small pots and carvings that she could easily fit into her suitcase for the flight home. She even found a shop that made special order saris, so she purchased two for herself and one for her neighbor, Helen. The cloth was delicate, with ornate patterns of flowers woven of contrasting threads. She also spent hours writing detailed emails to her friends and family back home. In them she described the sights, sounds, and smells of Mumbai and told of her adventures exploring Nave Mumbai on her own. She told of her escalating cooking skills, and even sent a recipe for the recipients of her emails to try. She purchased small jars of saffron to take home to her friends, as well as a large jar of the precious spice for herself.

One day she called Rajeesh, to come pick her up in the car. She asked him to drive her around the city, to show her other sections of Mumbai and any landmarks in which he thought she might be interested. Anna was amazed by the number of animals she saw walking along the same streets that they were driving. There were goats, dogs, pigs, ducks and many cows side-by-side with them in the traffic. She even saw a mother dog nursing her puppies in the middle of the street. Traffic, with horns blaring, was skillfully dodging around the little family. By the end of the day she had seen much of both the ancient and new sections of the city, and Rajeesh had given her a thorough history lesson in the process. She might have been alone in a strange city, but she had made the most of her time.

Chapter Thirteen: Time with Charlie

On the night of the fifth day, Charlie came home. He was filthy dirty and tired from five days of living without running water or electricity, but he looked good to Anna. He announced that he was off work and could spend the time doing whatever Anna wanted.

"I've been working so much that I haven't been a 'tourist' since I got here," Charlie said. "You figure out how we should spend the time."

This was more than she expected, so she hadn't even made any plans for what they might do when Charlie came home. She opened her laptop, searching for ideas, and soon had an agenda for the next several days.

For a special outing they took a bus to Darjeeling, home of the world famous teas. There were only a few people on the bus when they began their trip, so Anna thought it might be a peaceful journey. Soon the bus was filled with the sounds of the other passengers' snoring, belching and farting. Above the driver's seat was a small television, the volume blaring on high. There was nothing peaceful about the trip, despite the fact that the bus was thankfully air-conditioned. Anna was amazed to see that there were at least a dozen men riding on the roof of the bus, since the seats inside were all taken. At one point a man staggered to the front of the bus and spoke with urgency to the driver. The driver immediately pulled the bus to the side of the road, opened the door, and the man leapt out and vomited on the side of the road next to the bus. The motion sick man then proceeded to take down his pants and urinate in the same spot. He then pulled up his pants, wiped his face on his shirtsleeve, and climbed the steps back into the bus. The driver started the bus, pulled back onto the road and continued the trip as if nothing out of the ordinary had occurred. Anna watched all this in amazement, while Charlie slept undisturbed beside her.

Several miles later, the bus stopped in a small village, where vendors waited with food and drinks for purchase by the passengers. Anna inquired as to the location of a restroom and was pointed to a small shack a few hundred feet from the road. When she opened the door, she was greeted with a disgusting odor and millions of flies. She hesitated and then walked in. Imbedded in the ground was a porcelain toilet bowl, the bottom of which was centered over a hole in the ground. Not finding an alternative, Anna took down her pants and squatted on the toilet bowl over the hole. She looked around and saw that the walls and ceiling of the toilet room were covered with very active spider webs. She was horrified and could hardly wait to get out of there. When she was finished, she noticed a bucket of water and a pitcher next to the toilet, so she scooped the pitcher full of water and poured it into the toilet. She could hear the water running in a small ditch that had been dug from the hole in the ground and led outside, ending up she didn't want to know where. Anna vowed never to use one of these "squatties" again, no matter how badly she needed to go! She was glad to once again get on the bus, but she had lost her appetite and didn't eat the food that Charlie had purchased from the vendors. This would surely be one of her more memorable experiences of India, if not the most pleasant.

The rest of the outings she planned went well, and Charlie's time at home ended too soon for Anna. He announced that he was needed back in the field and would be there indefinitely.

"You should stay for the rest of the time you planned," he said, "but I have little hope that I will be back before you leave."

"I don't understand. Why can't you take some real time off? Are you so damned important that they can't do without you for a couple of weeks? I came all the way to India to be with you, not some driver I barely know. I was hoping things could be the way they were when we were first together. We were so much in love and we had such a wonderful life," she pleaded.

Charlie just stared silently into her eyes.

Anna's voice rose as she spoke, and she frantically wiped away the tears that were streaming down her face. "I want you to quit this damned job and come home to Taos. Surely you can find work there."

Charlie broke his usually calm demeanor and said forcefully, "You know, Anna, life seems too complicated in Taos. I'm not used to attending social events and doing chores around the house. You handle the finances, but even that seems too complicated. I don't want to have to deal with it all."

Charlie paused momentarily and lowered his voice, "In fact, life has become too complicated in India, too. I long for the days when life was simple: go to work, come home, go to work again. When I was working in Oklahoma, being in the field for days at a time seemed a welcome break. I lived in in the field and was essentially incommunicado with the rest of the world other than to talk to my workers. Although my position carried a great deal of responsibility, in those days I felt relaxed at work more than anywhere else. I'm the kind of man who prefers simplicity, and I'm only comfortable dealing with the present moment, rather than making elaborate plans for the future. I'm not sure what the future holds…for me or for you."

Anna took a deep, shaky breath. She knew she had to save this moment if there was going to be any hope for their relationship. She tried to be convincing as she said, "OK, Charlie. I understand. You keep your job here. I'll come and visit as often as I can. You're not comfortable in Taos, and there's no way I could live full-time in India. We'll just have to figure out how to make our marriage work long distance. We're both intelligent, reasonable people. We can do this!"

Charlie just nodded his head and picked up his field bag as he headed for the door. Anna ran after him and lightly kissed him goodbye.

After Charlie left, Anna paced the flat, walking round and round as she replayed Charlie's words in her head. Once her anger subsided, she knew that she believed what she had said to Charlie. She would do everything in her power to make their marriage work.

Finally, she realized that, once again, she was preparing to entertain herself and was forced finish her trip to India alone. She called Rajeesh and told him of her situation, asking him to figure out some places to see and things to do. He faithfully picked her up every morning for five more days, taking her around the city and telling her all that he knew about Mumbai and India.

The slums especially appalled Anna. Tiny children ran naked in the street begging for a handout as they drove by. Rajeesh explained that he had come from an area only a bit better than the one they had just seen. He had walked several miles to a free school, where the teacher had taken pity on him and invited him to come live with her. He learned quickly and well, and his benefactor had a friend who had a friend in the oil and gas industry. Because of this tenuous connection, Rajeesh had been able to get a job and had worked his way up to being a driver. By the time Anna met him, he was married and had a little girl, and he proudly found her picture in his wallet to show to Anna. They talked almost continuously as they drove, Anna asking questions and often telling Rajeesh about her life in the U.S. By the time the week was over, Anna felt that she had made a good friend in Rajeesh.

She still had another week in India, but Anna felt that she had seen and done enough of India for a lifetime. She called to change her flight reservations and, despite the change fees charged by the airlines, was relieved to know that she would be home in a few days. She left word for Charlie at his office and called Rajeesh for a ride to the airport. Rajeesh sounded heartbroken that she was leaving and immediately invited her to come for a meal at his home on her last night in the city. When she arrived, she met Rajeesh's family, a lovely wife and the cutest toddler she had ever seen. Her big brown eyes captivated Anna, and she wondered if David and Valerie might be going to have a little girl. Rajeesh's home was comfortable and clean, and the meal was simple and delicious. Anna recognized the spices in some of the dishes and enjoyed talking to Rajeesh's wife about the meal. When it was time to leave, Anna said her goodbyes and gave Rajeesh's daughter a big hug. The little girl smiled shyly and hid behind her mother's skirt, much as Bradley had done the first time he met Charlie.

Rajeesh sped Anna to the airport the next day, dodging motor scooters and water trucks along the way. Rajeesh skillfully drove around a cow that was sleeping in the middle of the traffic lane. *Luckily,* thought Anna, *we didn't come across any elephants lumbering down the road.* When Anna boarded the plane and settled into her seat, she breathed a sigh of relief. In so many ways her trip to India had been wonderful; but, all in all, she felt disappointed and depressed. Nothing ever turned out quite as one hoped, it seemed to Anna.

Chapter Fourteen: Anna's Family

Anna arrived in Taos tired, depressed and worried. She could feel her marriage slipping away, and she didn't know how to save it. Over the next few weeks, her anxiety over Charlie wasn't helped by the changing tone of his emails. They became more infrequent and focused mostly on his work and their finances. He said very little about the time they had spent together or the status of their relationship. She didn't have the energy to do much, so she settled into a quiet routine of weaving, reading, and preparing her garden for spring planting. After several weeks, she went back to El Rito and reunited with her friends there, discovering that she had sold more weavings. Several of her rugs had sold, and she decided to put the money from her sales into the special account she had opened when she sold her boutique. She wasn't sure what she would do with the funds, but she would save for something special.

Gradually, she felt her depression lifting, and she made a short trip to see David, Bradley and her grandchildren. She was amazed at how much Bradley's boys had grown in the few months since she had last seen them. They were busy with school and activities, so she saw little of them while she was there. They all seemed happy, enjoying the space of their larger new home. There was plenty of room for the swing set Bradley built in the side yard, and their dogs loved running through the small stand of trees in the back of the property. Anna laughed when the children squabbled. It brought back memories of Bradley and David as young boys fighting over their toys or which program was on the television. They were a pretty typical family, and Anna was thankful for that.

David and Valerie had given birth to a baby boy they named Jordan. When Anna held Jordan in her arms for the first time, she looked into his bright blue eyes and felt a special bond that she had never felt with her other grandchildren. She didn't understand why this baby was so special to her. Perhaps it was because of her concern for his welfare in the chaos of David's life, which was as unstable as ever. His job was tenuous and paid little. Valerie had quit working to stay home with Jordan, saying that she didn't make enough money to cover childcare expenses. They seemed to be adequate parents, but their drinking hadn't slowed down and Anna saw little affection toward their baby. Anna's concerns for Jordan's future were at the forefront of her mind when she left.

She stopped by to see her father, but it was an unhappy visit. He was a bitter old man, and he said little while she was there. He kept the blinds closed all the time, so the house was dark and smelled of old food, beer and cigarettes. Clearly, he spent his days sitting in his recliner, smoking and drinking. The ashtray on the side table was overflowing, as was the trash. Anna realized that nothing much had changed, except her father no longer had his store to get him out of the house. She asked about Jack, but received only a clipped response that indicated that Jack had left town "with some hussy" and her father had not heard from him in several years. As she walked down the creaky front porch steps, Anna knew in her heart that she would not return to that house until she came back to bury her father. The thought made her sad.

Her last two visits were not particularly uplifting, but Anna decided to call on Charlie's mother, who was finally packing to move to Tennessee. It was just a courtesy and she didn't plan to stay long. From what Charlie had always said about his mother, Anna was expecting another unpleasant visit. When she walked up to the old house, she could see how neglected the building had become. Paint was peeling and shingles were missing from the roof. She didn't know if the roof leaked, but she guessed that winter snows would bring with them many buckets to catch the melting water.

When she rang the doorbell of the old house, Charlie's mother answered with a broad smile and a welcoming hand waving Anna into the living room. This surprised Anna after all that she had heard about Grace over the years. Grace was dressed in casual slacks and a fresh blouse with loafers on her feet. She had even put pennies in the front of the loafers, and Anna had to laugh to herself that Grace had brought the '50's into the present time. But the '50's seemed to be everywhere, not just on Grace's feet. The furniture was in good repair but showed years of wear, and there were collections of nick knacks everywhere. On the mantle rested a dusty assortment of miniature teacups flanked by display boards holding tiny spoons. The side tables were cluttered with a variety of ceramic statues of birds and animals, especially cats; and the coffee table was strewn with magazines and other debris. Moving all of these items was going to be an enormous task, and she was secretly glad that she would not be a part of that process.

Anna sat in an upholstered side chair that had seen better days, and waited for Grace to begin speaking. After accepting Grace's offer of iced tea, Anna found herself conversing quite comfortably with Grace. Grace asked about the grandchildren, whom, she said, she seldom saw. She didn't sound bitter or nosey, but rather, lonely. She told Anna how much she appreciated the financial help Anna and Charlie had given her over the years. She talked about her past and how difficult it had been for her to give up the family farm. She had struggled when her husband died, she said, and her only consolation was her family. Because of that, perhaps she had become too involved in their lives. When she finally sensed their resentment, she had backed off and tried hard to find other interests to occupy her time. She joined a bridge group and volunteered at the local soup kitchen. Anna immediately thought of her mother and all the activities that had kept her living despite her abusive marriage.

Grace showed genuine interest in Anna's weaving and hearing about her life in New Mexico. Either Grace had changed dramatically, or the stories Charlie had told about her were not entirely true. When she left, Anna was feeling re-energized. This had been an unexpectedly pleasant experience and she was glad to have gotten to know Grace better.

The time she spent with Clare was the highlight of her trip. Clare had opened her gallery, which was slowly gaining a reputation for the quality of the work on display. Anna met Clare's professor and liked him in spite of her misgivings. He wasn't as old as she had imagined him to be, and he and Clare seemed to have a nice working relationship, as well as a personal one. When Anna told Clare of her success in selling several of her weavings, Clare immediately invited Anna to send one or two pieces for display in her gallery. Neither of them was sure how much demand there would be for southwestern artistry in a midwestern gallery, but it was worth a try. Anna felt closer to Clare than she had to anyone in a long while, and she told Clare of her misgivings about Charlie and their marriage over a long cup of coffee one morning. Clare listened sympathetically and said she wished she could help, but Anna knew that only she and Charlie could work this out.

The best part of the visit was having her own place to stay. She decided that buying Bradley's old house was one of the best decisions she had ever made, and she savored the peace and quiet of the little house by the lake. When she awoke in the mornings, she could look out the bedroom window and see the sunrise reflected off the water without even having to get out of bed. The kitchen was small but well-equipped, thanks to Bradley and Julie. Although most of the utensils and much of the furniture had come from thrift shops and garage sales, the house was comfortable and suited Anna well. Once again she marveled at the differences between her two sons. She knew that Bradley and David talked little and saw each other even less. David never would have taken the time to bring in all the things Anna might need.

Chapter Fifteen: Anna in Peru

When Anna returned to Taos, things felt more normal, and for the next several months she continued in her routine. Her garden brought her a sense of peace, and she spent her days doing what she wanted. There was no pressure on her to do anything else, and she enjoyed that feeling of freedom. Her only worry was her concern over her marriage; she was at a loss as to how to mend the rift that had grown between her and Charlie. She had asked him directly if he was seeing another woman, and he denied it consistently, saying that work was keeping him so busy he was unable to call or email regularly. He swore that there was nothing else going on. She finally decided that her only course of action was to spend time together to see if they could work things out. Charlie had mentioned that he hadn't had any time off in weeks, so she hoped he could take time now to be with her.

Once again, she went online to see what options were out there for them. She finally decided on a trip to Peru. The country sounded fascinating, with beautiful scenery, many opportunities for hiking and exploring, and, best of all for Anna, a thriving industry of weavers. She sent Charlie the details, asking him to join her and waited impatiently for his response. After several days he wrote back, saying that he had finally gone to a doctor about his breathing problems and had been diagnosed with worsening asthma. He was now on steroids and needed to use a rescue inhaler several times a day. His doctor had told him that, because of the altitude in Peru, he could not possibly make the trip. Anna was overwhelmed with disappointment, and she slammed her laptop closed, cursing both Charlie and his doctor. She felt so rejected and angry that she didn't even have any concerns about Charlie's health. She made up her mind to go to Peru alone, because she didn't need Charlie. But she knew in her heart that she was lying to herself. She needed Charlie very much.

One week later, Anna found herself in an airplane approaching the airport in Lima. This trip had been less comfortable than her trip to India, because Charlie's company was not paying for a business class ticket, and she was crammed into a seat between two large businessmen. One snored the entire trip and the other drank way too much, wanting to talk the entire time. She was more than ready to deplane. After checking through customs, she hailed a taxi and gave the driver the name of her hotel. From the back seat she could see that Lima was a large, modern city. She was surprised by the noise and pollution. She had been expecting a wholesome environment, but, clearly, Lima was just another big city. She realized, however, that it was nowhere near the environmental catastrophe that she had found in India. At her hotel, she made arrangements for transportation for the more than 600-mile trip to Arequipa, the next stop on her itinerary. She spent the evening walking the streets of Lima. There was no issue with altitude here, because Lima was on the coast. *Surely Charlie could have joined me for at least this part of the trip*, she bitterly said to herself. She knew, however, that before her trip was over she would be contending with much higher altitudes and she wondered if even she would feel the effects. Her thoughts vacillated as she thought, *Perhaps Charlie was wise not to have come to this mountainous country.*

Her main goal while in Lima was to locate Maximo Laura, an internationally famous weaver who was born into a long line of weavers. His studio was located just outside of the city, and Anna had made arrangements to observe him at work and, perhaps, be privileged to take some lessons. She found his studio, a very humble structure that housed his beautiful work, and introduced herself. He was gracious and kind, welcoming her with a warm smile and passable English. They spent several days together, she observing his techniques and him teaching her some of his not-so-secret tricks. This experience alone would make her trip worthwhile.

Traveling to Arequipa was long and arduous. Maneuvering through the airport to catch her flight took much longer than she had expected, and she had to run to the gate. As Anna handed the attendant her ticket, the woman glowered at her, but Anna moved on quickly and found her seat. She was out of breath and harried as she buckled her seat belt, just wanting the flight to get under way. The flight was unnerving as the plane bounced through the sky toward Arequipa. Anna, who seldom felt nervous when flying, found herself praying for safety and a wave of relief washed over her when she felt the wheels hit the runway. When she finally arrived at her destination, Anna was exhausted.

She found Arequipa to be as modern as Lima, if not as large and noisy. She stayed at a charming bed and breakfast, where she was treated to some South American dishes that seemed similar to, but slightly different from, the food she was accustomed to in New Mexico. After getting a good night's sleep, Anna's main goal in Arequipa was to tour the American yarn mill that was located in the city. The mill turned out to be a large, modern plant that turned out thousands of skeins of yarn each week. She was somewhat disappointed, as the mill offered nothing in the way of local charm or ancient weaving skills, so she moved on to Tarma, the next stop on her itinerary.

Tarma was an ancient village and more of a match to Anna's expectations. She roomed at a 300-year-old hacienda that had been owned by the same family through many generations. The owners' pride in their family history and the building itself were clearly evident in the immaculate gardens and whitewashed walls. Her room opened up onto a patio planted with lush flowers that thrived in the summer sun. She especially enjoyed bright blossoms when the sun shone on them early in the morning as she sipped her coffee. Anna knew that the winters in Tarma were severely cold, so she was glad to have come when the weather was welcoming. At a small café near the hacienda, she learned that the official name for Tarma was Santa Ana de la Ribera de Tarma, and the natives referred to their town as "The Pearl of the Andes". The town was laid out in the midst of an agricultural area in the foothills of the Andes Mountains and was at more than 7,000 feet in altitude. That was approximately the same altitude as Taos, so Anna wasn't bothered by it as she made her way up and down the quaint streets where she saw animals being herded right through the center of town. The most amazing sight for Anna, however, was the women who were spinning the Alpaca wool while walking down the street. They carried drop spindles with them, tossing the wool about eight feet ahead, spinning it skillfully as they walked that distance, picking up the wool, and repeating the process as they strolled through town. Anna didn't do a lot of spinning, but she was quite certain she could never master that technique.

As she traveled from Tarma to Cuzco, she noted the terraced hillsides planted with crops and dotted with alpaca. Arriving in Cuzco, she wondered at the ancient churches and cathedrals set amidst streets of stone so carefully laid that she couldn't see the cracks between them. She enjoyed watching the people, who seemed happy all the time in their colorful, traditional clothing. Anna was now at 11,000 feet and could tell that the altitude was taking its toll on her. She had to go to her room to lie down because she felt her heart beating fast and had a headache. The symptoms passed fairly quickly, however, but she knew that Charlie could never have made this part of the trip. She began to feel foolish for being so angry about his refusal to come along. She was surprised at how little she missed his company.

From Cuzco she went to Machu Picchu, where she marveled at the ingenious ruins left by that intelligent and wise culture so many centuries before. This was the heart of the Andes. She learned that the Quechua people in this area used backstrap techniques to create beautiful weavings, so she made arrangements to travel to Pisaq, which required going over a mountain pass. There she observed the weavers and went to a huge Sunday market where she purchased several unique weavings. *This alone,* she thought, *has made my trip worthwhile.*

She had packed a lot of traveling and experiences into two weeks, and it was finally time to return to Taos. Her time in Peru had been lonely, but she had encountered many wonderful people along the way, had learned so much more than she had even hoped about weaving, and was leaving with hundreds of wonderful memories of her time in that country. She planned to write many emails sharing her thoughts and experiences with Charlie and her family when she got home.

Chapter Sixteen: Fariha

Her name was Fariha. She didn't know exactly how old she was, but guessed she was about twenty-two. Her earliest memories were at her mother's knee around a cooking fire in a poverty-ridden village in Bangladesh, where she was born. She saw herself as a small child playing on the dirt floor next to the mat where she slept. Tall green trees and colorful flowers were a part of her memories, also, and rain pouring from the sky turning everything to sticky mud. She knew she had a brother younger than she, but she did not remember his name. She knew her father left every day to work in the fields where they grew crops to sell, and that, at times, she went to bed hungry because they had no food of their own to eat. She could remember being told she was a beautiful child as far back as her memory reached, and that was the curse with which she had lived every day.

When she was about ten years old, her family sold her to a man from India who said he wanted to give her a better life. Her family, recognizing Fariha's beauty, believed that this man would help Fariha become something special: perhaps a model or a movie star such as they had in the western world, or at least the wife of a wealthy Indian gentleman. Their dreams were naïve, of course, and Fariha was once again sold, this time into the sex trade where she was groomed to be a prostitute. Because she was so beautiful, she was given special treatment and was never beaten where it might show. A stern matron taught her etiquette and English, so that she could entertain wealthy clients properly. Fariha was bright and learned quickly. Even as a young girl, she recognized that the things she was being taught might be her only means of escaping the life into which she had been sold. By the time she was fourteen, the most powerful men in Mumbai were requesting Fariha's services. She learned quickly to hate her pimp, the fool who preferred to be called her "agent". She secretly laughed behind his back at his pretentiousness. Fariha knew exactly what he was, and she knew what she was.

She also learned to hate the men she serviced. In fact, she learned to hate all men, and assumed that every man's primary goal in life was to have sex with a beautiful woman. Her heart was hard, but she never let it show. She smiled and talked sweetly to her clients, earning extra tips that she secreted away in a crack in the wall of her closet. She had an upscale wardrobe and lived in a large house with the other women, but she considered herself far above her circumstances. She knew she was intelligent as well as comely, and she began to plan how she might escape the life in which she was trapped. Her plan began to become reality when her pimp beat her severely one day, shouting at her that she was too old to work the trade any more and that she had become fat and ugly. She knew this was not true; she was still quite beautiful. He told her she was no good for anything but taking care of the house, cleaning and cooking for the younger, more desirable women. Fariha knew that this tirade signaled the end of her work as a prostitute and she was repulsed by the idea that she was to become a servant to the other women in the house.

Fariha was hurt by his words, but she also saw this as an opportunity. Her mind quickly formulated a plan and she made a bargain with him. The bargain was that she could leave the house, taking her clothing and meager possessions with her. In return, she would repay her pimp the $25,000 within six months to buy her freedom. They both understood that, if she failed to deliver the money, he would hunt her down and she would not survive the consequences.

So, taking her money and clothes wrapped up in a pillow case, Fariha left the house in the old part of Mumbai and fled to Nave Mumbai where she thought she might have a chance of meeting a rich man. She moved into a shack with a kindly old woman who allowed her to share the tiny space in return for a small fee and Fariha's promise to care for the woman and her disease-ravaged body. Fariha largely ignored the woman and went about her business with no feelings of guilt that she had broken her word to the old woman. Within weeks, the woman was dead and Fariha greedily took over the shack as her own. She felt no sorrow at the kind woman's death; she only saw it as an omen that the gods were watching over her and helping her achieve her goal.

Every day she walked to a large apartment house many blocks from her shack. Although the building was not yet finished, there were several rich businessmen living there. She watched carefully from across the street and observed them coming and going for days. Some had families, and those men she paid little attention to. There were two men who seemed to be alone, however, and she studied their habits very carefully. One was short and fat; she found him repulsive and decided that she could not stand to make him a part of her plan.

The other, however, was tall and good-looking for a westerner. She studied him carefully, noting that he was often absent for days at a time, but always returned for several more days. He usually ate his evening meal at the little restaurant down the street and occasionally purchased food from the street vendors. Other than that, he seldom went out of his flat in the evenings, but he must have a job because he was always gone during the day. He would be her mark; she was sure he could afford to give her the $25,000 she needed. She knew she still had plenty of time left to make her plan work, and she felt excitement grow as she imagined herself a free and wealthy woman.

She began hanging around the lobby of the apartment building at the end of the workday, and several times she caught his eye as he came home from work. She even managed to get into the elevator with him and saw that he had pushed the button for the 29th floor before she told him she needed to get out at the 17th. Now that she knew where he lived, she was certain he was rich, because the construction workers had told her that the 29th floor was a large and luxurious flat. In fact, it was the only flat on that floor.

She watched and followed him for several weeks and was about to make her move when a woman arrived. She had an enormous suitcase and a bag strapped to her back like a pack animal. She was attractive for a westerner and had a nice body, but Fariha knew that she couldn't rival her own beauty. She wondered what the bitch was doing here and how long she would stay. Was she going to interfere with Fariha's plan? If so, Fariha would have to take her out of the situation. Foreigners were lost and killed by accident in India every day. It would not be too difficult to get rid of her if necessary.

The woman was with the man in the beginning, but then she seemed to be alone for many days. The man returned for a few more days and then left again. Fariha knew he was leaving, because she recognized the bag he carried whenever he was gone from the apartment for a long period of time. Two days after the man left again, the woman climbed into a black car. This car had picked her up before, and she recognized the driver as he put her suitcase and pack into the trunk. Fariha rejoiced that the woman was leaving, hopefully for good. As soon as the man came back to Mumbai, she would put her plan into action.

While he was gone, Fariha flirted with some of the construction workers and found out that the man's name was Charlie. He worked for a large Indian gas and oil company that paid for his fancy flat on the 29th floor. She thought Charlie was a ridiculous name for a man—or for anyone for that matter. But she didn't care what his name was. He was her target and she vowed to make him hers. For once she would be the master and the American would be her slave. She had been taught well and was confident that she had the beauty and skills to carry out her plan. She smiled broadly at the thought and waited for him to return to his flat.

Within a few days, Charlie returned to the apartment building. Fariha was ready. She rose early in the morning and watched him leave for work. Then she took the elevator to the 29th floor and sat on the floor by Charlie's door. When he returned at the end of the day, she was ready. As the elevator made its ascent, she rubbed her cheeks and nose to make them red and put a grain of salt in each eye. Her eyes began to water just as Charlie stepped off the elevator. He looked tired and surprised to find a weeping woman at his doorstep, but he bent down and helped her to her feet. Asking if she was all right, he opened the door and gestured her inside the flat. She noticed that it was refreshingly cool inside compared to the sweltering streets outside. He offered her a drink of water and waited patiently while she drank and composed herself. He asked again what was going on, and she proceeded to spin her tale.

"I live on the 17th floor, but my boyfriend has kicked me and my baby out. I'm a single mother, you see. My boyfriend is a violent man, so I left my baby with a friend and came back to the flat to get my things. While I was there, my boyfriend came home and threw me out again. He told me never to come back or he would kill me," she sobbed. "I was frightened and I needed a place to hide. That's when I remembered you from the elevator ride earlier and came to the 29th floor. I know my boyfriend would never think to look for me here."

As she told her story, she wept periodically and looked up at Charlie with soulful brown eyes.

Charlie believed every word she said. She was the most beautiful woman he had ever seen, and she must come from a well-to-do class of people, because her clothes were expensive. She obviously cared very much for her baby, a girl he was told, to hide her from her boyfriend. Charlie didn't think to ask if the boyfriend was the father of her child. Nor did he ask any other questions. He opened his arms to hug her, and she came to him, snuggling against his neck as she sniffled her despair. Charlie was beyond help and had no clue that he had just become a pawn in a game of wits that he was destined to lose. And halfway across the world, Anna had unknowingly become another player in Fariha's game. For once in her life, Fariha was in control.

Charlie and Fariha sat together on the couch and she told him how grateful she was that he had taken her in.

"Your flat is lovely," she gushed. "You have decorated it so tastefully, and I especially love the beautiful tapestry that you hung on the wall above the couch."

Then she tearfully told him her tale. She was careful to keep it close to the truth, having heard that lies based in truth are the most believable.

"I am from Bangladesh," she said, "and when a handsome Indian gentleman offered my father $25,000 as a bride gift to marry me, my father gave his consent. I had no choice in the matter, since I would have had an arranged marriage eventually anyway, as is the custom. So, at the age of 17, I left Bangladesh and came to India to be married. But no marriage took place. The 'gentleman' turned out not to be a gentle man at all, but, rather, kept me under strict control and I was more like an abused slave. He bought me beautiful clothes and took me to his business parties, introducing me as his wife, but we were never married. In the beginning he locked me in the flat while he was gone, but I eventually convinced him that I had nowhere to go and would not run away. So I lived with him for the past five years. I had his daughter three years ago."

Fariha continued her tale, saying, "I began talking to him recently about going home to Bangladesh to visit my family. They have never seen my daughter, their granddaughter. When I said this, he became irrationally angry and violent. He said he would never let me go back, that he had paid good money for me, and I owed him."

"I'm quite certain," Fariha continued, "that he has a new girlfriend in another building close by, because he is often absent for days and nights at a time. If I could just pay back the $25,000," she said, "I am certain that he would leave me alone."

Fariha wept as she told Charlie how humiliated it made her feel to know that she had been sold, as one might sell a cow or chickens. She was angry with her father for making such an arrangement, but she missed her mother and younger brother and wanted to see them again.

As Charlie listened, his heart melted and he felt such compassion for this woman that he vowed he would do whatever was necessary to help her. "Should we go to the police?" he asked.

She quickly insisted "My boyfriend has connections deep in the Indian government and such a move would be futile and dangerous. The only solution," she emphasized, "is to pay him off and hope that he will be done with me. But I have no way to get that kind of money," she sobbed. "My situation is hopeless."

After telling Charlie her story, Fariha seemed spent, so Charlie offered to let her stay the night. When he showed her to the bedroom, she took him in her arms and kissed him deeply. Charlie's heart and body responded to the kiss and, before he knew it, he was in bed with Fariha, making passionate love to her. She was amazing, he thought, satisfying him in ways that he never dreamed possible. It never occurred to Charlie to question her story or wonder where she learned her sexual skills. He was simply locked in the moment.

When they awoke the next morning, Charlie told Fariha, "Here is some money. Sneak out of the building, buy the clothing and other things you need, and then come right back. Be careful not to be seen and lock the door securely when you get back. I will figure something out and come home with a solution to your problem.

When Charlie closed the door to leave for his office, Fariha smiled and sighed in relief. Her plan was working, and she had little doubt that she would be a free woman very soon.

For the next several days, Charlie went to work and sat at his desk, but he could not concentrate on the papers in front of him. He had the means to help Fariha, so that was not a problem. The problem was Anna. Could he abandon her for another woman? He knew in his gut that, getting involved with Fariha was not going to be a temporary fling like the affairs he had in the past. Fariha was going to change his life forever, and he didn't know if he was ready for that. He loved looking at her, of course, and she was unbelievable in bed. Even more captivating was her ability to make Charlie feel interesting. She was able to discuss almost any subject and her interest in what he had to say about his work made him feel important. So, in the end, he decided that he would help Fariha. He wanted her, he needed her, and he would have her, even at the risk of losing everything else. Fariha was worth it.

He made arrangements to reduce his retirement fund contribution by $25,000. He took the money home, along with his regular paycheck, all of it in cash. Because he planned to travel to Bangladesh with Fariha and her child, he also kept money for that trip, sending Anna far less that he usually did to cover her expenses and the bills she had to pay. He went home to his flat and told Fariha that he had the money to buy her freedom.

"Oh, Charlie! I am so grateful!" she said, "I am now yours and will do whatever you want for the rest of my life!" The irony never occurred to Charlie that he was now buying her from her boyfriend. Fariha, of course, did not see the situation in that light.

Chapter Seventeen: The Payoff

Charlie gave Fariha the money in cash and she made arrangements to meet her former pimp while Charlie was at work. They met in an alley in a seedy part of Mumbai. Despite being daytime, the alley was dark and there were no other people around, although traffic noise from the street echoed off the walls. Fariha had brought a gun with her. She purchased the gun from a black market dealer on that first day when Charlie gave her spending money. The gun made her feel powerful. She was no longer vulnerable to the men in her life. She handed over the cash, telling the pimp that he must never contact her again. She would hold him to his promise no matter what it took, she said.

Following a harsh farewell, he turned and began to walk away with a victorious swagger. Fariha took the gun from her purse and fired two shots into his back. He staggered and turned toward her, and for a moment Fariha was afraid the bullets had not found their mark. As he stared at her, she saw blood begin to trickle from his mouth, his eyes clouded over, and he collapsed onto the filth of the alley floor. She quickly put the gun back in her purse and ran to his body, reaching into his pocket to remove the envelope containing the cash. She then straightened her dress and walked purposefully from the alley onto the busy sidewalk. No one paid any attention to her. The shots had sounded like a car backfiring and had been muffled by the noisy traffic on the street. Fariha felt no remorse and never looked back.

Fariha went straight back to the flat, carefully hid the money and her gun, took a shower, and changed her clothes. She wadded the clothes up into a bundle and was headed for the garbage when she spotted the beautiful tapestry on the wall. From the moment she first saw it, she knew that Charlie's wife must have bought it. It would be a reminder to him of his commitments back in the U.S. If Fariha had her way, Charlie was going to forfeit all of those ties.

She took the tapestry from the wall, bundled it up with her clothes, and headed for the trash bin next to the elevator.

To her surprise, Charlie never asked her about the tapestry, nor did he even seem to notice it was gone. She was almost disappointed, because she had thought of a creative story to explain its absence. At least that was one lie she would not have to tell Charlie.

When Charlie came home, Fariha told him that she had delivered the money and was now under no obligation to her former boyfriend. She gave Charlie no further explanation, but she rewarded him with a long kiss and led him to the bedroom. Charlie followed her lead without another thought for the family he was leaving behind.

Chapter Eighteen: The Child

Charlie kept asking about Fariha's daughter, saying that she was welcome in his flat. After all, he had an extra bedroom and Fariha would be able to care for her without worrying about her boyfriend any more. Finally, Fariha decided that she needed to show Charlie a little girl, so she took a taxi to one of the slums on the edge of the city. She got out, told the driver to wait for her, and walked about a hundred yards into the slum. She was repulsed by the stench and filth, but continued looking for the prize she sought. She saw rats running everywhere and let out a scream as one scurried over her shoe. The place was crowded with hovels made of cardboard and scraps of wood and metal. Women were sitting out front, staring with vacant eyes as she walked past. Their looks sent a shiver up her spine, as she knew that, but for her cleverness and ingenuity, she might be living in this wretched place herself. The smell caused her to gag, and she could see the evidence of human waste in the water along the side of the path where she walked. Finally, she stopped walking, as she spotted what she was looking for.

A female child about three years old was playing in the mud. She was a lovely little girl, with wide brown eyes and curly black hair that made a dark halo around her innocent face. She was filthy, of course, and naked except for a pair of boys' underwear that was too large and kept slipping off her little butt. Fariha thought she was perfect. She picked the child up and gave her a piece of candy, which the child greedily put in her mouth as Fariha quickly carried her to the waiting taxi. The little girl gave no protest as they drove away; in fact she never said a word. She just smiled at Fariha and held her hand out for more candy.

When the cab pulled up to the apartment building, Fariha bundled the little girl in a blanket she had brought along, paid the driver, and quickly carried the child into the building and through the lobby to the elevator. Thankful that the elevator was working that day, she entered the flat and headed straight for the bathroom. She ran the tub full of warm water, adding bubble bath, which she thought would make the child less frightened of being bathed, since she surely never had a bath in her life. Fariha discovered that she had picked out the perfect child. This one seemed happy to do whatever Fariha wanted and she willingly wore the new outfit that Fariha put on her. Smelling and looking like a little angel, the little girl waited with Fariha for Charlie to come home.

When Charlie opened the door and saw the little girl sitting with Fariha, he broke into a big smile. He took the child into his arms, gave her a big hug, and held her at arms' length to look at her.

"She clearly has your eyes and mouth," he told Fariha. "She's a beautiful child who will grow to be as beautiful as her mother!"

Fariha stopped herself from rolling her eyes at such nonsense. Charlie was truly a fool, although a generous one, and he clearly loved children.

Because the little girl smiled little and spoke less, there was not much interaction between her and Charlie that evening. When she did speak, the language was strange to Charlie, and neither he nor Fariha encouraged conversation. Charlie wondered why Fariha did not interact more with the little girl; but when Fariha joined him in bed, he forgot all about the questions he had regarding her child.

The next morning, after Charlie left for work, Fariha took the girl back to the slums and dropped her off in approximately the same place she had found her. She had no idea if the child's mother had missed her, nor did she care. Probably the little girl would find her way home again, if she even had a home. Fariha turned to look out the back window, and the child was staring after her forlornly. Fariha turned her gaze forward and never looked back. She was concocting the next story she would spin for Charlie. How would she explain her disappearing daughter? She would come up with something.

When Charlie came in from work, the first thing he said was, "Where is your daughter?"

Fariha was ready with her response. "When she awoke this morning, she was vomiting and quite ill. I took her back to my friend, because she is leaving for Bangladesh this evening and she will take the child with her. She will be cared for by my family until you and I make arrangements to join her." What she would tell him at a later date was that the child had actually been fatally ill and had died before she could be reunited with her mother. She knew that story would stir up sympathy for Fariha, the grieving mother.

Charlie accepted the story about the girl's return to Bangladesh with some misgivings for her welfare. Fariha was able to distract him from his doubts by saying, "Oh, Charlie. We can have our own children. They will be beautiful. Tall boys with your hair and beautiful girls with my looks."

Charlie quickly responded, "But Fariha, I had a vasectomy. I can't have any more children. Beside, I'm old enough to be your father. I don't think I could handle being the father of any more babies at my age."

Fariha never missed a beat. "You would be an amazing father, Charlie. The solution is simple. Have your vasectomy reversed. I've heard that it can be done quite easily. Then we can have all the children we want!"

"All right, Fariha. I'll look into it," Charlie reluctantly agreed.

The very next day Charlie, embarrassed to see his usual doctor, found a local clinic and made an appointment for the following week. He knew that, in a way, he was making some kind of permanent commitment to Fariha, but he reasoned that this was what he wanted for his life now and he would deal with Anna and the consequences of his decisions later. Charlie was to discover that later was to arrive sooner than he thought

Chapter Nineteen: Reunion

Anna was becoming worried…worried about her finances and worried about her marriage. Despite her constant emails to Charlie, he seldom responded and the money he had sent faithfully for so many months began to arrive late and was barely enough to cover their debts. In fact, she had to dip into their savings several times to cover all of the bills and buy food. Charlie was clearly distancing himself from her, but whenever she asked him if there was another woman, his response was always the same. He was just busy at work, spending more and more time in the field. Further, he claimed that the company was not paying him what they owed him, but he was trying to get the problem resolved. Anna should not be concerned, he said. But she was concerned. She knew in her heart that Charlie had found someone else, and she was determined to either win him back or, at worst, find out the truth. It was a risk she was willing to take.

So she wrote Charlie asking—no, actually demanding—that he meet her in Greece for two weeks together. She was worried about the cost of the trip but told him she very much wanted to work things out, that she was worried about their marriage and unhappy thinking that he had found someone else after 38 years. If he loved her at all, he would be willing to come to Greece to spend time with her. She had picked Greece, because it was at sea level and easily accessible, so she could see no excuse for Charlie not to come. To her surprise, he responded that he would meet her there and even sent money to pay for the airfare. She planned a romantic stay on one of the Greek islands, in a lovely little apartment she found online. In three weeks' time they would be together again, and Anna's hopes were high that her misgivings were unfounded and they could renew their relationship. She was filled with anticipation.

While she was waiting for the time to pass before her trip, David and Valerie showed up at her doorstep with Jordan in tow. They explained that David had lost his job and they were broke, so they had come to Taos in hopes that David could get work and they could start over in a new city. Anna knew that they had actually come for a free place to stay and to ask for money, but she welcomed them and set them up in her guest room. She would never have turned Jordan away, and she was hopeful that she could inspire David to do something about providing a stable future for his child. After a few days, Anna was so in love with Jordan that she would have adopted him as her own if that had been possible. He was a bright, curious little boy with an unending stream of questions and an engaging smile. When his mischief got him into trouble, he would look innocently at Anna and say, " I din't do nuffin." He had her wrapped around his finger in no time.

David and Valerie, however, were wearing on her nerves. Rather than looking for a job, David sat in the den and watched sports on television all day, while Valerie buried her nose in cheesy romance novels. Despite their claim that they were broke, they consumed cases of beer that Anna had not purchased. Neither of them ever offered to help out with buying food or doing anything around the house, and Anna couldn't wait for them to leave. Anna did feel a bit better about their relationship with Jordan, however. At times they were loving parents, and she stood in the doorway one day watching David play with his son. *Perhaps David will grow up along with Jordan,* she thought, hopefully.

The day was approaching for Anna to depart for Greece, and she didn't trust David and Valerie to stay in her house while she was gone, so she made them an offer. They could live in the little house by the lake if they would pay her what rent they could afford. She knew she wouldn't see a penny, but this would give them a chance to start over in a place where they already had friends and family and job opportunities were more plentiful than in Taos. After thinking it over, the couple agreed. They packed up their belongings and put Jordan in his car seat. As they drove away, Anna was heartbroken to see Jordan leaving in that car, but she knew she had to get her own life in order before she could help him.

She once again asked herself how her two sons could have turned out so differently. Bradley was a stable man with a wife and three children. He had a home of his own and held down a steady and respectable job. He and his family clearly loved her; they spoke often on the phone and Julie regularly sent her pictures of the boys. She felt close to them, in touch with their lives, and she loved making gifts for her grandsons. David, on the other hand, seemed only to want her for the resources she could provide. She didn't feel close to him at all, and it saddened her to think that he might not even be capable of loving her as she loved him. She knew that she didn't like him…but she did love him. And her concerns for Jordan's future were very real. Anna believed that David and Valerie would never harm Jordan, at least not intentionally, but they were nowhere near mature enough to give him the kind of life and upbringing that a young boy needed. She wanted so badly to intervene, but she was at a loss as to how to do that without destroying her relationship with her younger son. Anna's pain over the situation was palpable, and yet, she could think of no course of action that would fix things. First of all, she had to put her marriage back on track, and she had high hopes that would happen in the next few weeks.

Anna confided in her neighbors about her frustration with David, as well as the state of her marriage and her hopes for the trip to Greece. Helen and Lee listened compassionately and offered to help if they could, but there was little they could do. Helen, who had been a professional counselor, was an especially good listener but offered little advice. Anna supposed that good counselors did not give advice, but, rather, helped people figure out their own solutions. Helen seemed to be very good at that. When Anna told Helen of her plans to meet Charlie in Greece, Helen was very encouraging, urging Anna to be proactive about the situation, rather than always reacting to what Charlie did. They spent many hours together, knitting, sipping wine, and talking about Anna's problems with Charlie and her concerns about Jordan and David. After talking with Helen, Anna realized that the best course of action with David was to hold the line and not let him connive and manipulate her to get his way. She would stop sending him money, because she was enabling him to continue his shiftless lifestyle. She resolved to be strong when it came to David's requests for help, but she still worried about what all of this was doing to Jordan and how it would affect him as he grew up.

Over time, Anna, Lee and Helen had become closer than just neighbors. Helen was more like an older sister to Anna, and Lee an older brother (or even the father figure that her own father never was). They saw each other almost daily and gradually became a part of each other's lives. Anna had taken care of their little dog when Helen and Lee left town for their granddaughter's wedding, and they often helped each other out in small, neighborly ways. She knew that they loved Bella and were willing to care for her during her absence, so Anna asked them to take the German Shepherd into their home and to come to her house to feed Simba, change the litter box, and water her plants while she was in Greece. She felt like this was a huge imposition, but they had already done the same for her when she went to Peru. Anna had thanked them after her South American trip by bringing them an exquisite weaving, which they proudly hung in a prominent place in their great room. She would do the same this time, bringing them something unique and wonderful from Greece.

The snow was falling heavily when she left Taos for the airport in Albuquerque. Even Albuquerque was getting an unusual dusting of snow, but the weather had not delayed her flight and Anna boarded the plane with high expectations of the coming weeks in Greece. After an uneventful trip, she looked out the plane window and saw the sparkling waters of the Mediterranean Sea below her, the Greek Isles dotting their blue expanse. She deplaned, retrieved her luggage, and found her way to the ferry that would carry her to Folegandros, the Greek Isle on which she had rented a small apartment. As she looked over the railing of the ferry into the dark, choppy water, she could feel her nervousness growing. She gave herself a little lecture: She needed to be firm, to take matters into her own hands, to demand that Charlie tell her what was going on. But in her heart, she still hoped that this reunion would be sweet and romantic, rekindling the feelings they once had for each other. She didn't understand how their lives had reached this point.

Once the ferry docked, Anna asked directions to the apartment from a local fisherman whose English was as scant as her Greek, but she found her way. The apartments were like little cottages perched on a hillside and surrounded by flowering gardens. The owners, Cornelia and Dimitri, welcomed her like family and showed her to the room where she would spend the next two weeks. There was a sitting room with a tidy kitchenette and a compact bedroom and bath. The rooms were decorated with local artwork and fresh flowers, and the furniture had obviously been handmade by local craftsmen. Anna spent several minutes carefully examining several handmade rugs that gave warmth to the tile floors in the space. The best feature was a lovely balcony that overlooked the lush garden and the town below. The doors to the balcony were open, and Anna could feel the fresh breeze blowing gently in from the sea. The smell of the salt air was refreshing after the long flight to get here. All of the buildings in the village were painted white with blue trim. It was a charming scene, and Anna was delighted that she had picked such a lovely spot for her reunion with Charlie.

She unpacked her bag, stowing everything in the small dresser and being careful to leave room for Charlie's things when he arrived. He was not due until the next day's ferry, so she put on comfortable shoes and took a walk through the village. She saw cats everywhere and guessed that, since this was an island, the feline population would continue to grow since they were stranded here and unable to move on to other parts of the country. She also saw many burros, some being used for transportation, some carrying loads of produce to the marketplace, and some just wandering the streets with no apparent person to lead them. Feeling warm from the sun, she walked back up the hill to her apartment, where Cornelia greeted her with a glass of hand-squeezed lemonade and fresh baked cookies. Cornelia's English was excellent, and Anna sat with her, comfortably chatting for almost three hours. It was dinnertime, but Anna was beginning to get nervous about seeing Charlie and tired from her flight so, fortified with Cornelia's cookies, she decided not to go to dinner. She retired to her room, tried to read a book, and finally shut off the light and spent the night in a fitful sleep.

The next morning, Anna dressed carefully and walked down to the dock far too early for the arrival of the ferry. She found a small café and ordered coffee and a pastry to eat while she waited. When the ferry pulled up to the dock, she searched the faces of all the passengers, but did not see Charlie. She ran to the gangway and watched each departing passenger, but Charlie was not there. She didn't know whether to be worried or angry, but she was feeling both emotions as she walked back to her room. She could feel depression and anxiety reaching out for her, and she vowed to stay in control until she knew what was going on. She grabbed her computer and fired off an email to Charlie, asking him why he hadn't come as promised. His reply came an hour later. He simply said he had been delayed and would be there in four days, arriving on the morning ferry. Anna was furious. She paced around the little apartment and cursed Charlie and his life in India. She cursed herself for marrying him in the first place, and she cursed whatever it was that was keeping him away from her. She finally calmed down, and then the tears came. She cried until she was exhausted, wiped her face, blew her nose, and looked in the mirror. If Charlie could see her now, he would probably catch the next ferry to the mainland!

So she changed her rumpled clothes, put on her walking shoes again, and went into town to have lunch. As she was leaving her room, she saw Cornelia working in the garden. Cornelia noticed Anna's swollen face and red eyes and asked if something was wrong. Anna told her of Charlie's delay in coming, how upset she was, and about all the months she had been trying to resurrect her marriage. Cornelia absorbed Anna's story with empathy and gave her an encouraging hug, telling Anna that surely when Charlie came, everything would turn out all right. Anna wanted to believe her, but it was going to be a long wait until Charlie's ferry pulled up to the dock. She decided she had better find some ways to occupy her time.

She read books, swam in the pool, ate delicious seafood in town and became better acquainted with Cornelia and Dimitri. They were good listeners and very sympathetic to Anna's situation. They were almost as anxious for Charlie to arrive as Anna. One day, she rented an ATV, which seemed to be the most popular means of transportation on the island. Folegandros was a small island, with only two roads. One unpaved road ran to the north for six miles and the other ran to the south for four miles. She took the southerly road and began to explore that end of the island. Once she left the town, she found that the island was quite arid. This was a shock after the vegetation she had seen in the village. The brown, parched land reminded her of the familiar high desert ground of New Mexico, with few trees and only scrub brush and dry grass to keep the soil in place. She thought it surprising that such barren terrain could be found on an island in the Mediterranean Sea.

On day three she went to a nude beach on the north end of the island. While she didn't shed her clothing, almost everyone else had, and she found it rather disconcerting. At one point, an Italian couple that had been sunbathing entirely in the nude got up from their beach mats, put on their clothes and walked up the beach to the restaurant that catered to the nude bathers. What Anna couldn't believe was that the woman, who had donned a large straw hat and loose-fitting blouse, had neglected to put on any clothing below her waist! Anna just shook her head, laughed to herself, and told herself that she was definitely worlds away from Taos. But then she remembered that she had heard rumors of the same sort of behavior at some of the hot springs in the Taos area.

At last it was the day for Charlie to arrive, and, once again, she went to the little café to wait for him. This time, however, she could see his tall, lanky body amidst the crowd walking down the gangplank. She ran to greet him, giving him a big hug so that he almost lost his balance. He laughed at that and quickly hugged her back, grabbed his bag, and walked with her toward the apartment. Charlie had grown a beard, and Anna looked at it with disdain.

"Why the beard?" she asked.

"Just wanted a change," Charlie replied.

Other than that brief exchange, there was little conversation between them. They both felt awkward, but for totally different reasons. Anna didn't know how she would bring up the topic that was foremost on her mind, and Charlie was not anxious to tell Anna about his affair with Fariha. After unpacking his few belongings, Charlie and Anna went out to the balcony and chatted. Anna was frustrated by the small talk but was afraid to broach the subject that needed to be discussed. So she contented herself with Charlie's presence, but she was taken aback by the ways he had changed. She could smell cigarette smoke on his clothes. She decided not to say anything about the smoking, but before going to dinner, Anna told Charlie her worries about David and especially about Jordan. Charlie just smiled and shook his head.

"He's hit me up for money, too," said Charlie. "I sent him quite a bit over the last several months. I doubt if I'll ever see it again, even though he said it was a loan."

"That's what he told me, too," Anna replied. "I finally told him that I wasn't going to send him any more. He needs to learn to stand on his own two feet. I think we need to agree that we won't encourage his irresponsibility by sending him money all the time. We're just enabling him to get away with it."

"Enabling him? You sound like a psychologist!"

"I guess I learned that term from Helen. She and I have discussed David and his lack of motivation. She's been very helpful to me. Sometimes I need someone I can talk to, you know."

Charlie gave her a serious look. "Point taken," he said.

Anna continued, "I did offer to let them live in the lake house. I told them they could pay whatever rent they could afford. It seemed like a good solution at the time, but I haven't seen a dime in rent money. I guess I'm mostly worried about Jordan. He's such a great kid, and I hate watching him grow up in such an unstable home. It really troubles me!"

"I understand," Charlie replied. "But I think David will come around. He just needs more time to grow up. Some kids take longer than others. I will agree to stop sending him money, though.

I think you're right. Maybe if he gets desperate enough, he'll get his act together and get a real job."

At dinnertime they strolled into town. Anyone watching them would have thought that they were quite in love. They chatted and laughed and, at one point, Charlie took Anna's hand in his. After a delicious dinner in town, they walked back to the apartment and the tension between them was thick. Anna was thinking that, at last, Charlie would take her in his arms and make love to her just like the old days. She felt like a bride on her wedding night, nervous and expectant. When Charlie took off his shirt, Anna was stunned to see a tattoo on his left shoulder.

"You have a tattoo as well as a beard now?" she said accusingly.

"Yeah, just thought it would be fun to get it. It doesn't really mean anything."

"How long have you had it?"

"A few weeks is all."

"It just doesn't seem like something you would do. You've always been so clean cut and health conscious. I can tell that you've taken up smoking, too. I can smell it on your clothes," she scolded. "What's this all about?"

"I told you. It's not a big deal. Don't get so worked up about it," Charlie said, ending the conversation.

As Charlie continued undressing, Anna saw blood on the front of his boxer shorts.

Gasping, Anna asked, "Charlie, is that blood? What happened? Are you all right?"

Charlie was taken by surprise and stuttered a response. "Oh, it's nothing to worry about. I found a lump on my testicle and had it removed. That's why I was late getting here. I didn't tell you, because I didn't want you to worry about me."

"Should it be bloody like that?"

"Maybe it's gotten a little infected. I'll go back to the doctor when I'm back in Mumbai. Don't be such a worry wart."

"Shouldn't you have it looked at now? Waiting that long could be dangerous."

Charlie hesitated and then replied, "Actually, it won't be that long. I can only stay here for five days instead of the whole time we planned. I have to get back to India. They need me to help with an important new project they're beginning. I have to leave, because I am the only one in the company qualified to oversee the drilling of this new field. They're using experimental equipment to facilitate the entire process, and I'm the only person who knows how to operate it. I have to go so I can train the field workers to use it."

Anna was devastated by that news, and she was worried about Charlie's health. Once again, she was flooded by conflicting emotions.

She started firing questions at him. "Are you at risk of complications? Do you have cancer? Why can't they find someone else to start the project?"

"Slow down!" Charlie almost shouted. Then, calming himself, he continued, "The doctor said there isn't any cancer and I'm sure the infection will go away as soon as I take some antibiotics. You knew when you married me that I would be spending a lot of time on my job. That was the deal then and it's the deal now. Nothing has changed."

Charlie stopped for a moment, startled by how easily the lies had flown from his brain to his lips. He had changed. Anna was right. But he was too far-gone to go back now.

At that point, she let the topic drop and didn't raise it again. Anna didn't even ask Charlie about his deposits into their account being late or short on money. She just didn't have the energy. They barely spoke as they climbed into separate sides of the little bed, and the cool breeze coming off the water did little to mollify Anna's disappointment.

During his stay, Charlie left Anna each afternoon and walked down the path to the village with his cell phone to his ear. As he walked away, Anna could see the smoke from his cigarette drifting lazily in the air behind him. Most days, he would be gone for an hour or more, but on his final day in Greece, he was gone for over three hours. When Charlie returned to their apartment, Anna asked him about the calls.

Charlie told her that he was talking to his secretary, or to his co-workers in the office. Anna listened carefully, trying to detect any loopholes in his story, but she found none. The changes in Charlie were alarming, and she sensed that there was more going on than he was telling her. Then she chided herself for her distrust of Charlie and, once again, kept her thoughts of the possibility that he was seeing someone else private. Their relationship was rocky enough already. She didn't want to make things worse with unfounded accusations.

****

Charlie had intended to tell Anna everything while in Greece, but each time he looked at her, he was filled with an emotion he found it hard to identify. It wasn't remorse or regret, because he looked forward to being with Fariha again and continuing their life together. He was surprised at how easily he could spin lies to satisfy Anna. He was certain that she suspected his infidelity, but he continued down that path anyway. He knew that, by choosing Fariha over Anna, he was giving up his past life; he was also giving up his family—his daughter and sons, his grandchildren, his brothers, sister and mother. Every time he looked at Anna, his mind flashed back to the good times they had shared, the way his boys looked at him when he tucked them into bed at night, they way they all laughed about the flat tire that almost ruined their camping trip one fall, the way Anna looked wearing her apron while she fixed dinner or canned jelly—all the seemingly insignificant memories came flooding back.

He just couldn't bring himself to tell Anna what had happened in India. Perhaps it was cowardice. If so, he was beyond doing anything about it, and, when his five days were over, he walked back onto the ferry and away from Anna without looking back.

****

Anna's entire body slumped in despair as she watched the ferry pull away and eventually disappear over the horizon, taking her hopes for her marriage with it. She was positive Charlie was seeing another woman, but he wouldn't admit it and she had no proof. She felt stuck once again and was at a loss as to what to do about it.

Chapter Twenty: Bangladesh

Fariha had flown to Bangladesh at the same time that Charlie went to Greece. In the course of their phone calls while he was in Greece, she told Charlie that she needed time alone with her family, to grieve with them over the death of the granddaughter that they had never really known, and to try to mend her relationship with her father. She embellished this lie with some truth, saying that she felt like a prisoner in Mumbai, because Charlie was unable to be seen with her socially, since his co-workers knew that he had a wife in the U.S. Fariha painted a picture of the life they could have in Bangladesh. They could live handsomely on the money from his retirement account and no one would ever find him there. They could disappear together and be happy for the rest of their lives. What she didn't say was that she wanted his money, not Charlie.

Charlie agreed with Fariha's plan. He had already decided to escape India with Fariha. He was ready to be rid of the job, he was ready to be rid of his obligations to Anna and his family, and he was ready to be with Fariha to the end of his days.

Charlie returned to Mumbai and an empty flat. He had missed Fariha palpably while in Greece, and Anna's nagging and questioning had made him regret having even made the trip to see her. He could hardly wait to see Fariha again, hold her in his arms, and indulge himself in her sexual skills once more. After a little more than a week he had his finances in order and then, a month after Fariha went to see her parents, Charlie left Mumbai for Dhaka, Bangladesh. He left behind his flat with all the furnishings, he left behind his job with all its benefits and amazing salary, and he left behind the friends and co-workers with whom he had established relationships in the months that he had been there. But he left behind very few positive memories. The only memories he cherished from his time in Mumbai were the days and nights he had spent with Fariha. Charlie didn't tell anyone that he was leaving, nor did he leave any indication of where he was going. His plan was to disappear with Fariha. That way, he would never have to face his friends and family, and he certainly did not want to have to face Anna.

Charlie had never been to Bangladesh, so he was surprised when he saw the tall outlines of modern skyscrapers waiting for him on the horizon as his plane began its approach to Dhaka. He had done some research and knew that Dhaka was the eleventh largest city in the world with more than 160 million people; but, after reading about the political turmoil, low annual income, poor literacy rate and the genocide of 1971, he hadn't expected to see this modern city. When he deplaned, he found that Hazrat Shahjalal International Airport was as well equipped and sleek as any airport in which he had been. The signage was in English as well as Bengali, so he had no problem finding his way around. He followed the other passengers to the baggage area, claimed his bag, and proceeded through customs. He looked around for Fariha when he left customs, but she was not among those families waiting for their loved ones, and he just stood there for a moment wondering what his next move should be.

Just then his cell phone rang. It was Fariha telling him that she was running late and was on a bus that would arrive in 15 minutes. He was to meet her at the departing passengers lobby on the upper floor where the bus would drop her off. Charlie practically ran up the escalator and waited impatiently for Fariha's bus to arrive. He hadn't seen her in weeks, and he had missed her terribly. His time in Greece had been agonizing, and he had felt like a wanted criminal sneaking out of Mumbai.

Charlie was surprised once more as a bright red, double-decker bus, a remnant from the days of British rule, pulled up to the curb and started unloading its passengers. As Fariha came down the steps, Charlie thought he had never seen a lovelier sight. In Mumbai, Fariha had dressed in modern, western clothing. She looked stunning in the expensive wardrobe Charlie had bought her while they were there. But now she was dressed in a traditional sari. It was made from a soft, diaphanous cloth that made her look like a vision. It had brightly colored flowers and was embellished with gold thread. The loose garment could not hide the voluptuous figure that Charlie knew was beneath that cloth, and Charlie felt himself harden at the sight of her. She wore a matching scarf loosely around her head, and her shining black hair peeked discretely from beneath the scarf. She wore little makeup other than some color on her lips, and she grinned widely when she saw him staring at her.

She looked even more beautiful than Charlie remembered, and he was anxious and ready to get to their final destination at her family home in Tongi, a small township that was part of Savar, a commuter city north of Dhaka. Fariha had told Charlie during their long telephone conversations while he was in Greece that her family had left their farm in the countryside in favor of factory jobs in Dhaka. Her father and brothers made much more taka (money) by working in the factory than they had made selling their crops of rice and lentils, which were the staple of Bengali diets.

Charlie and Fariha walked slowly through the airport and down the escalator to the departing passenger pick up area. Holding hands as they waited for another red bus, they received admiring looks from people around them. Clearly, this was a couple in love that had only just now been reunited.

While they waited, Fariha cautioned Charlie, "Do not to mention my daughter to my family. My mother," she lied, "is distraught with grief and it would be better not to bring up the subject of the child and her death. Likewise," Fariha continued, " don't saying anything to my father about his having sold me when I was young. My father and I have made peace and come to a mutual understanding that the subject will never be discussed again." Charlie readily agreed, never suspecting that he had just become complicit in helping Fariha cover up the lies she had been telling him. In fact, Charlie was unaware that he was about to be the realization of her parents' dream of having Fariha marry a rich man.

As the bus wove its way slowly through the city, Charlie was once again startled by the modern buildings and indications of bustling commerce that he saw all around him. Bicycle rickshaws darted to and fro carrying families, tourists, and businessmen.

Dhaka was considered the rickshaw capital of the world, according to Fariha, who seemed proud and excited to show Charlie the city. Many people chose to travel on motor scooters, similar to those he was used to seeing in Mumbai. He caught a glimpse of a railway station, and there were many automobiles also. Charlie realized that he had become used to traffic moving in the left lane rather than the right.

If I ever do go back to the U.S., I will have some adjusting to do...but I never plan to go back there, he thought.

The plan was that he and Fariha could live very nicely on the money from his retirement account, although he had not told her exactly where the account was or how much money was in it. She mentioned that she, too, had some money saved that would help keep them in style in Bangladesh for at least a short time.

Fariha informed Charlie that Dhaka was considered one of the major financial centers of Southeast Asia, and Charlie could see that it bore some resemblance to the intensity of Wall Street that he had witnessed when visiting New York City. Fariha explained that there were many wonderful sights to see in Dhaka and the surrounding area, and, once she and Charlie had settled into their quarters at her parents' home, they would spend time seeing all that there was to see.

The bus finally arrived in Savar, where Charlie and Fariha stepped off. For the first time, Charlie noticed the humidity and heat of Bangladesh. He hadn't thought that it would be much different from Mumbai, but it felt more intense somehow. The sweat soaked his shirt in minutes, and he felt uncomfortable thinking that he would be meeting Fariha's family in such a state. Fariha didn't seem to notice either Charlie or the weather. She was frantically waving to a young man who was standing next to an ancient car. The paint had long since worn away, and Charlie wasn't even sure he could identify the make or model of the vehicle. Fariha explained that the young man was her younger brother, Akash, who had come to the bus stop to drive them to Tongi, where her family lived. Akash rushed up to them and shook Charlie's hand excitedly, nodding and speaking a heartfelt welcome in broken English. He then turned and proudly showed Charlie his car, a 1978 Ford Crown Victoria. Between Akash's broken English and Fariha's interpretation, Charlie learned that Akash had carefully saved his money from the factory for many months in order to buy the vehicle. It was his pride and joy, and was considered a symbol of great success among his peers. Charlie smiled and nodded, praising the beauty of the car and Akash's accomplishment in acquiring it. Akash put Charlie's bag in the trunk, slammed the lid, and gestured for Charlie and Fariha to get into the back seat of the car.

Charlie held his breath as they drove the distance to Tongi. Akash careened around corners and, it seemed to Charlie, came close to hitting several pedestrians along the way. Charlie nodded in agreement as Akash bragged about the speed and handling of his prized possession, Charlie closing his eyes when it seemed that they were about to crash into one of the big red buses.

As they drove, Fariha informed Charlie, "Tongi is part of the larger city of Savar. It is what you Americans would call a 'bedroom community'."

Charlie wondered where she had learned such an expression, but, before he could ask, Akash squealed up to a modest building, slammed on the brakes, and announced that they had arrived. Charlie breathed a sigh of relief and looked around. The area resembled a lower income housing district in the U.S., but the houses were very simple, one-story affairs set closely together with tiny yards. Some were built of wood, but most were built of cinder block, and none were painted. This gave the entire area a tone of gray, broken up only by huge trees and an abundance of flowers everywhere. There were flowers planted by the doorways, along the street, and in pots scattered throughout the small yards. The vegetation gave the area a colorful, joyful note. Clearly, this was the city-dwellers' attempt at bringing the tropical plants that grew in this wet region into their daily lives.

Fariha took Charlie's hand as he climbed out of the car and then ushered him into the house where her parents were waiting.

First she introduced him to her father, Nazeem. The man didn't seem inclined to shake hands, so Charlie shoved his outstretched hand into his pocket and greeted him with a courteous bow. He then turned to Fariha's mother. Her name was Chandni, and she smiled broadly at Charlie, nodding her head up and down and shaking his hand energetically. Chandni was lovely and looked quite young for her age. Charlie at first thought she must be in her 40's, given the ages of her children, but then he realized that she had probably married when she was still in her early teens and was much younger than he originally thought. Clearly, Fariha had inherited much of her beauty from her mother. When Nazeem saw Charlie looking at Chandni, he quickly grabbed Charlie's arm, turning him toward a long hallway. He said something to Fariha, and she walked down the hall, motioning Charlie to follow her. Charlie realized that he would have to be careful not to commit a faux pas by breaking any traditions or customs while he was there. He had a lot to learn, and he certainly didn't want to anger Fariha's father.

Fariha showed Charlie to a small bedroom. It was simply furnished with a small dresser, a desk and chair, and a single bed. Charlie looked at the bed, looked at Fariha and raised his eyebrows in a questioning gesture. Fariha laughed and explained that, as long as they were in her parents' home, they would not be sleeping together. Charlie was unable to hide his disappointment, and Fariha laughed again. Just then, Akash came in with Charlie's bag and hefted it onto the bed. Charlie wasn't sure where he might put his belongings, but he tried to hide his feelings and smiled a thank you at Akash. Fariha then showed Charlie the somewhat primitive bathroom across the hall and, with a meaningful smile, indicated that her bedroom was at the end of the hallway. Her parents' room, she said, was on the other side of the house, but Akash's room was between hers and Charlie's. Fariha seemed undisturbed by the sleeping arrangements, but Charlie was irritated. Fariha had forewarned him about many things, but not this.

After settling in and becoming better acquainted with Fariha's family over a traditional Bengali dinner, Charlie claimed exhaustion and went to his room. Fariha didn't even follow him to say good night, but she did blow him a kiss as he left the main room after saying good night to her family. His mind was spinning. Was Fariha planning to buy a different house for them to live in, and, if so, how soon? How far would his money go? He had several thousand dollars with him, and Fariha claimed to have some money of her own. He needed to gain access to his retirement account sooner than he had previously thought. Once he did that, his whereabouts would become known and that would cause serious complications in his life. He was in a situation that was beginning to feel out of his control. He decided that there was little he could do about it at that time, so he peeled off his sweaty clothes and climbed into the narrow bed. He wondered briefly about where he could do his laundry, and then smiled at the randomness of the thought, closed his eyes, and fell into a deep sleep.

Charlie awoke the next morning when Fariha knocked on his door and entered with a tray of steaming coffee. He didn't know what time it was, but the sun was up and the heat of the day was already pressing in on his little room. He took the cup gratefully from Fariha's hand and deliberately caressed her fingers in doing so. She just pulled her hand away and told him to dress, because they were going sightseeing.

"I have borrowed Akash's car for the day, and I don't want to waste a minute while you sleep in, you lazy man." As soon as she left his room, Charlie put the coffee cup on the desk and rustled around in his bag for a clean set of clothes. He would have to ask Fariha about a place to put his things and how he was supposed to do his laundry. He went into the small bathroom and found that it had running water and a working toilet, so that, at least, was a relief.

After cleaning up and putting on his clean clothes, Charlie found Fariha and her mother sitting in the main room having an animated conversation. Fariha seemed distressed and she was clearly trying to convince her mother of something. Chandni was stubbornly refusing to listen to Fariha's pleadings, however, and was sitting with her arms crossed over her chest and shaking her head from side to side. When Charlie entered the room, their conversation stopped abruptly. Fariha said a few brief words to her mother, went to Charlie and, taking his hand, led him through the door and out to the street where Akash's car was parked.

As Charlie climbed into the car, he realized that he was no longer wheezing as he had in Mumbai. The air away from Dhaka was clearer of pollution and his asthma had abated somewhat. He was still using the steroids the doctor had given him, but hadn't needed the rescue inhaler since he had been there. He made a mental note to see a local doctor to get his prescriptions renewed. He knew that, even in Dhaka, he would need to monitor his breathing.

They drove into Dhaka with Fariha at the wheel. She was a good driver, and Charlie was relieved to be able to relax and take in the sights. Fariha told him that Dhaka was located where the Ganges and Brahmaputra Rivers met, forming the lower Ganges delta. The soil was very rich for growing crops, but flooding was a problem. They drove by Dhaka University, where the brightest of the privileged class went to school. Charlie thought the campus was beautiful, but he wondered about all the intelligent, lower class young people who would never have a chance to receive higher education there. Next, they drove around the historic quarter that was located right on the banks of the Buringanga River. Charlie was fascinated by the ancient buildings and decided that he would have to study the rich history of this city when he had more time.

As they drove, Charlie noticed many parks and public areas, green with the lush vegetation that grew everywhere in this wet, tropical climate. Fariha pulled Akash's car to the curb at Ramna Park, and told Charlie to get out. She opened the trunk and retrieved a large basket covered with an embroidered cloth, and motioned Charlie to follow her. They walked over the thick lawn and sat on the grass under a large tree that provided refreshing shade from the heat of the noon sun. Fariha removed the cloth from the basket and began taking out its contents. First, she unfolded a small tablecloth and spread it on the grass. She then brought out several containers of food, utensils, cups and a jar containing tea. They sat in companionable silence as they ate their lunch, and then Fariha put the containers back in the basket and replaced the cloth over the top.

Charlie was still sitting, so she came to him, knelt down, and kissed him deeply. Charlie's heart melted and his body responded immediately, but they were in a public park and he knew there was nothing he could do to satisfy his need for her. Fariha then lay on the ground with her head in Charlie's lap and, as they talked, Charlie toyed with her silken black hair as it fell onto his thighs. Their conversation drifted from the sights they had seen that morning, to Fariha's family, and finally to their plans for the future. Fariha told Charlie that they would soon have a house of their own not far from her parents. Her family had located a suitable place for them to live and it was to be a gift. Charlie was relieved to think that he and Fariha would have some privacy in the not too distant future, and he relaxed, just enjoying their quiet time together. It didn't occur to him that Fariha's family did not have the money to buy a second house. Their house was modest at best and in a less than desirable neighborhood. How much money could her father and brother make toiling away in a factory every day? But then Charlie looked at Fariha and became lost in the moment and the peaceful atmosphere of the park. They remained sitting on the lawn this way for quite some time before Fariha announced that they should be going. So they rose, picked up the basket, and walked back to the car hand in hand. This was the most content Charlie had felt in several months.

Fariha continued the tour by showing Charlie the Three Leaders Mausoleum, which was strikingly modern. It reminded Charlie a bit of pictures he had seen of the Sydney Opera House, with its soaring white domes. Then, returning to Old Dhaka, they saw the Baldha Garden. Charlie was astounded by the way Dhaka went from old to new instantly, with modern skyscrapers next to ancient buildings in the city center. Finally, they drove by the headquarters of Grameenphone, the country's largest telecom operation. Charlie was impressed with the company's campus and beautifully manicured grounds. This organization obviously employed many of Dhaka's citizens. At last, Fariha said it was time to head back to Savar, because her family was expecting them for dinner.

When Charlie sat down with the family for the evening meal, with Fariha translating he thanked Chandni for the nice lunch she had sent with them on their tour of the city and also thanked Akash for the use of his car. Akash told Charlie that he expected Charlie to purchase his own vehicle before many more days passed. Charlie was somewhat taken aback by Akash's stern tone of voice, but he decided that the young man was just trying to demonstrate his manhood to his sister.

After this exchange, the mood around the table seemed to shift, and Charlie sensed tension mounting. Finally, Nazeem stood, spoke in broken English and stated that the time had come for Charlie and Fariha to wed. The house they were going to move into was a wedding gift. It would bring shame on their family if Fariha were not married to the man who had obviously been living with her for the past several months. They were no longer in Mumbai, and the rules were different in Bangladesh. Nazeem finished his statement, nodded once at Charlie, and sat down firmly in his chair at the head of the table.

Chapter Twenty-One: The Wedding

Charlie was stunned, but before he could say anything, Fariha began translating for Chandni who excitedly said that the wedding was only two days away and had been in the planning stages for weeks. All the preparations were in place, Fariha's wardrobe was ready, friends and family from near and far had already been invited, and the food was being prepared as they spoke. Charlie just nodded dumbly and tried to smile, but Fariha could see that there was no joy in his eyes. They all finished the meal in silence, and at last Charlie excused himself, saying that he was tired from the long day of sightseeing and needed to relax in his room.

Fariha followed him down the hall and entered his room behind him. Charlie knew that Fariha had been aware of her family's plan all along and had not said anything to him about it, and he was angry. Fariha could see his mood in the set of his jaw and the intensity of his posture, so she went to him and put her arms around his neck, moved in as close as she could, and gave him a lingering kiss. Charlie immediately responded, and, in the same instant, he realized that if he were ever to have Fariha as his own, marrying her was the only way he could accomplish it. He relaxed as she began to massage his shoulders and snuggle up to his neck, and all logic and reason began to fade away at her touch. At last he nodded, kissed her soundly, and told her that he would marry her as planned. Fariha sighed in relief that her plan had worked, kissed him once more, and slowly backed out of his room, confident that Charlie was hers and her goal had been accomplished. Soon she would be a wealthy woman, married to a decent man. She had successfully escaped the life to which she thought she had been doomed. *So much for destiny,* she thought. *Surely one makes one's own destiny through cleverness and perseverance*
.

When he awoke in the morning, Charlie found Fariha and Chandni busily talking about the wedding ceremony and he was being ignored for the most part. He decided to go for a walk despite the heat and humidity. Perhaps he could get a look at this house that Fariha's family was giving them. He was curious to see what it was like. He headed in the direction of the home, and found it a few blocks away. It was almost identical to the one in which Chandni, Nazeem and Akash lived. He supposed it would do, at least for the time being, but it was hardly as nice as the places to which he had grown accustomed. Once he got his hands on his money, he could afford to buy them a much nicer home, and one in a better neighborhood. As he looked around, he realized that he thought the area was suitable for Fariha's family, but that he and Fariha would not be happy living here. He began to walk quickly back to Fariha's house and went straight to his room and his computer.

Despite the fact that he would be giving his location away, he emailed his former company and asked that they forward him whatever paperwork was necessary to access the money in his retirement account. He knew that this process might take several weeks, and he hoped that the nest egg Fariha claimed to have, along with the few thousands he had brought with him, would keep them until he could get his hands on his own funds. In the meantime, he would have to go along with the wedding plans and become Fariha's husband. Once that happened, neither her family nor Fariha herself could refuse to allow him to sleep with her. He had been deprived of her for too long…it had been almost two months now…and if getting married were the means to that end, he would get married. What could be the harm? His marriage to Anna was over long ago, except for the paperwork. Besides, he never planned to go back to the U.S., so who was to know and who was there to care? He was starting a new life in a new country with a new woman. This is what he wanted and his dreams were about to be realized. He didn't know what a Muslim marriage ceremony was like, but he would try his best to enjoy every minute of it. And he knew for sure that he would enjoy his life with Fariha afterward.

The next two days were a whirlwind of preparations and instructions. Charlie never dreamed that a wedding could be so complicated! He thought back to the simple ceremony he had shared with Anna. For a few moments he became wistful as he remembered how happy they had been back then. He wasn't sure where or when things had started to change, but he knew that his being away so much had been part of the problem. He enjoyed sex and felt justified in filling the empty time with the pleasure of other women. Toward the end, it seemed to Charlie, Anna had only wanted him around to do chores and fit into her lifestyle. She didn't value his career and reputation in the oil industry, as Fariha did. She didn't make him feel important, as Fariha did. She only seemed to enjoy the life that his paychecks provided for her, and she was quite content with her life without him. He reasoned that she really didn't need him at all. Their sons were grown men with lives of their own, despite the fact that David was still asking for money up until the time Charlie left India. Anna would be just as well off without him, he reasoned. He would continue to send her money each month, and she would have no need to know where he was living or that he was married to someone else. His conscience clear, Charlie allowed himself to be moved through the pre-nuptial activities without protest. He even began to enjoy being the center of attention, in Fariha's shadow, of course.

Nazeem told Charlie in no uncertain terms that it was time for him to leave Fariha's home and live in the new house on his own. Even though Charlie had no family to represent him in the upcoming ceremonies, Nazeem had recruited several friends who would act as Charlie's family and would live with him in the house that would become Charlie and Fariha's new home once the wedding was completed. Once again, Charlie felt that he was in no position to argue, so he acquiesced and moved his belongings into the other house. The men that Nazeem had assigned to be Charlie's "family" spoke no English and seemed to be less than friendly, so Charlie stayed to himself as much as possible.

Charlie learned quickly that the wedding was not just a one-day affair. It would take place over several days, with many different rituals and ceremonies. Despite the circumstances of Fariha and Charlie's relationship, this wedding would include almost all of the traditional steps. Because the situation did not quite fit with tradition, there had been no *Ghotoks*, or matchmakers, involved. Likewise, the *Paka-dekha* also had not occurred. Normally, this event involved both sets of parents meeting to set the wedding date and agree to any demands made by the bride's parents to ensure that the bride's future would be assured. Fariha's parents were quite certain that Charlie's wealth would ensure Fariha's future, and Charlie's parents were not available, so they concluded that skipping this tradition was allowable.

Thus it was that Charlie and Fariha's engagement began, as any arranged marriage was to begin, with an announcement of formal consent accompanied by trumpeting on a conch shell. There was a large crowd of people, mostly women, present for the ceremony. Following the trumpeting sound, the elder women present began making a sound that was strange to Charlie's ears.

Fariha explained, "This ceremony normally takes place six to eighteen months before the wedding. Clearly, that time has long past, but it is acceptable to announce the marriage plans even up to the day of the wedding, so it is all right. The women, who must be married, are making a sound called *jululudhvanis* as a part of the traditional announcement. It is something they do with their tongues in the back of their throats. I know it sounds strange, but it is a very important part of this ceremony, Charlie, so just smile and nod as if you're enjoying it."

So Charlie smiled and nodded. As a matter of fact, Charlie smiled and nodded through each of the ceremonies that took place over the next several days. He felt as if he were taking part in some kind of theatrical drama, having been cast in the lead role but never having seen the script. He was overwhelmed and tired, so he just followed whatever directions Fariha or her family gave him, nodding and smiling at every opportunity.

Next came the Turmeric ceremony, which was so foreign to Charlie that he almost told Fariha the entire wedding should be called off. But he didn't say that; instead, he allowed himself to be guided through the steps of this very elaborate and unfamiliar ritual. Called the *gaye halud* ceremony, this one involved Charlie by himself, rather than with Fariha. Charlie's "family" took a Rohu fish, dressed as a bride, along with Fariha's wedding dress and assorted sweets to Fariha at her house. Charlie was not allowed to go with them, but, while they were gone, a group of women came to him and applied turmeric paste to his face and hands. An interpreter told him that the same was being done to Fariha. The paste was intended to make their skin soft. After they left, Charlie looked in a mirror and was alarmed to see that the turmeric had turned him a ghastly shade of yellow! He assumed that it would have the same effect on Fariha. With hopes high, he went to the bathroom and showered vigorously.

When the day arrived for the wedding, Charlie was picked up in a car and accompanied to Fariha's home by several men. Charlie was wearing the best suit he was able to find in Dhaka, but the other men were dressed in traditional Bengali attire, which made Charlie feel somewhat out of place. Once they arrived at Fariha's home, Chandni came out and washed the wheels of the car, while the other women welcomed him with the sound of conch shells and the same ululations Charlie had heard previously.

Next, to his surprise, Charlie was clothed in traditional clothing. His wedding attire included a silk shawl, or *jore,* and *topor,* a headdress made of pith and zari. From Nazeem's broken English and gestures, Charlie understood that he was to wear this attire during all of the remaining wedding ceremonies and rituals. The actual ceremony began with the Kabin ceremony of registering the bride and groom and presenting them to the family and community. After that, Charlie was led through a number of rituals that he neither understood nor wanted to participate in. He was weary of all the ceremonies and just wanted to take Fariha to their home. He didn't protest, however, but allowed himself to be guided through each phase of the wedding without enthusiasm. Each ensuing ceremony included elaborate dress, especially for Fariha, who wore several beautiful white saris accented in gold with her arms and body adorned with gold jewelry. Charlie wondered where all the gold came from. If Fariha's family had all this gold, why were they living in near poverty in a questionable part of the city? He was certain that he would never completely understand her culture and religious practices.

There was much gift giving back and forth, and, finally, Charlie was told to present Fariha with a silver tray on which was another beautiful sari and assorted pieces of jewelry. This, Charlie understood, symbolized that he was now to take care of Fariha. He wasn't certain, but he thought that they were finally married at last.

Charlie found out quickly, however, that there was still one more ceremony to be completed. *Bou Bhaat* was a huge reception with hundreds of people in attendance. Once again, Charlie wondered how Fariha's family could afford all of this luxury and splendor, but he went along with each action that was demanded of him and, at last, he was officially married to Fariha. He breathed a sigh of relief and waited for the time when they could be alone together at last.

Finally, Charlie and Fariha went to their new home, which had been furnished in a manner similar to her family's dwelling. After living in Fariha's house for so long, Charlie felt comfortable there and was glad that her family had provided them with a private place in which to live. When dusk fell on their first night together, Charlie gently led Fariha into their new bedroom. To his surprise, the bed was covered with flowers. He found it a bit disturbing to think that Fariha's family and other people had been in their bedroom without his knowledge. Putting those feelings aside, Charlie made sweet, passionate love to Fariha. He had waited so long that it was difficult for him to hold back, but each time he looked into her eyes, he knew once again how much he loved and cherished her. She was now his to make love to wherever and whenever he wanted. She was his forever now, and he vowed to treat her like a queen.

Fariha enjoyed their lovemaking. Charlie was skilled and satisfied her own need as much as his. She was content and felt that she could live out her remaining days with Charlie. He would be an excellent provider. He had promised her that his wealth was vast and would be all hers. Her plan had come to completion and she was now a new woman. And Charlie was hers.

Chapter Twenty-Two: Disappearance

When Anna returned from Greece, it was fall and Taos was beginning to shift into winter mode. The aspen trees were turning golden as they stood on the mountainside amidst the green pines. The air was cold at night and remained chilly all day. There seemed to be a growing atmosphere of excitement throughout the town. Soon the winter tourists would be arriving to ski Taos Mountain, and the nearby slopes of Angle Fire and Red River. The town would be bustling with shoppers looking for unique gifts to take home to their loved ones. Merchants were already displaying Christmas trees in their shop windows and hanging garlands and twinkle lights around their stores. Signs announced that merchandise was on sale, despite the fact that the prices remained the same as before. And, as always, the odors from the restaurants announced the flavors of the season. Posolé was Anna's favorite. She loved the stew made with pork and hominy-like corn, flavored with red chilé. Tamales were standard holiday fare, and there would also be biscochitos everywhere. Anna loved baking the cookies, flavored with anise and sprinkled with cinnamon sugar, that were always a favorite around the holidays.

The festive atmosphere began to lift Anna's spirits. She had spent hours talking to Helen over their knitting and glasses of wine. It made her feel better to have a friend to confide in. Helen didn't chide her for her misgivings about Charlie. In fact, she seemed to agree that things appeared to be amiss. She encouraged Anna to get on with her own life and see how things played out.

"Sitting around the house feeling depressed, frightened and angry is not doing you any good and is not changing the situation," Helen said. "I'm not sure there is anything you can do right now."

Anna agreed and set her resolve to get on with her life. She planned out all the Christmas gifts she would buy or make for her family. She bought lovely silver and turquoise jewelry for Julie and Clare. She even found a pretty necklace to give to Valerie. She finished knitting a sweater that she had started for Bradley. It was his favorite color and soft wool that would keep him warm during the cold midwestern winter. She also found a silly hat with ear warmers that made her laugh. She put that in the package with Bradley's sweater. For David she bought a hand-tooled leather belt with a silver buckle. As she shopped, she realized that she hardly knew David any more, and she resolved to remedy that situation as soon as she was able.

Anna had the most fun making and shopping for the gifts to give her grandchildren. She bought toys and games for the younger ones, CDs and DVDs for the teenagers, and she knitted sweaters for each of them. For each family she made a special gift. She chose nine photos of each family, picking out those that showed each person doing something interesting or funny. Each photo brought back memories of good times she had shared with her family. Her heart was full of love as she framed each set of photos in a collage. She hoped that these projects brought her loved ones as much pleasure as they had brought her while making them.

Shopping, making, wrapping and mailing all of the gifts kept her busy for several weeks, and, by the time her Christmas preparations were complete, the snow had begun to cover the town. Snow on the adobé buildings made Taos look like a picture postcard. Everything seemed clean and fresh. Anna loved walking from her home into town and just strolling through the shops and around the plaza. She loved the sounds of happy people, excited about something special they found in a store; she loved the smells of fresh-baked pastries, cookies and dishes spiced with red or green chilé; she loved the clean mountain air of her town. This had become her town, she realized, and she vowed never to leave Taos. This was home.

Anna spent many hours in her weaving studio making a special rug for Helen and Lee. They had been good friends and her main support as she fretted about her husband and her family. She had brought them small gifts from Peru and Greece, but she wanted to do something especially nice for them for Christmas. As she wove, the rhythm of the shuttle was calming. She kept a fire going, sipped a glass of wine, and watched as her animals slept peacefully nearby. Anna felt an unusual contentment creeping into the chaos that usually filled her mind. This loom was her therapy.

There was one more gift that Anna wanted to buy, but she hadn't found just the right thing yet. It was for Charlie, and needed to be perfect. After searching several stores from top to bottom, she wandered into a jewelry store in which she hadn't been before. It was small and quaint. The shelves were a bit dusty and the ancient wooden floor creaked when she took a step. The owner might have come straight from the pages of a Charles Dickens' novel. Old and stooped, he sported a long, white beard beneath a large nose and a balding head. He looked up at her with sparkling eyes, and Anna immediately thought of Santa Claus.

She greeted him and said, "I'm just looking, thank you. I need a Christmas gift for my husband."

"I have just the thing!" the old man replied, leading her toward the rear of the store.

He stood on tiptoe and reached up to the top shelf, retrieving a dark blue velvet box. Snapping the lid open, he held it up to the light and Anna's breath caught. The old man was right! This was the perfect gift for Charlie. It was beautiful and it was masculine. The box held a silver bracelet, unique from any she had ever seen. It was heavy and about one inch wide. On each side were small braids of silver, next to these were strips of black leather woven together like a rope, and in the center was a plain band of gold. The bracelet shone in the light and, when she took it from the box and slipped it on her wrist, it seemed to radiate warmth all the way up her arm. Without even asking the price, Anna told the shopkeeper that she would take it. He smiled knowingly and hobbled up to the front where an ancient cash register guarded the front door. Anna paid the price without protest and left the shop with her prize, hearing the bell on the shop door jingle as she left. She smiled victoriously, like this had been an almost otherworldly experience. Picking up her pace, she headed for home, welcoming the sound of her boots as they mushed through the slushy snow.

That night, by the light of a warm fire, Anna took the bracelet out of the velvet box, put it on her arm, and watched the firelight dance on the shiny metal. Taking it off, she kissed it tenderly and placed it back in its box with loving care. In the morning, she would wrap it and send it on its way to India. She hoped that Charlie would feel the love emanating from the bracelet when he put it on his own wrist. She went to bed with a hopeful heart.

The first of December arrived and Anna's money from Charlie had not been deposited in the bank. She had all those bills to pay, and she began to panic. Calming herself, she reasoned that the money had been late before. Charlie was probably out in the field, unable to wire the money at the usual time. She went to the credit union and withdrew enough from her savings to cover their expenses and groceries for herself and the animals. As she did this, she realized that she hadn't heard from Charlie in several weeks, and worry began to gnaw at her stomach. Still she told herself that this had happened in the past. Surely there was nothing untoward going on.

Sure enough, a week later, she found that money had been wired into her account. It was not as much as usual, which was a concern, but it was enough to pay back most of what she had borrowed from savings. She still hadn't heard from Charlie, but, since he had wired the money, he must be all right. She hadn't spoken with him since he left Greece, and she wondered about his health. She had sent him several emails over the past few weeks, but he had not responded. Nor had he answered his phone the few times she had tried to call. This was very concerning. She resolved that, if she didn't hear from him by weeks' end, she would contact his company. She knew that, if she did so, Charlie would be very angry with her for treating him like an errant child. But as her worry grew, she increasingly felt the need to take some sort of action.

Finally, she called Charlie's company, but the person she spoke with said that she had no information about Charlie. Anna wasn't sure that he understood the urgency of the situation, so she decided to call Rajeesh. Surely he would have seen and talked to Charlie recently.

It took several days to get in touch with Rajeesh, who said, "I have not seen Mr. Charlie in weeks. I'm assigned to another person as driver. I will ask questions and get back to you, Mrs. Charlie."

Anna tried to wait patiently for Rajeesh's return call, but it was difficult. Her impatience grew, and with it her concern about Charlie and her anger with him. How could he do this to her? She called his brother and his mother. Neither of them had heard from him for over a month. She talked to Bradley, who had no idea what was going on. When she called David, he seemed nervous. Anna felt that he was hiding something, but he denied having talked to his father and said he had no idea if there was a problem or not. Finally, in desperation, she called some of Charlie's former co-workers in Houston to see if they were aware of what Charlie was doing. They, too, claimed not to have heard from Charlie in months.

Anna had spent enough time in Mumbai to know that, despite its modern appearance, it was still a hostile and dangerous environment. She let her imagination go wild, picturing Charlie lying injured next to a gas rig while the workers gathered around and watched him die. She pictured him lying in a hospital bed, unable to communicate with the medical workers who did not know who he was or where he came from. And, finally, she pictured him holding another woman in his arms. The woman was without shape or substance, but Anna could sense her there, stealing Charlie's heart as she leaned into him. These images came to her at all times of the day and night, and Anna truly believed that she was going mad.

In desperation, she even called the Taos police to report Charlie missing. The officer who answered the call had a hard time hiding his laughter after she explained her reason for calling. "I'm sorry, m'am," he said. "We cannot follow up on a missing person's report in Taos if the missing person is in India!" Anna became irate. She was on the edge of despair and this desk cop was barely concealing his amusement at her situation. Her temper exploded and she cursed at the policeman, telling him that if something bad happened to Charlie she would sue him and the Taos Police Department. He apologized meekly, but insisted there was nothing he could do. His apology didn't mollify Anna in the least, and she called him "worthless" and "uncaring" and hung up the phone. After Anna hung up, she felt foolish for having made the call. Perhaps she shouldn't have lost her temper, but she was at wit's end and had run out of ideas.

To add to the feelings of madness creeping in on her, one night she had a strange vision. She was not asleep, but was wide-awake with her eyes open. She saw Charlie beside her bed. He was dressed in his favorite, ratty, old sweatshirt and he was smiling at her. Her breath caught in her throat and she blinked her eyes. When she opened them, Charlie was gone and her room was lit only by the moonlight coming through her window. She didn't understand. She was not a mystic. She had never had a vision before. Had she even seen what she thought she saw? Was this God's way of letting her know that Charlie was alive and well? Did the smile mean that he was happy? Did he want to come home but was unable for some reason? She was baffled. Unable to get to sleep, Anna got up, went to the kitchen, and fixed herself a glass of wine. She sat at the kitchen table for the rest of the night, sipping her wine and thinking back over all that had been going on. Bella, hearing Anna get out of bed, came and sat beside her. Anna stroked the dog's soft fur and puzzled over what had happened.

Then she suffered another devastating blow. Charlie's health insurance company sent a statement that had been returned to them marked "addressee unknown" and they had forwarded it to Anna's address. She opened it with trembling fingers, fearing that he had been injured on the job…or worse. When she read the words describing the procedure that had been done, she felt her chest tighten. Charlie had been to a clinic in China for a vasectomy reversal. She was stunned. She checked the date of the procedure and realized that it was done just before Charlie met her in Greece. *That explains the blood on his shorts and the so-called infection,* she thought. She was more than just angry. She wanted to smash something, put a hole in the wall with her fist, or throw something through a window. Charlie had lied to her the entire time they were together. Then she scolded herself for being so trusting. Had she closed her eyes to the truth, blindly hoping that her fears weren't true? *If I ever get my hands on Charlie I'll kill him!* she swore.

By then it was nearing Christmas and Helen and Lee, in their concern for Anna, asked if she would like to accompany them to the Taos Pueblo for Christmas Eve.

"It's an old Taos tradition," Lee said. "For days prior to Christmas, you will hear people around town greeting each other, saying, 'See you at the Pueblo'. Actually, it is so crowded that you often do not see anyone you recognize, because, in addition to the townspeople and the puebloans, many tourists come to watch the ceremony."

Anna considered their offer. She had been a nervous wreck for weeks. Could she take time away from her troubles to enjoy the native culture? Finally, she told them she would go with them. Early on Christmas Eve afternoon, the three of them piled into Lee's Suburban to drive to the pueblo. They were bundled from head to toe in headgear, earmuffs, gloves, down parkas, ski pants, and snow boots. Lee had warned Anna that they were in for a cold night in the open air. They had all come prepared.

As they drove, Lee explained the history of the area and the ceremony itself to Anna. "The Taos Indians were originally called the Red Willow People," he explained. "Their religion was a form of pantheism, a belief that all things, both animate and inanimate are spiritual in nature. When the Spanish came in the 17th century, they imposed Catholicism on the Native people. They were forced to attend Catholic church services and take on Spanish surnames in place of their Native American names. Eventually, the Red Willow People staged the Pueblo Revolt and drove the Spanish from New Mexico. The Spanish influence remains to this day, however, as the Native people still use the Spanish surnames and practice both Roman Catholic Christianity and their Native religion. This dual faith became the focus of the Christmas Eve celebration that we are going to see tonight."

Anna began to put her situation at home aside for a few hours and looked forward to the events for which they were headed. The big vehicle lurched over the rutted road to the pueblo and Anna could see that, despite their early start, many people had arrived before them. They exited the car and joined hundreds of other Anglos and Hispanics who waited outside the small chapel on one side of the huge pueblo plaza. The Red Willow People were holding a Catholic mass inside the little building. The crowd was mostly silent and Anna could hear the faint murmurings of the vespers, blessings and prayers being said and sung inside. Occasionally, a cough, or someone stomping his boots on the slushy ground to get the circulation going in his toes broke the silence. The night was dark early, being the winter solstice, and the air was wet and cold from the recent snow.

Anna then saw men from the pueblo moving around the area lighting huge bonfires built on log structures similar to log cabins. Some of the smaller fires were only six feet high, but the larger fires reached twenty feet or more. Soon the smoke from the fires was overpowering, and people began to cough, their eyes watering and tears running down their faces. Anna jumped when she suddenly heard a gunshot. Armed pueblo men pushed through the crowd firing rifles into the night sky. They cleared a wide path as they walked in a meandering pattern through the visiting crowd. That is when the procession began. First came a priest, who blessed all the people attending the ceremony. Six men carrying a litter on which was a large statue of the Virgin Mary followed him. Next, a group of carolers paraded by singing familiar Catholic Christmas hymns. Finally, dancers dressed in traditional Native dress led the parishioners from the chapel through the plaza to the light of the bonfires. Anna strained her eyes to see the wonder of the procession as it passed by, but she was careful not to move too far away from the warmth of the nearest bonfire, even though it was shooting out sparks and embers that could easily burn holes in her parka.

As the crowd dispersed, Anna noticed some of the visitors being greeted by pueblo people who had invited them into their homes for a traditional Christmas Eve supper of posolé or chilé. Helen, Lee and Anna were not so fortunate as to know any of the

Native people, so they trudged through the slush back to their car. Lee turned the heater on high and they slowly drove along the rutted road with the rest of the crowd back toward Taos.

This night would be a memory Anna would cherish for a long time. It was a beautiful evening steeped in ancient tradition and had provided her with a much-needed respite from the stress of her life. She was grateful to Helen and Lee for encouraging her to attend.

A few days later Rajeesh called. Anna trembled as he told her what he had learned. Charlie had failed to come to work over a month ago. When people at his office had become concerned, they began looking for him, but were unable to find him anywhere. He had not paid the rent on the flat for over three months, so the owner of the building had sold all the furnishings and contents to make up for the unpaid rent. Charlie had disappeared without leaving a trace of where he was going. Rajeesh assured Anna that Charlie's co-workers had called all the hospitals and morgues in Mumbai. Charlie was not dead or injured. He was gone.

Anna was at a loss. She didn't know whom else to call, but finally she realized that Charlie, being an American citizen who had gone missing, might be a concern to the American Consulate. She placed a call to them and, after being sent from one person to another and still another yet, she spoke with a young woman who seemed to understand her concern for her husband. She promised to look into the situation and get back to Anna as quickly as possible.

What if Anna never found Charlie? What if his disappearance remained one of those unsolved mysteries seen on television? She couldn't wrap her mind around how she had come to be in this situation. Enough time had passed that all of her bills were due again, and there was no money to pay them. Even her savings account would not cover all of their expenses. Anna could think of no other recourse, so she tried to put her anxiety aside, took some extra medication, drank some extra wine, and determined to continue her life as best she could.

By selling some of her precious collection of South American antiquities, she made her house payment and the payment on Charlie's mother's house. David had sent some money for rent on the lake house, but, rather than making that payment, she used the rent money to buy food. She did not pay on the land they had purchased. She knew that, if this pattern were to continue, she was going to lose everything before too long, but she was desperate and didn't know what else she could do.

Finally the woman from the Consulate called. Her words were chilling to Anna's heart: "You realize, don't you, that if your husband does not wish to be found, I cannot tell you where he is."

The next day, she received the box hat had contained Charlie's Christmas bracelet back in the mail marked "Addressee Unknown". That was the final blow. Anna knew that Charlie had deserted her and she was entirely on her own. In some ways, this knowledge was freeing. As much as it hurt, at least Anna knew where she stood. Now she wouldn't needlessly wait around for word that wouldn't come or money that would not be deposited. She was on her own and would have to figure out how to survive. There was no one who would come to her rescue.

Chapter Twenty-Three: Depression

The weeks that followed brought one difficult decision after another. Her money was running out at a frightening rate. She had sold one more piece of weaving, but that bit of income made almost no dent in the mounting stack of bills she needed to pay. She sold the rest of her antiques and art collection, but it brought in very little. She stopped paying the mortgage on her house and Grace's new home. She called Grace to explain, and Grace seemed to understand her predicament, although she was worried about Charlie and at a loss as to where she was going to live next. Anna made no more payments on the land they had purchased for their retirement home. She did continue making the payments on the lake house, however, and demanded that David be forthcoming with some rent money. The payments on the lake house were the least of any of their bills, and, if worse came to worse, she could move back there and try to find a job. She was in survival mode, she was hurt, and she was angry. If David took the brunt of her mood, that was too bad.

She called him, saying, "David, I can't afford to let you stay in the lake house without paying any rent. In fact, I may have to move back there myself. Either send me what you owe or get ready to move out!"

David's reply was predictable. "Sure, Mom. I'll send some money as soon as I can. Just hold your horses."

When she hung up, Anna knew that no money would arrive from David.

Anna slowly sank into a deep depression. She fought it as hard as she could, but her situation seemed hopeless and her medication didn't help. She spent days in the house, but didn't touch her loom. She took care of Bella and Simba, but barely took care of herself. She ate only a few crackers with cheese each day, drank coffee, and didn't even dress most days. She had a gun, and it crossed her mind to use it to put an end to her troubles. This thought frightened her, so she called Helen, who came over immediately. As they talked, Helen felt that she wasn't getting through to Anna, but Anna was listening and absorbing more than Helen realized. The one phrase that hit home for Anna was when Helen said, "You know, Anna, suicide is a permanent solution to a temporary problem."

Somehow that resonated with Anna, and, through the fog of her hopelessness, she began thinking about what she had to live for. First came Jordan. She still wanted to somehow give her grandson a better life. And what about Bradley and his family? Bradley had been a good son to her and had made a nice life for himself, Julie and the boys. He didn't deserve to have to deal with a messy death. Even though they didn't talk often, Clare would be devastated if Anna ended her life. Even Charlie's mother and brother would grieve for her. There were Helen and Lee, who had stood by her, counseled her, and loved her ever since the first day they met. She thought about all the friends she had made in El Rito at the weaving school, as well as her friends in Taos. Then she looked at Bella, who was lying at her feet. What would happen to her and Simba? She saw her loom sitting in the other room. It was gathering dust, but it had provided her with hours of pleasure as her talent created beautiful weavings. Outside her window she saw her garden. How she enjoyed pruning and babying the plants along, and how rewarding it was when they finally bore their bounty of vegetables!

She recognized how important all these things were to her, and slowly the fog in her brain began to lift. She saw that she had made a life for herself. Charlie hadn't even been a part of that. She began to see herself in a new light: as a capable, independent, smart woman whom many people loved. It took more than a week to recover, but at last the depression was beaten down and she was able to move forward.

She found work at a local art gallery, but that ended abruptly when the owner's daughter came home from college without a job and her mother made her a partner in the gallery. Desperate, Anna finally landed a job at a souvenir shop on the plaza. The shop primarily sold cheap tourist junk and the inventory met with Anna's disapproval, but the owner was kind and easy-going. She enjoyed chatting with the tourists who came in, and loved telling them about the area and the various attractions they might want to see. After a few weeks of working there, she decided it wasn't so bad, and at least she could put food on her table and dog food in Bella's bowl.

She sent letters, emails, and made phone calls to her mortgage company trying to get them to reduce her house payment until she could get money from Charlie somehow, but they were unrelenting in their demands. She knew that she was going to lose her house before this was over, and it made her even more angry and depressed. She cursed Charlie, wherever he was, with her first breath each morning and her last breath each night.

Chapter Twenty-Four: The Truth

Anna walked slowly away from the mailbox with the latest stack of bills dunning her for money. She entered her kitchen through the back door and dropped the mail on the counter. Going to the coffee pot, she poured herself a cup, even though it was like sludge left over from breakfast. She needed the buzz from the caffeine to make it though opening the mail. She opened third and fourth notices that her various mortgages were due, along with a note from the bank saying that they were going to put the mountain property into foreclosure.

The next envelope was from her cell phone carrier, and she hesitated to even open it. But when she did, she was surprised to see that the bill was in Charlie's name and was for his cell phone number, not hers. Apparently they couldn't find him either. She started to put the bill in the stack that was headed for the trash when she saw a series of numbers repeated on the bill. Charlie had called the same number many times over a few days' time. When she checked the dates, she realized that these were the calls he had made while they were in Greece. The dates matched exactly. From the looks of the number he was calling, it was an international call, but she could not tell where. She only knew that the numbers were quite different from the ones she used to call Rajeesh and Charlie's company in India. She knew that she could find the location by checking the number with the telephone company, but she could do that later. At that moment, she just wanted to know who Charlie had been calling.

With trembling fingers, she dialed the number. At first she thought the phone was dead or the call was not going through. Finally, after a series of clicks and static, she heard ringing on the other end of the line. After several rings, a woman answered, saying, "Hello. Who is this?"

"Let me speak to Charlie," Anna demanded.

She could sense the woman hesitating, heard a male voice in the background, and then Charlie's voice saying into the phone, "Who is this?"

Anna lost her voice for a moment. She was shaking all over. She had found him! She didn't know where he was, but she could figure that out. Finally she said, "It's Anna. Where are you?"

Charlie's answer was brief. "I can't believe you found me! I can't talk now. Please, just leave me alone." Then he hung up the phone.

Anna stared at the phone in disbelief and, after a few seconds, pushed the "end" button. She didn't know whether to be relieved that Charlie was alive or murderously angry that he was alive...and living with a woman...and still wouldn't tell her where he was. She sank to the floor, spilling her coffee all over the unopened mail on the counter, and began to cry softly. Her anguish increased with each new breath and she was sobbing uncontrollably when she heard a soft knock on her back door.

Helen peeked through the window and saw Anna on the floor. She took in the spilled coffee and Anna's tear-stained face in one glance and let herself into the kitchen, going quickly to Anna and asking if she were all right. Anna just gulped back more tears and tried to catch her breath. Asking again if Anna was okay, Helen heard Anna mumble the word "no". She helped Anna to her feet and over to a stool at the counter, made sure she was steady, and ran some water into a glass. After placing the glass in front of Anna, Helen sat on one of the stools and just waited for Anna to speak. Clearly, whatever was wrong was emotional, not physical, and Helen would wait all day if necessary to find out what was going on.

Finally Anna was calm enough to speak. She haltingly told Helen what had taken place with the mobile phone bill and her subsequent call to the mysterious number. Helen did not question her when Anna said she recognized Charlie's voice on the telephone, nor did she disagree with Anna's conclusion that Charlie was with another woman somewhere in the world. She encouraged Anna to take some time to get herself pulled together and then to come up with a plan. Did she want to find Charlie? That would mean finding out the details of what could be a devastating truth. Did she want to just let him go? That would mean giving up, and Anna was not one to give up on anything. Did she want a divorce? Clearly, Charlie did not want to be her husband any more. Would a divorce free Anna from her emotional ties to Charlie, or would it make her life more complicated? If Charlie was unwilling to continue supporting Anna, how was she going to survive? Clearly, she had many issues to consider, and she realized that she needed to think things through thoroughly when her head was clear and she was less emotional. When she left, Helen gave Anna a huge bear hug and told her to come over that evening to talk things through if she wanted to. Anna thanked her and watched her walk down the sidewalk toward her own home. Right at that moment, it felt as if Helen was the only line left to grasp on the sinking ship that was her life.

She took Bella for a long walk and thought over her options. Thoughts were tumbling in her head. *Clearly, Charlie doesn't want to be married to me any more, so maybe a divorce is the best course of action. If I ask for a large settlement from him, I could be set financially and perhaps could avoid losing my home and Charlie's mother's house. Do I still love Charlie after what he has done? Can I just dismiss all those years of marriage as easily as he has? Could Charlie really do this to me? To his mother? Does he even realize all the consequences of his actions? Is he willing to throw away his entire family--children, grandchildren, siblings--for some woman he barely knows?*

As she walked, these questions kept circling around in her mind, and she began to feel even more confused. *What I need to do,* she decided, *is have an actual conversation with Charlie. I need to know for myself exactly what is going on, and only Charlie can give me that information.* She picked up her stride and urged Bella to walk faster as they made their way back home. The first step of her plan was clear to her now.

Once she got inside and gave Bella a fresh bowl of water, Anna sat down at her computer and wrote Charlie a long e-mail. She had e-mailed him before, of course, and he hadn't answered. But now things were different. She had found him, even if she didn't know exactly where he was. She wouldn't let him know that, of course. She wanted him to think that he was no longer safe from being pursued. She posed to him all the questions she had been asking herself during her walk. She told him that she was about to lose her home and about his mother's home going into foreclosure as well. She told him stories about their children and the grandchildren, hoping that his heart would melt when he thought about those little ones. She counted on his love of children to change his mind. Finally, she resorted to begging. She begged Charlie to come home and talk things over, to give their marriage another chance, to try to work things out. She told him that she still loved him and wanted to reconcile, no matter what he might have done. She read the e-mail over and hit "send". There was nothing else she could do now. She just had to wait to see how Charlie would respond, if he ever did.

Chapter Twenty-Five: Charlie's Doubts

Meanwhile, in Bangladesh, things were becoming frayed at the edges in Charlie's life with Fariha. When Anna's telephone call came, Fariha went berserk. She screamed and yelled at Charlie, accusing him of trying to get back together with Anna. If he hadn't told her where he was, how else could she have found out? Charlie denied having any communication with Anna since he and Anna had been together in Greece, but Fariha was frightened that she might lose Charlie and decided that she needed to tighten the reins on him. She demanded that he give her all the details of his finances. Charlie reluctantly did so, but he never told her exactly where his retirement money was being kept. Instead, he showed her that he had filled out a request for access to his funds and that seemed to placate Fariha's anger a bit.

But then Charlie decided to ask a few questions of his own. It seemed to Fariha that his personality had changed. Instead of the easy-going man she had married, all of a sudden Charlie had become assertive. His passive nature seemed to have disappeared, and she was even more frightened that her plan might go off course. Charlie questioned her about the "nest egg" she had told him she had when they came to Bangladesh.

She defensively retorted, "I spent it. How do you think my parents paid for the house that you and I are living in? Surely you aren't fool enough to think they have the money to buy two homes. And what about the lavish wedding that had just took place? I used my money to pay for all of it, from the food, to the clothing and jewelry, to the fees paid to the priests and musicians. I am broke," she said despondently. "I was depending on you to take care of me as you promised," she accused. She acted as if Charlie had betrayed her, rather than that she had been dishonest with Charlie about her own finances.

Charlie was speechless. He looked at the woman he loved and realized that he truly didn't know her at all. Was this all about the money? Did she even love him as much as he loved her? He needed to figure out how to get out of this mess. He was married to two women, he had almost no money in hand, it seemed his old company was dragging their heels about giving him access to his savings, and Fariha's money was gone. As much as he loved her, he guessed that, in the end, money was the final, all-important factor. He left Fariha standing in their house with her hands on her hips and a furious expression on her face. She was not the least bit apologetic about her own dishonesty, but was upset with Charlie because he hadn't been able to get to his money. This whole situation seemed unbelievable.

Charlie walked for miles and, when he had calmed down, he returned home. He found Fariha waiting for him. The house was fragrant with cooking and Fariha came to him with a contrite attitude. She was no longer angry, but, instead, she apologized for her earlier words.

"I'm sorry, Charlie," she said meekly. "I was just frightened about our future. I need to feel secure after what I've been through in my life. I love you, Charlie. Please don't be upset with me."

She had fixed his favorite meal and put on his favorite sari. She led him to the table; and, after their meal, she led him to the bedroom. Once again, Charlie succumbed to Fariha's skills in bed and decided that, perhaps, he had been the one in the wrong. *I should have planned better before leaving Mumbai and quitting my job,* he thought. *I acted impulsively. It was my responsibility to provide for Fariha, and I have let her down. She has lived through difficult times since she was very young. No wonder she's afraid of what the future holds.* He drifted off to sleep vowing to fix things the next day.

Chapter Twenty-Six: Anna's Plan

Anna was surprised when she had an e-mail from Charlie within two days of sending her plea for reconciliation. She had given up hope that he would write her back. In the e-mail he said:

>I'm not going to change my mind and I have no intention of coming back to
>Taos. The house there is your home, not mine. It is not my responsibility.
>I don't love you any more and I have no intention of trying to save our
>marriage. As far as I'm concerned, our relationship is over. I will hold up
>my end of the deal. I promise to send money whenever I can, but I don't
>know when or how much that will be. I don't want to leave you broke,
>but I'm almost broke myself and need what money I have.

His words were cruel, and Anna felt her heart rip in two. But this time she didn't cry. Instead, she poured herself a glass of wine and made a list of things she needed to do next.

First on the list was a call to Charlie's brother, Rick. She had gotten to know him well in the process of finding and buying Grace's home, and she had talked to him several times when Charlie disappeared. Of all the family, she had the closest relationship to Rick and believed that, if anyone could help her, he would be the one. When he answered, Anna recited all the most recent events, including her phone call to Charlie, the e-mail she sent Charlie, and his e-mail response. Rick was quiet for quite a while, and Anna wondered if he was going to tell her that he was unwilling to help her out. Instead, Rick finally said that he had an idea that might help.

"It may seem strange," he said, "but I have an acquaintance that spent some time in jail for computer hacking. He is out now and working as a computer security analyst for a local insurance agency. I wonder if, using Charlie's e-mail to you, he could figure out Charlie's precise location. You know from the telephone number that he's in Bangladesh somewhere, but it would be good to know exactly where he is!"

Anna's heart began to beat more rapidly and she peppered Rick with questions. "Do you really think that's possible? Would he be willing to do that? Would it jeopardize his job? Would it be illegal? Could he find out what Charlie's doing in Bangladesh?"

Rick chuckled at her response and then cleared his throat. He certainly didn't want Anna to think he wasn't taking her problems seriously. In fact, her problems were also his problems, because Grace would be moving in with him and his family once her house went into foreclosure.

"I'll look into it," he said. "In the meantime, forward me both your e-mail to Charlie and his e-mail to you. I'll call my friend tomorrow and see if he thinks he can help."

Anna thanked Rick profusely, feeling hope rising to the surface at last. She forwarded the e-mails to Rick and leaned back in her chair, feeling for the first time that she had been able to do something proactive about her situation.

While she waited for Rick to get back to her, she continued to hound David for some of the rent money he owed her. Her requests went unheeded, and she finally gave up on the idea that he would help her out. She continued working at the souvenir shop, using the money to live on, but it wasn't enough to pay the mortgage on the lake house and she began skipping those payments. She still occasionally sold one of her weavings, and the extra money from that always seemed to come at an opportune time. The foreclosure threats continued to come from the banks that owned her house and the mountain property, but there was no way that she could afford to pay on them. She was getting deeper and deeper in debt, her credit cards were maxed out, and Charlie had not sent her a dime. She was getting desperate and she was angry.

Anna had another long talk with Helen, who helped her sort through her options. She clearly could not continue things the way they were. When she looked at her assets, she realized that there was some equity in her house. If she could sell the house, the equity money could tide her over for a short time, but that would mean leaving Taos and moving back to the lake house. It made her sad to think that this was her last course of action, but she called a realtor that night and set up an appointment for the following day.

When the realtor came, he assured her that, because the house was in a desirable section of town and had been very well maintained, it would sell quickly if the price were right. They talked over the figures and agreed on a selling price. If she could get that price, she would walk away with a few thousand dollars. No fortune, but enough to move to the lake house and find a job there. While the house was on the market, Anna would make arrangements to sell most of her things. She also needed to get Charlie off the title to the house so that she could have the equity money when it sold. She called David and gave him the news that she was coming back.

"David, I am out of options. I will be selling my house in Taos and moving back to the lake house by the end of the month. You and Valerie will have to find somewhere else to live. I'm sorry it's come to this, but your father has left me with no other options."

David took a moment to respond. "Yeah, you always did blame everything on Dad, didn't you? Now you're in a fix and you're going to take it out on me and Valerie by kicking us out of our house. We've put our own money into that house. It hasn't been free to live here, you know! I mean, we just had the propane tank filled! That cost us a bundle!" Then, after a thoughtful pause, "What about Jordan? Don't you care about him at all? You're shoving him out in the cold along with us!"

Anna couldn't believe her ears. She had been letting David and his family live in the lake house for free for all these months without a single thank you. And now he was blaming her for "kicking him out" of *his house*. On top of that, he was heaping guilt on her about Jordan. She began to shake.

"You ungrateful, worthless man!" She shouted into the phone. "How dare you try to put a guilt trip on me! You are so much like your father. I'm not going to let you ruin my life the same way he has. You have 30 days to get out, or I'll have you evicted by the sheriff. If you don't believe it, just try me!" After hanging up, she flung her phone across the room. *Why should I feel guilty?* she fumed.

But she did feel guilty. Surely, when all of this was over, she would be able to find a way to make it up to Jordan, her sweet grandchild. She realized that she had a desire to mend her relationship with David, too. Perhaps she had misunderstood his attitude. That was the good thing about moving back to the lake house. She would be closer to Jordan and her other grandchildren, as well as David. She could reunite with Clare and get to know Bradley and Julie better. Perhaps she could even spend some time with Charlie's daughter, Christine, and get to know her and her children again. Now that her marriage was disintegrating, Anna felt a deep need to connect with the rest of her family. She didn't want to be alone.

Next she called Bradley. "I plan to sell my house in Taos and move back into the lake house. I just can't afford to keep up both places now that your father has disappeared."

"That sounds like the best thing you can do, given the situation." Then he added,
"Because of my job and the boys' activities, there's no way I can come to Taos to help you with the move."

"I can handle that part," she assured him. "What I need you to do is make sure that David and Valerie move out and, once they do, have the locks changed so they can't come back and damage the place any more than they already have. Just keep an eye on the house until I get there."

Bradley reluctantly agreed, but added, "Okay, but the lake house is not very close to my house and it won't be easy to be running over there all the time."

Disappointed in his response, Anna ended the call by saying, "Well, just do the best you can, please. I need you to help me out with this." After she hung up, she wondered, *Is Bradley abandoning me, too? He didn't even sound glad that I was coming back. Maybe I'm more alone in this than I thought. But I don't see any other options right now. I'll make it work somehow. I have to!*

Next, she sent Charlie another e-mail. Without revealing any emotion, she told him that, because of her financial situation, she needed to sell the house in Taos. She reminded him that, because of his lack of support, this was her only option. She attached papers for him to sign giving up his right to the proceeds of the sale of the house. Finally, she reminded him that he did have some responsibility for her situation and he owed her at least this much. She didn't say she loved him, she didn't beg for reconciliation, she didn't plead for anything. She just laid it out in plain, simple language and worded it in such a way that Charlie would understand that she intended to do what she said.

Then she called an estate sale agent and asked her to come over and look at the things she had to sell. She would keep only the basic furniture that she needed to furnish the smaller lake house. She planned to keep her looms, however. She couldn't bear to part with them, so she would pack them into the truck and move them, storing them in the garage until the time when she might be able to move to a larger place and put them to use again. When the estate sale lady came over, Anna was disappointed to learn that she didn't have enough items for an estate sale. She had sold so many things just trying to bring in enough money to survive, that almost all of her valuable possessions were gone. The things she wasn't taking with her would have to go into a garage sale and were likely to bring in very little money.

Surprisingly, Charlie responded to her e-mail the next day, attaching the necessary signed papers. Anna couldn't believe it. Charlie just wrote, "Here are the papers you want," another word.

Well, what did I expect? She thought. *He certainly wasn't going to sign the e-mail with "Love you forever"!*

Anna was elated and called her real estate agent right away to share the good news. The financial end of the sale was really not his business, but she considered him an ally, and she wanted him to know that Charlie had acquiesced to her demand. Perhaps, she thought, he was beginning to soften. What else might she be able to get him to do?

She had already explained her situation to her boss at the souvenir shop, and he had been very understanding. In fact, he had assured her that, should she return to Taos, she would be welcome to come work for him again. Anna realized that he had become another one of the many friends she had made in Taos. She was going to miss this town so much.

Helen and Lee came over to help Anna get ready for the garage sale. They set up tables and displayed her items in the most appealing way possible. Anna had little hope of making much money, but at this point, anything that came in would be helpful. As they were leaving, Helen approached Anna with a sly smile on her face.

"My nephew is unexpectedly coming into town tomorrow, and Lee and I already have plans for tomorrow evening. Would you mind taking him to dinner in town? He's never been to Taos before and he loves New Mexican food. It would be a huge favor to us. Do you mind?"

Anna was taken aback. She really was in no mood to entertain, especially not anyone of the male gender. But Helen and Lee had been such good friends, how could she refuse? "Of course. I'd be happy to take him to dinner. It would actually be good to get away from all of this for an evening," she conceded.

Helen nodded and smiled knowingly. "Great! Come by about 6:30 and I'll introduce you before Lee and I have to leave. Thanks, Anna. You're doing us a big favor."

The next evening, Anna put on one of her nicer dresses and arrived at Helen and Lee's at the appointed time. When Helen answered the door, she looked stunning, and Lee was standing behind her in a suit and tie.

"Where are you two going?" Anna asked. "You both look fabulous!"

"We've been invited to a private showing at the new gallery in Arroyo Seco. It's a formal evening, which is quite unusual for around here. I forced Lee to put on a suit and tie, and he fussed the entire time!" she giggled. "Oh, here's my nephew, Mark. He's from Washington D.C. Mark does something mysterious for the government that he can't talk about, so I hope you two can find a topic of conversation during dinner!" she said proudly.

Anna saw Mark coming into the entryway behind her good friends. He was nice looking, a few years younger than Anna, she guessed, and was dressed casually in slacks and a sport shirt.

"It's nice to meet you, Anna," he said politely. "Aunt Helen has told me a lot about you."

"Not too much, I hope," Anna replied quickly. "Well, let's get going and leave these young folks to their evening out," she joked.

Mark showed Anna to his car, a shiny black Porsche, and held the passenger door open for her. Anna felt awkward, but had to admit that it felt good to have a man pampering her a bit. Mark followed Anna's directions to the restaurant where they enjoyed traditional fajita dinners and delicious local wine. Anna even splurged and ordered flàn for dessert. She laughed when Mark wiped a bit of the rich custard from her cheek. She found herself blushing and wondered, *Am I actually flirting with this man?*

Mark drove to Anna's house, jumped out of the car and ran around to open the door of the luxury car for her. As she was getting out, Anna's hand brushed Mark's, and she felt a shock of electricity go up her arm. They locked eyes, Anna nodded, and Mark followed her into her house. They enjoyed more wine in front of a fire, with Bella and Simba snoozing beside them. The conversation became more relaxed, and, finally, Anna told Mark about Charlie and her situation. She began to curse Charlie, and Mark took her into his arms, rubbing her shoulders and helping her calm down.

When Anna regained her composure, Mark kissed her gently on the top of her head, then tilted her face to his and kissed her on the forehead and on her nose. Then he looked her in the eyes and kissed her tenderly on the mouth. All of Anna's anger and frustration left in the midst of that kiss. She felt valued for the first time in many months. She took Mark's hand and led him to the bedroom, where they shared a night of lovemaking that she would remember in the lonely months to come.

Mark awoke early, kissed Anna once more, and said his good-byes. He was kind and gentle, but this was clearly a one-night stand in his mind.

Anna languished in bed for another hour, drifting in and out of sweet dreams. Finally, she rose to face the harsh reality of the coming day and her impending trip to the lake house. She felt no regrets about sleeping with Mark. In fact, she decided that a little revenge sex was just what she had needed. Then it occurred to Anna that Helen and Lee's event at the gallery had been a bit too convenient. *Were they complicit in my brief sexual encounter with Mark? Did Helen and Lee know that was going to happen all along? Exactly what did they tell Mark about me? Perhaps my good friends are more devious than I thought!*

Chapter Twenty-Seven: Anna's Move

Anna made just enough money at the garage sale to rent a trailer and pay for fuel and food during the drive to the lake house. Anna packed her things into the U-Haul trailer and hitched it to her truck. She made the drive without help, and was glad for the company of Bella, who sat quietly and watched the road from the passenger seat. Simba was carrying on in his crate for the first 100 miles, but finally settled down and slept most of the way. She saved money by sleeping at a rest area in a sleeping bag in the front seat of her truck. Even with Bella sleeping on the floor beside her, the idea made her nervous, so she slept very little. She kept checking to make sure the doors were locked and that the tire iron was close at had on the floor near her feet.

She managed to tow the trailer without mishap, except for one incident. She was leaving a truck stop after fueling up and ran the trailer over a curb. The trailer was stuck and the tire was flat. She got out of the truck and was looking the situation over when a trucker, who had seen the whole incident, strolled over and asked if he could help her out. Anna was leery of accepting help from a total stranger, but she knew that she couldn't free the trailer and change the tire on her own. The trailer was packed to the brim and she just wasn't that strong. Besides, Bella was an intimidating sight, even if she was really harmless. That thought reassured her somewhat.

So she accepted the man's offer. Anna was thankful that the trailer had come with a spare, because at least she didn't have to buy a new tire. The trucker went back to his rig, pulled some tools from the back of the cab, and came back to where Anna was waiting. Within minutes he had the spare tire installed. He asked her how much farther she had to drive, and, when she told him, he assured her that the spare should make the rest of the trip as long as she drove at a reasonable speed. Then he climbed into her truck and gently drove the trailer off the curbing on which it had been stuck. When he had finished, Anna thanked him profusely and offered him what little money she had in her wallet. The man thanked her for offering, but refused the money.

He shook Anna's hand and said, "If my wife was stuck somewhere like you were, I'd sure want somebody to help her out." Then he turned around, strode back to his own truck, and started the big engine.

Anna was so grateful she almost cried. He was like an angel that had been sent to her rescue at just the right moment. Was this a sign that things were going to turn out all right after all? She certainly hoped so!

The rest of her drive passed without any problems. Once she reached the lake house, Bradley came over with the keys, and he and her grandsons helped her move her meager furnishings into the house. She was grateful for their help; she could not have moved all of those things on her own. Her looms would not fit in the small house, so she carefully put them in the garage. She wondered what kind of condition they would be in after sitting all winter on the dirt floor of the building that was detached from the house itself. There was no heat out there, and the freezing temperatures would be hard on the fragile structure of the looms.

She had brought barely enough furniture and decorations to make the small house comfortable; but when she opened the front door, she realized that she had a lot of work to do before the house would feel like her own. David and Valerie had removed every stick of furniture and every piece of household goods, including the pieces that had been left by Bradley originally. The carpet was filthy from David's dogs. Clearly, no one had taken the time to housebreak them. There was grime on the walls and the doors, and the linoleum in the kitchen and bathroom was torn and filthy. Anna wasn't surprised to see that the sinks, toilet and bathtub were dirty beyond using also. There were even holes in the walls, and the closet door was nowhere to be found. After Bradley and the boys left, Anna sat down on a kitchen chair and wept.

She planned to pay David for whatever propane was left in the tank, since he had made such a big deal of it on the phone. If she could get the money, perhaps several hundred dollars would appease him. She went out and checked the meter. The tank was empty! Obviously, in his anger at having to leave, David had let all the remaining propane out of the tank. She was broken-hearted to think that her own son would stoop to such a level. What might have been a windfall for David had become another liability for her. Clearly, he was his father's son. She was certain that David and Charlie had spoken, because she was sure that David had continued to ask Charlie for money. She began to wonder if David's nervous manner on the phone was because he knew more about Charlie and his whereabouts than he was telling her.

She stopped and assessed her finances. She had only enough cash left to partially fill the propane tank. It would take at least that much to clean up the house enough to live there. She didn't see how she could survive without at least cleaning the carpets and painting, plus the entire place needed a good scrubbing from top to bottom. She could wait to replace the furniture David had taken until she found a job. The few things she had brought from Taos would have to do. In addition, she needed to buy food for herself and the animals. She decided that the propane could also wait until she found a job and had some extra money. In the meantime, she would have to make do with cold water and cooking in the small microwave that she had brought from Taos.

On her way back inside, her phone rang. It was her realtor telling her that she had an offer on her house. The offer was the only interest anyone had shown, and it was considerably under the asking price. Did she want to accept the offer? Reluctantly, she said, "Yes." She didn't have time to wait for a better offer. She was dead broke. Her realtor told Anna that he would e-mail the paperwork that afternoon and closing should be in about two weeks. It was a cash offer, so there was no waiting for financing. All they had to do was go through the inspection and make any minor repairs that were necessary. He told Anna that he didn't expect any roadblocks to a quick closing, at which time Anna would receive a small check for the remaining equity after closing expenses were paid. Anna hung up and wrapped her arms around Bella. Her hug was promptly returned with big, wet doggy kisses that wiped away Anna's tears. Simba just looked up from where he lay in a shaft of sunlight on the floor, gave them a feline look of disgust, and put his head down again.

She called Bradley to give him the news. She didn't tell Bradley how broke she was. She was too proud to admit to him that she needed any help. At the same time, however, she wondered why he wasn't more concerned about her finances. He knew the reason she had moved back. He was aware that she had lost the house in Taos. She reasoned that he was too busy living his own life to be concerned about hers, and she hung up once again feeling deserted by all of the men in her life.

Then she called Helen and Lee. They wanted to know who had bought the house, but Anna didn't know anything about the buyers. She told them she hoped the new people would be good neighbors and once again said how much she missed them. The conversation made her even more depressed, and she hoped Charlie was having his own problems, wherever he was.

His e-mails had indicated that he was strapped financially also. Anna didn't understand how that could be. Charlie had made a huge salary at the Indian oil company. He couldn't possibly have spent all that money. And what about the retirement account? Anna knew that it had at least $2 million in it and had been earning interest. Charlie couldn't access that until he retired, of course, but that certainly bode well for both of their futures. Half of that money was rightfully hers, since Charlie had earned it during the course of their marriage. She began to wonder if Charlie was even still working. None of the people she had contacted in the oil industry seemed to know where he was. Her curiosity was growing with each new fact she discovered.

After weeks of searching, Anna finally got a job as a barista at a local coffee shop. She thought the job would be easy, since she occasionally went there for a special treat herself. She found, however, that the vocabulary and pace were too much for her.

Maybe she was getting old, but the job became so difficult that she was fired after two weeks. Anna's career in the coffee industry was brief and unsuccessful. That bad news was just the beginning, however. Try as she might, Anna was unable to find another job anywhere. The economy was so depressed that no one was hiring. In fact, the town she grew up in and the neighboring communities had begun to look like ghost towns with both mom and pop stores and huge warehouses sitting empty.

Unable to pay the bills, Anna had given up her cell phone account. Neither did she have money for an internet connection. She kept her computer and went to the local library when she needed to send e-mails or go online.

As she sat in the library one day, she had a thought. In order to do something positive with her time, Anna volunteered to help at the library. Anna loved to read, but she found the library quite boring. She was not challenged in the least by shelving books and mending broken bindings. She was able to get a peek at the latest best sellers when they came in, but she was not allowed to check them out herself until they had been available to the public for at least two weeks. She wasn't even getting paid for her time, and she was about to quit when she had another thought that might make her feel worthwhile.

Her idea was to start a "Children's Hour" on Saturday mornings, and, as it turned out, it saved Anna's sanity. This was Anna's project, and the head librarian allowed Anna to advertise the activity for three to five year olds by placing posters in the library and ads in the local paper. Anna picked out a book to read each Saturday morning. She would practice reading the story at home. Bella and Simba did not make a very responsive audience, but Anna would try different voices for different characters in the books. These sessions were the highlight of her week, and the library staff was impressed by the number of families who began using the library for the first time as a result of Anna's efforts.

Anna, too, was amazed at the positive response she received. Her biggest thrill was that Jordan came. She had imagined

Children's Hour as a special time she could share with her grandson. David and Valerie brought Jordan to the library on Saturday mornings, dropping him off without talking to Anna. They seldom allowed Jordan to see Anna otherwise. She would call them, asking permission to pick Jordan up, but their response was usually that they had other plans and Jordan would be too busy to go. She knew this was a lie, but she had no recourse other than to say, "All right. Maybe he can go next time." Occasionally, Jordan was allowed to go on a picnic, to the park, or to the local indoor swimming pool with Anna. When they went on these outings, Anna was overjoyed and made sure that Jordan had a wonderful time. *My relationship with David is far from perfect, but at least I'm able to show Jordan how much I love him. I'll have to work harder on my relationship with his father,* she thought.

Then Rick sent her an e-mail. She had almost forgotten about Rick's friend, the hacker, and her hopes that he would be of help. She was dumbfounded when Rick told her that Charlie was on the outskirts of Dhaka, Bangladesh. His friend had also discovered that Charlie had been fired from his job in India and was living in a small town outside of Dhaka. The most amazing news of all was that Charlie had married a Bengali woman in a Muslim ceremony hosted by the woman's parents. This shook Anna to her core. Charlie was a bigamist? What on earth was he thinking? After recovering her composure, Anna e-mailed Rick, thanking him and asking him to thank his friend on her behalf. Although this news was not encouraging, it was interesting.

Anna put Bella on her leash and went for a long walk around the lake while she tried to digest what she had just heard. Once she got past the hurt and anger, she began to try to think of how she might use this knowledge to her advantage. Once again, she had many options to consider, including what her next move would be.

Chapter Twenty-Eight: Destitution

The sale of Anna's home in Taos was complete. But the money from the house would last her only a few weeks, even if she were extremely careful. She missed Taos and the life she had made for herself there. Her life now felt temporary. Her family, if not helpful, was kind to her with the exception of David, but she got the feeling that much of their caring for her was out of pity for her situation without Charlie. She had not let anyone know how desperately broke she was. Besides, they lived far enough away that she seldom saw them. Now she couldn't even talk to them on the phone. She didn't feel the same kind of genuine love as she received from Helen and Lee or her other friends in New Mexico. They had made a concerted effort to stay in touch with her after she moved away and were still concerned about her welfare.

She began to wonder if she had made a mistake by moving back to the midwest. At least in Taos she had a job waiting for her, and there might be other opportunities for additional work, too. Here, the economy was so depressed that even the lowest-paying job was impossible to find.

But Anna was in no position financially to move back to New Mexico. She managed to keep her cupboards stocked with enough food to survive, but she was eating mostly beans and Raman noodles. She fed Bella and Simba whatever she could get from the grocery store butcher, who was generous with meaty bones and day-old fish that was scheduled for the dumpster.

Without realizing how quickly time had passed, winter was upon her. She still hadn't filled the propane tank. She just didn't have the money. So, not only was there no heat in the house, but the pipes froze and she had no water either. Eventually, the power company shut off the electricity for lack of payment. She scavenged what wood she could from her property and made fires in the oven of the stove to keep herself warm. She slept in her sleeping bag on the kitchen floor in front of the open oven door with Bella cuddled close to her side for warmth. Finally, she ran out of fallen branches and resorted to burning what furniture she could. In the end, she began tearing her looms apart and burning the pieces for warmth. Occasionally, she would melt some snow water by the fire and use it to wash herself as best she could. *I might as well be homeless,* she thought. *At least then I could go to a homeless shelter.*

That gave her an idea. She couldn't afford gas for her truck, so she bundled up as best she could and walked the mile into town for a free hot meal at the town's shelter. She begged the woman at the counter to give her some extra food for Bella and Simba, and the woman grudgingly handed her a bag of bones and a few cans of dog and cat food. Anna was humiliated, and when she arrived back at her house, she swore she would never stoop that low again. But Bella and Simba were glad for the food, and Anna wondered how she would be able to care for her pets beyond that day.

She had stopped doing the children's hour at the library, and she could feel the signs of depression closing in on her. She had thoughts of suicide, but remembered Helen's words from months before. Besides, she couldn't leave Bella and Simba to fend for themselves. They would miss her, even if her family wouldn't. Then she thought of Jordan and knew that she had to keep going for his sake, if not for her own. Somehow she would figure out a way to survive this life she had been thrown into.

Despite her resolve not to return, Anna went to the shelter almost every day after that. She offered to help in the kitchen just for the joy of being in a warm room. After the first week, Anna was allowed to help on the serving line in order to "pay" for the food she took home to Bella and Simba. After another week, the director of the shelter offered to pay Anna a small amount if she would stay to sweep up and clean the kitchen after meals. At last, Anna was able to make a bit of money and she carefully saved every penny she could. She was grateful to have a roof over her head, even if it was a cold one, but she knew she had a job waiting for her in Taos if she could just get herself back there.

Anna's anger at Charlie grew as her resources dwindled. She sat in her kitchen and thought, *Where is he and what is he doing? And what about That Woman? What about her is so wonderful that he chose to disappear from my life in order to be with her? What does she give him that I can't? Does Charlie even intend to come back? Will Charlie ever send any money? What made Charlie so heartless that he could do this to me? To his family?* Anna tortured herself with these questions as she tried to keep warm in front of her little fire.

By the time winter had passed, Anna was sick of the midwestern weather. The snow had piled up around the lake house, and she shoveled constantly to clear an opening to her front door. She even had to climb a ladder to the roof and shovel the snow away so that the weight wouldn't cave the roof in. The sky was always gray, even when it wasn't snowing. She seldom saw the sun for weeks and she found that wearisome. And the cold, because of the humidity, seemed to seep into the marrow of her bones. In Taos it snowed, but it felt different. The air was dry and crisp, and the sun shone almost every day. She realized how much she had missed the blue skies of New Mexico. She also had not seen mountains for many months. It would be refreshing to once again see the piney slopes on the horizon, rather than flat land disappearing into nothingness.

All through the winter, Anna had been getting notices from the mortgage company regarding the lake house. The last notice informed her that she hadn't made a payment in months and they planned to start foreclosure proceedings immediately. Soon, Anna realized, she really would be homeless. Very well. Let them have the house. It was a wreck now anyway, and when the pipes burst with the spring thaw, there was no telling how much damage would be done.

Anna phoned her former boss at the souvenir shop from a pay phone at the shelter and asked if she could come back to work there. He was delighted. The young woman he had hired in Anna's place had not worked out. "You spoiled me, Anna. I've never had an employee who was as dependable and capable as you were. I'd be happy to have you back. I'll even give you a raise! When will you be here?"

Anna told him she would get back to him once her plans were complete, hung up the phone, and felt quite relieved. She felt the coin return bin on the phone to see if anyone had left any coins there, but was disappointed to find it empty. Then she opened the old billfold where she had been stashing her money from the shelter and carefully counted it up. If she drove straight through and bought only the gas she needed for her truck, she probably had just enough to make it back to Taos. She really didn't need to buy food, and she could stop at a rest area and nap if she needed to. The more she thought about it, the more her excitement grew. She felt as if she were going back home, rather than leaving the place where she grew up.

Almost before she knew it, Anna was driving away from the lake house. She didn't need a trailer this time, because she had nothing left. Charlie had left all of them without anything, and she felt that simmering anger when she thought of all the people he had hurt. Grace's house had already been foreclosed, and she was living with Rick. Charlie's grandchildren didn't even know who he was, and his children didn't seem to care that he had disappeared from their lives. But Anna knew that he had heaped the most painful hurt on her, and, once again, she asked herself what she had done to deserve this?

Was I too complacent with my nice life? Did I not appreciate Charlie enough for working long hours away from his family. NO! I did appreciate what I had, and Charlie's career was his choice. He was the one who wanted to go to India. He was the one who didn't make an effort to spend time with me when I made the arrangements for us to be together. It's Charlie's fault...all Charlie, and I will see him rot in hell for what he's done to me.

The angrier she became, the faster she drove. Catching herself approaching 90 miles an hour, she jerked her foot off the accelerator and shook her head. Yes, she had been suicidal at times, but she wasn't going to let Charlie kill her on this highway.

She believed with certainty that he would eventually get his due. The thought made her smile briefly, and she continued down the interstate back to Taos. She still didn't know what she was going to do about Charlie, but she knew she wouldn't just let the whole thing drop. He had "done her wrong", as the old song said. She knew that she was tenacious enough to want some kind of closure to the madness that his actions had wrought on her life. Anna didn't know what that was going to look like, but somehow she would even the score. She just hadn't figured out how yet.

Chapter Twenty-Nine: Charlie's New Job

Things had taken a turn for the worse in Charlie's life.
Charlie was alarmed at Anna's phone call. She obviously knew
where he was, and his plan to just disappear without a trace had
backfired. Fariha was understandably upset that Anna had re-
inserted herself into Charlie's life. As a matter of fact, Charlie's
relationship with Fariha had suffered greatly. Although their sex life
was still amazing, Charlie realized that there was no longer much
trust between them. It felt as if they were simply going through the
motions of a genuine relationship. Most worrisome of all, however,
was their financial situation. What little money Charlie had would
not last long. He did feel a sense of responsibility to Fariha. He had
promised her and her family that he would provide for her, and now
he was unable to do that. Fariha's father and brother would not be
merciful if he let Fariha down. Besides, he was in love with Fariha
and wanted to spend the rest of his life with her.

Then it hit him. He had also made the promise to love and
provide for Anna, and he had let her down in a big way. According
to her e-mail, she was on the verge of losing everything they had
accumulated during their marriage. Charlie began to replay
memories in his mind. He saw the boys as they were when they
were young. They were cute and inquisitive, willing to learn, and
held him in high esteem. Now, though, things were different. He
never even communicated with Bradley, and David seemed to view
him only as a source of money. Christine had also become a
stranger to him, and he really didn't even know his grandchildren.
Anna claimed to still love him and be willing to reconcile. She was
ready to forgive him, if only he would come back to her. The
question was, did he still love Anna? He quickly decided that he did
not. They had grown so far apart over the years that there was
nothing left between them. It wasn't his fault, Charlie, rationalized.
It was just the way things had turned out. Once he was able to turn

his finances around, Charlie would send Anna money once again, he decided. That should help to make her feel better about the situation.

Charlie realized that he needed to take some action and find a job. He got out his laptop and updated his resume, leaving out the details of his departure from the Indian oil company. After reading it over, he made a few minor changes and sent it out to several companies in Asia and Australia. He was careful to avoid sending it to any companies that had close ties to the U.S. He knew the oil industry was a tight-knit community, and he didn't want word getting out that he was job hunting.

In the meantime, he received the e-mail from Anna saying that she was selling the house in Taos. *Good riddance!* thought Charlie. That house was never his home, and he was glad that she had finally come to her senses and was getting rid of the place. It was too large, too expensive, too...everything! He gladly agreed to let her have the profit from the sale. Perhaps that would get her off his back about sending her money. Surely her financial situation wasn't as dire as she was making it out to be. When he hit "send" and the e-mail was on its way back to Anna, Charlie felt justified. He had done her a huge favor by agreeing to those terms on the sale of the house. She should be grateful to him. Maybe now she would stop harassing him to send her money.

Afterward, though, Charlie began to question his action. He was still waiting to hear back from the oil companies to whom he had sent his resume. Fariha was becoming increasingly agitated about their finances, and Charlie was not sure what he was going to do. The money from the sale of the house would have been a much-needed windfall. But, if he had insisted on sharing in the profits from the sale, Anna and everyone else would know for sure where he was. He just couldn't have that. So letting Anna have the proceeds was the only wise thing to do. Charlie was certain that someone out there needed his expertise and would hire him before too long.

The wait was actually shorter than Charlie thought it would be. Within a week of sending out his inquiries, Charlie heard back from an oil company in China. They were opening new exploration in northern China and would be happy to have Charlie and his experience to help with the project. Charlie was excited. He found Fariha at her parents' home and told her the good news. Fariha, however, was less than thrilled. She had planned to stay in Bangladesh, she said. She didn't want to leave her aging parents, and she had established a new life for herself there. Charlie was startled to hear her refer to her parents as "aging". In fact, they were actually quite a few years younger than Charlie! He was disappointed in her reaction, and he told her that this was his last and only option.

"If you don't want to come to China, Fariha, you can stay here. I will come visit as often as possible," Charlie said.

"I'll have to think about it, Charlie. I would miss you and I don't think I want to stay here without you," was her tepid reply.

Fariha's mind was racing. *Charlie is once again in touch with Anna. How much of a threat to my relationship with Charlie does Anna pose? Can Charlie and I maintain our relationship if we are thousands of miles apart? Wasn't Charlie and Anna's separation what made it possible for me to insert myself into Charlie's life to begin with? Charlie loves sex, and if I am not available, I have no doubt that he will fill his need elsewhere. If Charlie were so far away, how could I be sure I would get my share of his money? Who will oversee his finances, monitor his paychecks, and make sure that I have access to his funds?* The answer was clear. She needed to follow Charlie wherever he went.

Within a day, Fariha went to Charlie and told him she would come with him to China if that was what he wanted. She didn't mention her concerns about the money; instead, she told Charlie that she loved him so much she wouldn't be able to stand being without him. Charlie was flattered. Fariha's response made him feel valued and loved, and he began to look forward to moving away from Bangladesh and Fariha's ever-watchful family. This would be an opportunity for Fariha and him to start over and make a new life for themselves.

Charlie exchanged e-mails with the Chinese oil company over the next week. They discussed his salary and benefits, his options for health care, his long-term investment opportunities with the company, and what his living situation would be. He would be working for Sinopec in the Daqing oil field. The company wasn't used to hiring employees with families, so, when Charlie insisted that he would be bringing his wife along, they dragged their feet. Finally, though, they agreed to help Charlie with the paperwork and governmental procedures necessary to bring Fariha into China. Getting a work visa for himself was problematic enough. Charlie was thankful to have the help of his new employer to run the maze of red tape necessary to allow Fariha to accompany him. Had they not been married, there was no way that Fariha would have been allowed into China.

The plan was for Charlie and Fariha to get established in an apartment in the city of Shenyang. Charlie would commute to the field from there.

Charlie and Fariha packed their necessary belongings and prepared to leave for China. Charlie told Nazeem to sell the house for whatever he could get for it and to forward the money to them once they were in China. He doubted very much that he would ever see any money from the sale of the house, but he was in no position to question Nazeem's honesty. Fariha's farewell to her family was long and tearful. Charlie wondered at that. In such a short time, how could Fariha have become so attached to the family that had sold her as a child? She had clearly forgiven her father for his actions and she had become quite close to her mother, so he guessed that it was natural for her to go through a grieving process at the thought of having to leave them. Fariha, on the other hand, was trying to play all of the cards in her hand. Yes, she was going to China with Charlie, but she wanted to keep her family in Bangladesh as a backup plan. She wasn't sure how things would go in China. *What if I hate it so much that I decide not to stay? What if Charlie's job doesn't work out? What if my marriage to Charlie doesn't last?*

She had learned the hard way that things didn't always go as planned. Fariha wanted to leave her family with a desire to have her return, just in case she needed a place to go. In actuality, she found her father detestable and her mother a simpering servant to her father. Her brother had shown some fortitude, but he was still living at home, so what did that say about him?

Akash drove Charlie and Fariha to the airport in Dhaka, unloaded their suitcases from the trunk of his car, and watched them walk into the terminal building. He had his doubts about Charlie. As a matter of fact, he had doubts about Fariha. She was his sister, and he supposed he loved her, but he sensed a coldness about her. To be honest, he was glad to see her leave. He didn't want her to hurt his mother or his father, although he could understand why she and her father weren't close. Even more, he didn't want her usurping his place in the family. Even though Fariha was older than he, Akash had been treated as the first born for as long as he could remember, and he wasn't happy about giving up the status of that position now. Hoping that they were gone for good, Akash climbed into the driver's seat and drove away without looking back.

Fariha and Charlie boarded their flight to Shanghai and squeezed into their seats. The only other time Fariha remembered flying was when she flew tourist class to Dhaka many months before, but Charlie was used to flying first class. He was a tall man and felt crammed into the tiny space that was available for his legs. He had an aisle seat, so that was helpful, because he was able to angle his legs from the knees down and encroach on the space in the aisle a bit. Fariha was in the center seat, but she was a small woman and seemed not to mind the close quarters. Charlie sighed and looked forward to the day when he would once again be able to afford flying first class—or at least business class.

Fariha didn't drink alcohol, but she ordered a soft drink from the steward. Charlie ordered a bourbon and Coke, hoping it would take his mind off of his nervousness about starting a new job in a new country with a new company. He really didn't know what to expect. He had adjusted to India quite easily, because his company had given him an English-speaking driver and many of the employees spoke and understood at least some of the language. Charlie didn't know what he was going to find once he reached China. *The recruiter I talked to on the phone spoke passable English, but I suppose that was a requirement of his job. How will I communicate with the workers in the field? How will I communicate with my superiors? What will the living conditions be?* And then he thought of Fariha. *She knows no Chinese either. As far as I know, she has never been anywhere except Bangladesh and India.* Charlie vowed that he would do whatever was necessary to make the move easy for her, although he wasn't sure what that meant.

When they landed in Shanghai, they had little opportunity to look around. They had a close connection with their flight into Shenyang Taoxian International Airport. Fortunately, signage in Shanghai included English, so they were able to find their gate and board their flight without much trouble. They didn't have time to eat anything, and they hadn't eaten in many hours, so they asked the steward if he had any sandwiches or snacks. They received a curt reply in the negative, so they resigned themselves to trying to nap in order to make the flight time seem shorter. When they landed in Shenyang, Charlie's discomfort grew exponentially. Not only was he hungry, but the airport seemed confusing and there were no English signs. No one even seemed to speak English. Fariha was grouchy from hunger, and Charlie began to wonder if the entire plan to work in China was a mistake. Without any other guidance available, the two of them gathered up their things and followed the crowds to baggage claim and customs, successfully guessing where to go and what to do next.

When they emerged from the security area, Charlie looked around and was relieved to see a young man holding a sign with Charlie's name on it in English. He told them in broken English that his name was Xun and he would be their driver for the day. He explained that he would take them to their hotel and then Charlie was expected to meet with his new supervisors later in the afternoon. *At least there's a plan*, thought Charlie. He settled into the back seat of the car and looked out the window to get his first real view of his new home country.

Charlie's mind was bombarded with images as they drove along. As he had discovered in Dhaka, Shengyang was a conglomeration of the old and the new. The roads, laid out in a perfect horizontal and vertical grid, were crowded with cars, bicycles, buses, and pedestrians. As a matter of fact, "crowded" seemed to Charlie to be the operative word for this city. He knew that China's population had exploded, but he wasn't prepared for the feeling of being crammed into a city with more than eight million people. The main thing Charlie noticed was the pollution. He thought the air quality of Mumbai was not good, but Shenyang had air that didn't even justify the word "quality". He could feel his chest and throat tightening and he began to wheeze from the moment he stepped outside the terminal building. Once inside the car his wheezing subsided a bit, so he tried to relax. He was well aware that stress had a negative impact on an asthma attack. Charlie saw that many people wore masks over their noses and mouths to protect their lungs from the damaging air. Perhaps he would have to take the same precaution.

Fariha, on the other hand, rode silently and had her eyes closed. She seemed to be unconcerned with where they were going or the sights, smells, and sounds around her. Charlie hoped that she was just tired and hungry. Sometimes her anger took the form of a hard-edged silence that could make him squirm with discomfort. He decided it best to say nothing and just wait to see what would happen when they reached their hotel.

Xun pulled the car in front of a modern-looking hotel. The sign said that it was a Marriott; but, while checking in, Charlie learned quickly that the Marriott group did not run the hotel, despite the name, as were other Marriott hotels around the world. Apparently, because of a dispute over finances with the Chinese government, the Marriott management had relinquished the administrative work to the Chinese. Xun helped translate what the desk clerk had to say and then took Charlie and Fariha to their room. He explained to Charlie that he would return for Charlie in two hours, so Charlie could rest, freshen up, and change clothes before meeting his new employers. Xun was about to leave when Charlie stopped him and asked if there was any food available, since they hadn't eaten since early the day before. Xun apologized energetically, saying that he should have realized their need. He walked briskly to the room phone, punched in some numbers, and spoke in rapid Chinese. Hanging up the phone, he told Charlie that the hotel's room service would bring up a meal shortly. He added that Charlie should simply call the front desk if there were any other things that he or Fariha needed. Then Xun quickly bowed to each of them and left the room, quietly closing the door behind him.

Xun's hospitality was certainly a godsend, but Charlie felt helpless. He could no more communicate with the front desk than with an alien from another planet. Charlie was the alien, he realized, and he wondered how long it would take to feel comfortable in this ancient country that was so new to him.

Fariha remained quiet as she began to unpack her suitcase and put things into the drawers provided. She told Charlie she was going to shower and, taking her fresh clothes with her, went into the bathroom and softly closed the door. Charlie still couldn't tell if she was angry or not, but he hoped that the room service food would help her mood.

Fariha had just stepped out of the bathroom when there was a knock on the door. Fariha looked refreshed and was smiling, so Charlie felt relief flood his body as he went to the door. The hotel attendant wheeled in a cart containing a pot of tea, two cups, a small tureen of soup, two bowls, and a plate containing two peanut butter and jelly sandwiches. Charlie had to laugh. Apparently Xun had emphasized that the meal was for some American guests. They sat at a small table and ate ravenously. The soup was fragrant and delicious. Charlie didn't recognize exactly what it was, although he identified mushrooms and cabbage as part of the ingredients. They wolfed down the sandwiches and then sat back to enjoy their tea at a more leisurely pace. When Charlie asked Fariha how she was feeling, she replied that she was excited to find a place to live and begin their new life in China. Charlie, relieved that there was no crisis looming in her attitude, said that he hoped to find out what the plan was at the upcoming meeting. He tried to sound confident, but inside his stomach was churning with doubts about this move and how things would work out for them.

Charlie was waiting in the lobby when Xun pulled up in front of the hotel. Fariha had fallen asleep almost immediately after eating, and he didn't want a knock on the door to wake her. He had rolled the room service cart out into the hallway and quietly slipped out of the room without her knowing he had left. This time he climbed into the front passenger seat of the car so he could have a better view of the city around him. Once again, he could feel himself starting to wheeze, so he pulled his rescue inhaler out of his pocket and took three deep puffs. Xun looked at him questioningly but didn't say anything. Charlie just smiled and turned his attention to the scene outside his window.

When they reached the restaurant, Xun let Charlie out in front and then drove around the side of the building to park the car. As he stood waiting for Xun to return, Charlie again began to feel nervous about this meeting. He was surprised at his feelings. Usually, where his work was involved, he was confident and on top of any situation. Perhaps his nerves were a result of his desperate need for money. He had to succeed at this job; there really were no other options for him. He decided that he was just feeling the pressure and would relax once he became acquainted with his co-workers and the job itself.

Xun returned and they walked to the rear of the restaurant where Charlie was invited to sit at a large, round table with six other men. As Charlie's interpreter, Xun sat beside him and made the introductions. Everyone smiled and nodded, but no one said anything for a few minutes and Charlie's nerves began to get the better of him. At last, one of the men, who had been introduced as Hao, asked Charlie in surprisingly good English if Charlie would like a drink. Charlie said, "Yes," and, after that, things began to get interesting. A waiter brought out a case of 40-ounce beers that he placed on a lazy Susan in the center of the table. He put a small glass in front of each man, bowed, and left the area. Hao opened a bottle, passed it around, and each man filled his glass. Then Hoa offered up a toast that, although Charlie could not understand exactly what was said, was clearly in honor of Charlie. Charlie lifted his glass to the other men and downed his beer. This process was repeated two more times with different men offering toasts each time. The entire group downed their beer and waited for the next toast. After the group finished saluting Charlie, the bottles were distributed around the table and large bowls of food and rice took their place on the lazy Susan. The men continued to offer up individual toasts as they piled food from the large bowls into saucers at each place. Xun translated the Chinese toasts for Charlie, but Charlie was surprised that many of the men seemed to speak understandable English. This knowledge put him more at ease and he began to relax and enjoy the meal, along with the company of the men seated around the table.

After everyone was full, Hao began the business meeting. He outlined the terms of Charlie's contract with the company, noting that Charlie would be required to spend at least two weeks of each month in the field, and possibly even more time at the beginning of the project. He explained that the company would pay for Charlie's hotel for two more days until he and Fariha had located a suitable apartment, and then the company would pay for the apartment. Charlie would have to furnish the apartment with his own money, however. Charlie would also retain Xun as his driver/interpreter, and Fariha was welcome to use Xun for her own purposes when Charlie was in the field. He outlined Charlie's other benefits, including a more than generous salary, and an investment plan. This plan, Charlie concluded, was similar to the one he had in India. It was a part of the company but was actually administered by the Chinese government. Charlie would also have health benefits. The company required that Charlie must have a complete physical before he began working, and Charlie was glad to hear that. He hadn't seen a doctor since the infection following his vasectomy reversal, and his asthma had become much worse. A visit to a physician was a good opportunity to get that under control. All in all, Charlie was very pleased with the contract and happily signed the papers that Hao passed to him.

Charlie felt that he had finally put his problems behind him. He didn't actually start work for another week, and he and Fariha had two days to locate an apartment to her liking. He would let her choose their living quarters since she would be the main person living there. Once again, he would be the absentee husband, as he had been with Anna. He hoped that he wouldn't be tempted to cheat on Fariha as he had on Anna. He felt a twinge of guilt as he thought about the women with whom he had affairs over the years of his marriage to Anna. But then he thought about Fariha's beauty and sexual skills. He decided that he would never need to cheat on her.

By the time Xun dropped him off at the hotel, Charlie was feeling excited about the future. He went quickly to their room and told Fariha all about his meeting and his new job. She seemed to catch his excitement and they talked long into the night about what sort of place they wanted to live in and all the things they wanted to see and do while living there. Xun was scheduled to pick them up early the next morning to start looking at apartments. Charlie went to bed feeling exhausted but relieved. He had a feeling that, at last, things had turned around and his future with Fariha was assured. He had managed to fix their financial problems and he would be able to provide for her as he had promised. He fell into a dreamless sleep and was surprised when the alarm woke him the next morning.

Xun picked them up right on time and they began searching the city for an apartment. They told Xun their requirements. They wanted a large apartment with at least two bedrooms, a modern kitchen and bathroom, and it must be close to shopping, restaurants and entertainment. Xun listened to their demands without expression and told them about Shenyang. The city covered a large geographic area and was comprised of five different districts, plus an additional three counties. Each area had its own personality, so Xun took them to the area that seemed to best fit their needs. Getting around the city would not be difficult for them, as there was a grid system, as well as several loops that made access to the various areas quite easy. In addition to the language barrier, the only other problem was the traffic, which was heavy at all times. Xun's services as their driver would be invaluable, but they could use the bus system. There were also high-speed trains that could take them out of the city if they wanted to go sightseeing elsewhere. Xun seemed quite proud of Shenyang and its modern transportation systems.

Xun drove them into the Tiexi District, the section of Shenyang that was noted for blocks of residential complexes as well as shopping strips. As Charlie and Fariha looked around, they saw high-rise after high-rise, all apartment buildings. At street level, there were a variety of restaurants and shops. This area seemed to fill their requests quite nicely. After looking at several vacant apartments, they became discouraged, however. The apartments were so tiny! Charlie especially, being a large man, felt like Gulliver. Each place seemed designed for the smaller stature of the Chinese population rather than for accommodating someone Charlie's size. Charlie was beginning to worry. If they didn't find an apartment soon, he would be expected to start paying for their hotel. He had no money to do that. On the second day, however, they found a place that would do. It had a small living room that would be large enough for a sofa, end tables, and a television. There was no dining room, but the kitchen would hold a small table and two chairs. The kitchen itself was tiny. It was equipped with a hot plate rather than a stove, and the refrigerator would hold little more than a bottle of milk and a few vegetables. There was a small sink, of course, but no dishwasher, no oven, and very little cupboard space. Likewise, the bathroom was small but adequate. The apartment had only one small bedroom, but it had a large window that looked out over the street and had a distant view of a park a block away. This was apparently the best they could find, so Charlie had Xun contact the landlord and he negotiated a deal. They would rent the apartment for a year to begin with, at the company's expense, of course.

Charlie and Fariha packed their suitcases and checked out of the hotel the next day. Even though the apartment was empty, they were anxious to settle into their new home. Fariha said she wasn't comfortable living in a hotel. The truth was that she was afraid they would come across someone Charlie knew in the oil industry who would question their relationship and Charlie's marital status. Charlie hadn't actually started working yet, so they had almost no money. Buying furniture was out of the question until Charlie's first paycheck arrived. His credit cards were at their limit, so all Charlie had was the last bit of cash in his billfold. Hopefully, this would buy enough food to last until he was paid. Fariha was a surprisingly good sport about all of this. Her good mood was a mystery to Charlie, who expected her to be unhappy with the whole situation. In Fariha's mind, however, she had come that much closer to achieving her goal. She was married to an American and would soon be a rich woman, especially once she somehow gained access to Charlie's retirement account. After all she had endured in her life, she could be patient for a few more weeks until Charlie's paychecks started arriving.

The only down side she could see was that Charlie had aged considerably since she had first met him. He had put on weight and his once ruggedly handsome features were starting to look somewhat haggard. She reasoned, however, that in her culture, young women almost always married much older men, so her situation was not unusual. Even if she were no longer physically attracted to Charlie, she certainly was attracted to his money and would do whatever it took to protect the progress that she had made toward achieving her goal. So she put a smile on her face and pretended that their present circumstances didn't bother her that much.

Since they could not yet afford to buy furniture, Charlie and Fariha sat on the floor to eat and made a makeshift bed with a blanket that they had "borrowed" from the hotel, along with a single towel and cloth that they used for bathing. Fariha carefully doled out their skimpy supply of cash to buy the barest essentials for the kitchen. At a street market she purchased two plates. Chopsticks were everywhere and they were free, so she and Charlie learned to eat using the bamboo utensils. She purchased the least expensive food items she could find, and their diet consisted primarily of rice during those first three weeks. Neither she nor Charlie were happy with their living conditions, but they made do and both of them felt that the sacrifice would be well worth it in the long run. Fariha was about to achieve the culmination of what seemed to her to be months of planning and hard work. Charlie was looking forward to being independent and alone with Fariha without having to worry about money or family. Clearly, their goals were very different.

The first thing Charlie was required to do before he could begin his actual job was get a physical. He made the appointment and saw the doctor as soon as he could. When he entered the waiting room, he was surprised at how modern and well equipped the clinic seemed to be. Xun had come inside with him to translate, but there was no need, because the receptionist, the nurse, and the assistant doctor all spoke English. The assistant doctor checked Charlie's vision, hearing and reflexes, nodding his approval of the results. Then he listened to Charlie's heart and lungs. He told Charlie that his lungs didn't sound normal, and Charlie explained his long history of asthma and how it had become much worse since coming to China.

"I am not surprised," the doctor commented. "The air here is not good for someone like you. It is not good for anyone, really."

He then wrote out a prescription for a daily dose of steroids that would help Charlie even when he wasn't having an asthma attack and encouraged him to continue using the rescue inhaler as needed.

"Other than the asthma you are in excellent health. I will fill out the forms that your company requires to let them know that you are fit and ready to go to work."

Charlie thanked the doctor, got dressed, and he and Xun left the clinic. Charlie was happy that this step on the road to employment had been completed. He was now free to begin work within the next few days. This was indeed the start of a new chapter in his life, and he was excited to begin.

Charlie began working the next week, and Fariha found herself alone in the apartment most of the time. She walked the area around the apartment, gradually increasing the distance she went in each direction. Because she couldn't read the signs or speak the language, she had to guess from looking in the windows what each business was. She found many restaurants, which was excellent, she thought. She didn't plan on cooking a single meal in that miniscule kitchen once they had money again. She found a variety of shops, similar to those in Mumbai, that carried everything from clothing and jewelry to electronics and household goods. Most people appeared to shop for groceries each day, buying what they needed for the next meal only. She could understand that, given the size of the refrigerator in her kitchen. But, once again, she reminded herself that she didn't plan to do much cooking in the future anyway.

She realized that she was quickly becoming bored and vowed to find some way to entertain herself while Charlie was at work. As she walked down the street, she was aware that people were staring at her. At first, she thought it was simply because she wasn't Chinese. She was wearing western dress, rather than her Bengali saris, but most of the Chinese women she saw were also dressed as she was. It made her uncomfortable and self-conscious until she began to wonder if they were looking at her because she was beautiful. It seemed to Fariha that the men especially constantly caught her eye as she wandered the streets exploring the neighborhood. Her mind began to work on an idea, and she decided to test her theory. She knew she was still beautiful and, therefore, desirable. She began making eye contact with the men who made eye contact with her and found her looks being returned in a hungry way. In a society where women were traditionally trained to be modest and refrain from looking directly into another person's eyes, she found this very telling. It amused her to think that she still wielded sexual power over men. She hadn't used her sexual skills on anyone but Charlie for a very long time.

Within a week, Charlie received his first paycheck. It wasn't as large as his future checks would be, but it was plenty to buy furniture and get them back on their feet. Fariha took the check from Charlie and, with Xun's assistance, opened an account in a local bank. She brought home the forms to have Charlie's checks automatically deposited into the account, and she made arrangements for the statements to come to their apartment in her name, not Charlie's. She took a moment to rejoice, knowing that she now had at least partial control of Charlie's money. The end game was near.

Once the apartment was furnished and Fariha had money to spend, she began a new routine. Charlie had gone to the field and wasn't expected back in the city for several weeks. Fariha was left up to her own devices for entertainment. She began each day by eating breakfast at one of the local restaurants. Then she went shopping, buying whatever caught her fancy. She bought new clothes and jewelry; she bought trinkets to send to her mother in Bangladesh as proof that she was enjoying free rein with Charlie's money. She bought items to decorate their small apartment and she bought a television and state-of-the-art stereo system.

The television was an unnecessary luxury, because neither she nor Charlie could understand what was being said. Besides, she knew that whatever was broadcast had to meet the Chinese government's strict approval. She probably would not even turn the TV on, but it added a sense of prosperity to the look of the place. For a decorative item, she purchased a large painted tapestry to hang above the sofa. She thought it was pretty and the colors were soothing, but the main reason she bought it was as an obscene gesture to Charlie's wife and the tapestry Fariha had destroyed when she and Charlie first met.

She not only ate breakfast out, she began eating all of her meals out and decided that she would probably never need to cook again. She found that she enjoyed the food in the various restaurants, many of which were owned and operated by Koreans. One of her favorite dishes was called *suan cai* and was made with stewed chicken and mushrooms. She also enjoyed what was known as meat pie. The Korean restaurants served rice cakes and cold noodles, which Fariha grew to like as much as the traditional Chinese dishes she found in the Chinese-owned establishments. The tastes and smells were unique, and she had never had the opportunity to eat out often. While she and Charlie were in Mumbai, she was basically in hiding and ate almost all of her meals in the flat. In Bangladesh, they dined at her mother's table for almost every meal. She had never had such a variety of food from which to choose.

Fariha walked everywhere, despite the fact that she could have called on Xun to drive her wherever she wanted to go. The area surrounding her apartment had plenty to offer now that she had money to spend. She enjoyed eating out and shopping, of course, but she also spent hours sitting in the park near her apartment just watching the constant parade of people who streamed by. She had never seen so many people at once in her life, and she couldn't get over how crowded everything was in this new land.

She soon noticed the same man walking by her each day as she sat in the park. At first, he simply nodded his head as he walked by. He wore a well-cut suit of expensive-looking fabric and Fariha thought he must be a very successful businessman. With each day that he passed by, his look lingered a bit longer. He gave her a smile on the fifth day and she smiled in return. On the sixth day, he paused and indicated that he wanted to share the bench on which she was sitting. Neither one spoke, and after about five minutes he stood and walked away. On the seventh day, he finally spoke to her. Fariha was surprised to hear him speak English with a British accent, because he was clearly of Chinese descent.

"I notice that you sit here in the park every day," he said.

"Yes, I find it quite pleasant," she replied.

"Does the pollution bother you when you're outside like this?"

"No, I'm quite used to it. I have always lived where the air is unclean."

"Oh, really. Where is that?"

"I have lived in Mumbai as well as Dhaka. I have only been in Shenyang for a few weeks."

"You are here by yourself?"

"No, with my husband." And then she deliberately added, "He works out of the city most of the time."

The man nodded knowingly and said, "I see. Perhaps it is lonely for you."

"At times it is. I keep myself busy exploring the area around our apartment. It is only two blocks from here."

"Perhaps you could show it to me sometime," he suggested.

"Would you care to see it right now? It is a short walk away," Fariha invited.

"Of course." The man stood and held out his hand to help Fariha rise.

They walked toward the small apartment without touching or talking, but they both knew where this was headed. The only thing that remained to be said was how much this rendezvous was going to cost the man. Fariha decided that he could probably afford even her highest rate from her former career in India. She made up her mind to be bold and demand the highest price ever. The worst that could happen was that he would turn her down and walk away. But he did not do that. He gladly paid her price and, when their tryst was completed, he asked when he could see her again. Fariha smiled a shy smile, but inside she was laughing. Men were such fools! And she was still able to ply her trade; only this time the money wasn't going to anyone except her. China was a wonderful place indeed!

The man's name was Yu, which, he said, meant "rain" in Chinese. Fariha thought that was appropriate, since he was going to rain down money on her. He was from Shanghai originally but had been educated at Oxford University and other schools in England from the time he was a young boy. His parents were successful import/export dealers and had sent him to boarding school early on, because they felt the education he would receive in China would not serve him well in the future. As things turned out, they were correct. He came back from England as a well-educated gentleman and took over his father's business. Eventually, he bought out several other companies and had become independently wealthy at the young age of 35. He knew the best people and had many friends in government who had helped him out along the way. He had done them favors in return, of course, and had ended up a very powerful man. He was in Shenyang every few weeks on business and hoped to see Fariha whenever he was in the city. He said he found Chinese women unattractive and Fariha's exotic beauty fascinated him. Fariha knew she had a steady customer if she chose to continue the relationship.

Fariha soon worked out a system with Yu. If Charlie was out of town and she was available, she would sit in the park during the noon hour. Yu would walk by that same bench at noon whenever he was in Shenyang. Their meetings became more and more frequent and they got to know each other quite well. Eventually, Yu asked Fariha if she were interested in entertaining other gentlemen of his class. She replied that she was, and she slowly built a steady clientele of men who paid for her services whenever Charlie was out in the field.

Charlie naively never suspected anything. When he came home, Fariha was always there waiting for him. He noticed that she had new clothes and they looked expensive, but she justified them saying that she was very efficient at handling money and had saved enough from Charlie's pay to purchase the new items. She still thrilled Charlie in the bedroom, and he was always so glad to be back in her arms that he never questioned her. In fact, he left all money matters to Fariha. He was busy at work and chose not to be bothered with their finances. As long as he was making money and Fariha was happy, he asked no questions.

Their lives in China settled into a comfortable routine. Charlie was in the field for two weeks, and then home for one week. This pattern made it easy for Fariha to schedule appointments for her side business without worrying about Charlie arriving unexpectedly. It wasn't long before Fariha's closet was filled with new clothing and she began to grow weary of shopping. She realized that her new sideline gave her the perfect opportunity to insure her future without any contribution from Charlie, so she opened a savings account in her name only. She was delighted to see that her regular deposits were rapidly growing into a substantial retirement account of her own. That, along with Charlie's money, would see her living comfortably well into old age.

One day, as Fariha was dressing to meet Yu in the park, she noticed that her skirt fit more snugly than usual around the waist. She was able to zip the garment, but it was quite tight. She didn't think she had gained any weight, so she went to the full-length mirror that Charlie had mounted behind the bathroom door and took a long look at herself. She saw nothing unusual and decided that she had better cut back on ordering when she ate out. Within a few days, however, she knew that overeating wasn't her problem. Her waistline continued to expand and her breasts felt swollen and sore. Despite all of her precautions, she was pregnant. Due to the government's efforts to curb the exponential population growth, birth control was easy to obtain in China, and Fariha had been meticulous with her own protection, as well as that of her clients. But she had missed her period and was late once again. She had also been feeling nauseous in the mornings, although she hadn't actually gotten sick. The smell of garlic cooking especially bothered her, and she had always loved that odor before. She had no idea who the father was, of course, and because chances were that the father was of Chinese descent, there was no way she could fool Charlie into thinking that the baby was his if he were not the father. Her options were few and simple. She would get an abortion.

She found a clinic not far from her neighborhood and scheduled an appointment. This particular clinic did abortions frequently as a part of the accepted practice in China to help keep the population explosion under control, so no one questioned Fariha or asked embarrassing questions. It appeared to be just one more routine procedure for the medical staff. Following the procedure, Fariha took a cab home and stayed in the apartment to rest and recuperate for a couple of days. She tried to tell herself that it was no big deal. But she went through a hard time emotionally for a few days.

She wasn't grieving the loss of the baby. She truly didn't care about that. But she decided that the risk to her overall plan was too great. If Charlie ever suspected that she was seeing other men, he would cast her aside without another thought. She had no doubt about that. The thought of losing Charlie didn't upset her any more than the thought of losing the baby, but the thought of losing Charlie's money sent her into a tailspin. She had worked too hard and too long to let another pregnancy or Charlie's discovering her liaisons ruin her achieving her goal. She was on the final lap of this race, and nothing was going to stop her. Despite the elation she felt whenever she deposited more money into her private account, she knew she had to stop seeing her clients. It was too dangerous and she might risk not reaching her end goal…having access to all the money and leaving Charlie high and dry once she had it.

She met Yu in the park one last time and they went to her apartment as usual. This time, however, they didn't have sex. Fariha told Yu that she was ill with uterine cancer and would no longer be able to perform her services. She told him that she would be having extensive medical treatments and might even have to go to America or somewhere else in order to survive. She worked up tears to accompany her sad tale, and Yu was more than sympathetic. He didn't love her, but he had grown fond of her. She looked sad and frightened. He offered her money to help pay her medical expenses and she reluctantly accepted his offer. He wrote her a sizable check, kissed her on the cheek, and bade her goodbye.

Clearly, Yu did not care to be involved in the messy details of her treatment or recovery. He was done with her and would move on to someone else, which suited Fariha just fine. When she heard the elevator doors close behind him, Fariha smiled, wiped her tear-stained face, tucked the check into her purse, and headed to the bank. This unexpected money would more than make up for the business she was losing. She thought about how amazing things could turn out if a person were clever enough to turn a bad situation into a windfall such as this. She no longer had to deal with the piggish men who came to her with their tales of cold-hearted wives and lonely hearts. She didn't need them any more. She had managed to put herself in a position to be independent of Charlie if need be, but she planned to see her plan through to the end. Charlie wasn't so bad to be with; besides, he was only home one-third of the time anyway.

When Charlie did come home, he was usually tired and spent the first couple of days just enjoying Fariha and their apartment. They ordered food from nearby restaurants and ate in the apartment at the little kitchen table. Sometimes they stayed in bed most of the day. Although Charlie was getting old in Fariha's estimation, he still had an insatiable sexual appetite and was never ready to do anything else until his desire for her had been satisfied. By the third day, however, Charlie was usually ready to enjoy doing some sightseeing and taking in the local entertainment.

After quitting her other business, Fariha often called Xun to drive her to places of interest throughout Shenyang, so she was quite familiar with what the city had to offer in terms of entertainment. She toured the Mikden Palace, the former imperial palace dating all the way back to the early Qing dynasty. She attended several dances at the Dawutai Theater, famous for its Er Ren Zhuan and Chinese skit performances. Without understanding the language, she was able to understand and appreciate the humor. She thought it felt good to laugh, and she realized that there had not been much laughter in her life over the years. She had even spent a glorious weekend at Qipan Mountain in the Shenbei District. This recreational resort in the northeast part of Shenyang was a much-needed get away from the crowded city and her small apartment. She also enjoyed the Shenyang Botanical Garden, but her favorite was Shenyang Meteorite Mountain Park.

Located southeast of Shenyang, the park was the site of a 4.5 billion year old meteorite that had fallen to earth 1.9 billion years before. Fariha was staggered by those numbers. They reinforced her belief that what she might do or not do really didn't matter in the big picture of things. She was in a particular place at a particular time, but in terms of the entire universe, what she did was inconsequential to anyone other than herself. Therefore, she didn't need empathy from other human beings and she didn't need a conscience. She was a speck in the scheme of creation. She would live for her own pleasure while she existed and, beyond that, she didn't know what would happen. She didn't believe in God or follow any particular religion. She simply was; the earth simply was. There was no room for speculation about what might come next. Today, this moment, was the only thing under her control. That was the credo by which she lived her life.

After many months, Fariha was feeling quite comfortable with her life in China. She had secretly laid aside a great deal of money; she lived in a decent apartment by Chinese standards and owned a fabulous high-end wardrobe; her husband was loving and attentive when he was around, which, she thankfully realized, was not that often; and she had freedom to do whatever she wanted when he was away. She had to be prepared to tell Charlie how she had spent her time, of course; but that was easy, especially once she quit her side business and was doing nothing of which Charlie wouldn't approve.

Chapter Thirty-Two: A New Development

Fariha called Xun to take her to a shopping mall in another of Shenyang's districts. She had heard that the shops were unique and had items not available in other areas. She didn't really intend to buy anything; she just wanted to see what was there. On another day, Xun drove her to Middle Street, a shopping area that featured many western-style stores and restaurants. She was amazed to see the Wal-Mart and Pizza Hut, especially when she realized that in Shenyang, Pizza Hut was a fancy restaurant. She enjoyed shopping in the Louis Vuitton flagship store. There was even a Haagen-Dazs retail store on Middle Street. In addition, she wandered the large shopping mall also located on Middle Street. The mall featured products from all around the world. It was interesting to Fariha to see items from India and Bangladesh showcased in stores in Shenyang. It was definitely a small world.

Following one of these outings, as Xun drove across the city toward her home, Fariha was startled when he turned the car into a side street and parked. He seldom spoke, other than to tell her about the sights of the city, but this time he had a different agenda.

"I know about the men you have been seeing," he said in a matter-of-fact tone.

Fariha remained silent, waiting for him to continue, although she could guess what was coming next.

"I will give you two choices. Either you pay me to remain silent or I will tell your husband what you have been doing during his absences. If you pay me what I ask, I will not come back for any more money. I want to move to Shanghai and study at the university there. I have already been accepted. This money will make it possible for me to do that. You will never see or hear from me again. If you don't pay, I will tell him the whole story. I know that you meet men in the park and take them to your apartment. I also know that you were pregnant and chose to have an abortion. How would he feel if he thought you might have killed his baby?"

Fariha's silence continued for a few more moments, and then she agreed to do as Xun asked. "I will give you the money," she said. "How much do you want?"

"Twenty-five thousand will take care of my needs. I swear that is all I will ever ask of you."

Fariha had to smile. There was that amount again. It seemed as if her entire life hinged on the same $25,000. The amount just moved from one person to another, but it was always there to haunt her. "All right," she finally replied. "I will give you the money, but it will take me some time to get it. A week, perhaps. You can come back a week from today and I will have the money for you."

"Excellent! That will give me just enough time to move to Shanghai before school begins. I will come in one week."

The negotiation completed, Xun started the car, pulled back into the never-ending traffic, and drove Fariha the rest of the way back to her building. She got out of the car without Xun's usual assistance, shut the door firmly, and walked into the building without saying a word to him. She had the money. That would not be a problem if she had intended to give it to him. But she was determined that Xun would never see his plans work out. She was not going to give him any money, nor would he ever attend college in Shanghai. She had one week to come up with a plan of her own.

She fixed herself a pot of tea and sat on the sofa. She came up with several ideas, but discarded them immediately as being impractical or too dangerous. Finally she hit on a plan that she thought would work nicely, although it might be somewhat risky. She called one of the men who used to frequent her apartment. She knew from their conversations that he had connections in the Shenyang underworld, and she needed his help in recruiting someone to help her. When she told him that she was being blackmailed and needed someone to help her discourage the blackmailer from bothering her, he quickly agreed. He gave her a name and phone number, and, wishing her good luck, he disconnected the call.

She immediately called the number. When the man answered, she said a code word that she had been told would let him know who had given her his information. The man's tone changed from guarded to curious, and she explained that she wanted to hire him to fix a problem for her. They arranged to meet the next day at a teahouse quite far from Fariha's apartment. It was in another district entirely, but Fariha thought that was a good thing. She didn't want to be seen with this gang member anywhere near her home.

She spent the rest of the day planning. First, she went to the bank and withdrew $5,000 from her private account. She didn't know how much this person would demand to do the job, but she figured it wouldn't be more than that amount, especially when she came with cash in hand. Then she spent the rest of the afternoon studying the bus schedule to figure out how to get to the teahouse using public transportation. By noting the bus lines designated in different colors on the map and then matching the symbols, she was able to determine a route, even though she still did not know how to speak or read the Chinese dialect spoken in Shenyang.

To her surprise, the teahouse was quite upscale and in a good district of Shenyang. This made Fariha feel more comfortable. She hadn't known what to expect and had been afraid that she herself might be at risk during this meeting. When the man arrived, he didn't look at all as she had expected either. He was nicely dressed and well groomed, not at all the stereotypical gangster. They sat on the floor cushions and were served a traditional tea ceremony by a lovely Chinese woman who never said a word to either of them. When she left, Fariha told the man what she wanted.

"I need this person to disappear," she said. "He is already planning to leave the city and move to Shanghai, so there are time constraints. On the other hand, his absence will not be questioned since he has already made arrangements to quit his job and move."

"That is perfect, then. The cover story will be simple. It has already been put in place by this man himself. How do you plan to pay me for my services?" He asked.

"How much do you want to be paid for those services?
"

"I would need $3,000 up front, and another $3,000 when the job is completed," he stated.

"What if I gave you all the money, in cash, up front? Would there be a discount? It would reduce your risk if you never had to meet with me again. I should tell you, though, that if you fail to complete your assignment, I will have my contacts hunt you down and you will pay for trying to cheat me," she warned.

He looked at her appraisingly. "I consider myself warned," he said with a hint of a smile. The ruthlessness in her voice made him believe that she would certainly follow up on her threat if necessary. "If I were paid in cash up front, I could do the job for $5,000. That is quite a bargain, I might add."

Fariha held out her hand and he shook it. She was a cool character, he thought. Her hand was warm and dry, showing no signs of nervousness. She had a firm grip and seemed quite self-assured.

"It is done, then," she said while taking the envelope containing the money out of her purse and placing it on the table. Then she rose, nodded to the man, and calmly walked out of the teahouse.

The man smiled broadly. This was quite a woman. If he had the time and the energy, he might have pursued her. She surely would have given him a run for his money. She knew exactly how much he was going to ask and had come prepared. In the envelope with the cash, she had placed a note with all the information he needed in order to complete the job. Along with the note, she had included instructions for him to burn the note and the envelope as soon as he had memorized the necessary information. No detail had been omitted from her plan, and he admired that. He also had no doubt that, if he failed to do exactly what she hired him for, she would make good on her promise to have him hunted down and punished.

He put the envelope inside his jacket and whistled a happy tune as he left the teahouse. He enjoyed doing this kind of work. The intrigue, planning and excitement kept him energized, and he got a mysterious thrill when he watched the life drain from a person's eyes. He didn't understand it, he didn't question it, he just enjoyed it. The money was an added benefit, of course. This job was just one of several that he had on his to-do list, but working for this particular woman gave the job priority somehow. Besides, the victim was about to leave the city, so the man mentally moved him up to the top of his list and headed for home to plan out his actions.

Charlie called Fariha two days later. He rarely called from the field, so at first she was alarmed. *Does Charlie somehow know what I have done? Has Xun told him of my betrayal already? Has Charlie been injured, or, even worse, has he been fired?* All of these thoughts ran quickly through her head before she heard him continue to speak.

"I just called to let you know that Xun quit his job," Charlie said.

"Oh, really?" she replied calmly, feigning surpris   "Yes. He's leaving Shenyang for Shanghai. He's been accepted at one of the universities there. He turned in his resignation as of the end of the week."

"I just saw him a few days ago when he took me to a shopping mall across the city. He never mentioned a word of this to me," she lied.

"Apparently it's a done deal," Charlie said. "I called to see if you want to have another driver. I can arrange that from here, since

I won't be home for another week. Will you need a driver before then?"

"That's so thoughtful of you, Charlie," she gushed. "I think I can do without a driver for a week. I'm not planning to go anywhere. But it would be nice to have a replacement for Xun by the time you come home. I have been planning where we should go and what we should do the next time you're in the city. There are so many things to see here."

"OK, then, I will make sure that we have a new driver by next week. I'll see you in seven days. I love you."

"Love you, too," she said. Then she disconnected the call. She was getting nervous. She wouldn't know if her plan had worked until Xun did or did not show up for his money on his way out of the city in five days. Charlie would be home two days later, so, if Xun were still around by then, he could easily contact Charlie to tell him of her deceit. She had no intention of paying Xun the money he had demanded. If the man she had contracted with did not come through, she hoped she could quickly come up with a backup plan.

She decided that if Xun did contact Charlie, she would calmly tell Charlie that Xun had made advances to her and she had rebuffed him. He was telling Charlie lies to get back at her for embarrassing him and hurting his ego. Surely Charlie would believe this story. Charlie seemed to believe whatever she told him. She had never met a man who was so easily swayed. He seemed to bend whichever way the wind was blowing at the moment, with little thought about what might happen as a result. This made it much easier for her, of course, but she wondered how he had come to be so malleable and passive. She didn't care, but she was curious.

Xun never came to collect the money he had demanded of Fariha, so Fariha took that as a good sign that the man from the teahouse had kept his word. Charlie was delayed by three days, but when he came home from the field, he had interesting news regarding Xun.

"Apparently Xun said his goodbyes at work and drove off in the company car, promising to take it back to the firm's transportation depot the next day when he boarded the train for Shanghai. The car was never returned, however. People became concerned and contacted the university in Shanghai. Xun had never shown up to enroll. It seems that Xun simply disappeared with the company car. There was no one left to contact, because Xun had no family, and the few friends who were questioned seemed to think that he had gone to Shanghai as planned. Where he is and what he is doing are a mystery to everyone!" Charlie explained.

Fariha acted as puzzled as possible by this news. That meant that her plan had worked and the man had done his job. Not only had he been paid for his work, but he had also ended up with the car that, she assumed, was already disassembled and the parts sold on the black market. The man was obviously smart, and she just hoped that he was smart enough to believe her threats if he came back to her about any of this. Then she decided that there was no use in worrying about something that might never happen, so she put a smile on her face and walked into Charlie's waiting arms.

There had been a small wrinkle to deal with, but she had ironed it out and things were back as they should be. Charlie heard her sigh and thought that she was relieved that he was home. Fariha was thinking how quickly things could become complicated, but how easily they could be dealt with. It was her intelligence rather than her beauty that had saved her this time.

Chapter Thirty-Three: Another Plan

Fariha was not completely satisfied with how things were progressing. It was beginning to look as if Charlie's former employer was never going to release the money in his retirement account. She wanted more than just his regular income and the money in her private account. When she asked Charlie to get his vasectomy reversed, she was hopeful that she might become pregnant with his child. She had become pregnant, of course, but she was quite sure that Charlie was not the father, since she hadn't become pregnant sooner. Her plan had been to have Charlie's child, because there would then be no doubt about who might get his money if something were to happen to him. Since that hadn't worked out, she decided on a different approach.

One evening after Charlie had been home for a day and was well rested and relaxed, she cuddled up to him on the couch and put her next idea to the test.

"Charlie, I've been thinking," she said gently. "You are a few years older than I am and, although I hate to think of living life without you, it is reasonable to think that your life will be over many years before mine."

"That's true," he said. "I've had the same thoughts myself from time to time."

"Well, I hate to bring up such an unpleasant subject, but I worry, Charlie. What will happen to me when you are gone? I don't want to go back to Bangladesh, dependent on my family to take care of me. I know you have been putting some money aside, but I don't know if that would be enough to last for the rest of my life. I'm afraid of the future, Charlie," she pouted.

"I understand, but I don't know what to do about it. I can't make myself any younger," he said, trying to make light of the topic.

"I have thought of something that you could do to assure my future, Charlie. It could be as simple as signing your name."

"What do you mean?"

"We could get a life insurance policy for you. It wouldn't cost that much, but it would make me feel much better about what will happen to me once you are gone. I will miss you, Charlie, but I'd rather miss you with money in the bank than living in poverty. It would ease my mind to know that my future is secure."

"Of course, Darling. I can easily do that. If it will make you feel better, I can get the paperwork started tomorrow. I know my company has insurance plans available to its employees. I just never thought about it before now. Now, come here and kiss me. I've missed you, you know!"

"I've missed you, too, Charlie," she replied as she moved in closer, but she was thinking how easy that had been. The conversation had gone just as she had hoped.

At the office the next day, Charlie went to the human resources department and asked about life insurance plans. He decided that $500,000 would be a nice buffer for Fariha once he was gone. The thought of dying didn't appeal to him but he hadn't minded that she had brought it up. He was enjoying his life and, while he didn't know what would come in the afterlife, he believed that there would be something. Perhaps he would be reincarnated as a lizard in India or as a tiger in Bangladesh. He certainly wasn't going to worry about that now. But he was going to make sure that Fariha was taken care of. He glanced through the paperwork and came to the last page where he was required to fill in some of the blanks. He wrote in the date and printed his name just above his signature.

Then, as he looked further down the page, he saw the section where he was to list his beneficiaries. On the first line he wrote Fariha's name and filled in her information. But there was another line to list a second beneficiary in case the first beneficiary was unable to collect the money. It had never occurred to him that Fariha might not outlive him, but one never knew, did they? On impulse, he quickly wrote in Anna's name and address. He wasn't sure why. Perhaps it was a way of trying to make up for his behavior without having to actually do anything. Perhaps he still cared about her, at least a little. At any rate, she was unlikely to see any of this money and would probably never even know he had written her name on that line. He gathered up the sheaf of papers, handed them to the administrator, and left the office without giving it another thought.

That evening he told Fariha, "The insurance policy will be in effect in a couple of days. You could stop worrying about your future. Five-hundred thousand dollars will go a long way toward taking care of you for the rest of your life."

She went to him and kissed him long and hard. Charlie reacted as she expected and she led him to the bedroom. As usual, she had gotten her way and achieved another goal.

Chapter Thirty-Four: Anna's Return

Anna's life in Taos quickly returned to the way it had been before she left for the lake house, with the exception that she had no money at all, and it looked as if Charlie was never going to send her any. When she drove into town, she headed straight for Helen and Lee's house. When Helen answered the door, she could tell immediately that Anna had suffered while she was gone. She had lost a great deal of weight and her hair hung limply around her face. Anna's color wasn't good either. She was very pale and looked as if she had been very ill. Helen invited her in and offered her a cup of coffee, which Anna gratefully accepted. After letting Bella into the yard and watching Simba settle into a familiar feline ball on the couch, Helen invited Anna to sit down and talk.

Anna began guardedly, but, sensing Helen's accepting spirit, she eventually told her about her terrible winter in the lake house. As she talked, Anna kept her tears in check, and Helen listened empathetically as she related the entire, horrible experience. When Anna confessed that she had no money, Helen offered to let her stay in their guest room until she could save enough money for a place of her own.

"You would do that?" Anna questioned.

"Of course." Helen replied. "We're your friends. In fact, we're as close to being family as you can get. You are welcome to stay here for as long as you need to."

Anna was so relieved that she wrapped Helen in her arms and just held on for dear life. Finally, she went out to the truck and dragged in her few belongings. When Helen saw how little Anna had, she was startled. The physical change in Anna had been alarming, but to see her brought this low was staggering.

Anna returned to her job at the souvenir shop, which paid her well, considering the type of work she was doing. She was able to save enough over the first few months to put a deposit on renting a place of her own. She couldn't bring herself to impose on Helen and Lee any longer than absolutely necessary. She went to the library, did a search and found a small apartment for rent several blocks away from the plaza. By living there, she could save money by walking to work and paying as little rent as possible. How much space did she need anyway? Simba took no room to speak of, and she would make sure to walk Bella twice a day and take her to the mountains or desert to have a good run on her days off. She wouldn't have room to entertain, or even to set up her loom; but then she realized that she didn't even have a loom or furniture any more. She could always go to El Rito and use their looms to do her weaving.

She and Charlie had exchanged occasional e-mails over the months since she first re-established communication with him. The content of those messages was totally predictable. She would ask for money and he would say that he wasn't able to send her any. She did learn two additional things, however. First, he revealed that he was working once again and was in China somewhere. Second, he led her to believe that That Woman had total control of Charlie's finances.

Anna never asked Charlie That Woman's name, and he never volunteered it. Anna just thought of her as That Woman. In Anna's mind, That Woman didn't deserve a name, because she was less than human. *Who would do what she has done to me? What about all the other people she has hurt? How many people's lives has she destroyed or harmed? The list is surely too long to count.*

Anna didn't find it too hard to believe that Charlie had allowed That Woman to take over his life so completely. When she thought about it, she could see how easily Charlie was influenced by whatever was occurring at any given moment. He never did seem to have much concern for the consequences of his actions. *Perhaps he's incapable of looking into the future and visualizing what will happen as a result of what he does today. He disgusts me as much as That Woman disgusts me. She is obviously a conniving, money-*

hungry bitch, and Charlie deserves what he gets. But, Anna thought bitterly, *I do not deserve what I have gotten. Neither does my family or Charlie's mother.* Anna did believe in karma, however, and that Charlie would suffer the effects of the negative karma that was surely coming to him. She prayed the same for That Woman. At times she would dream up plots to get even with Charlie. She was so hurt and angry that she felt she would gladly murder him with her bare hands if she ever had the opportunity.

Anna stayed very busy with her job, her dogs, and trying to get to El Rito to weave as often as she could. She had many friends and frequently went to their homes for lunch or knitting sessions. She enjoyed following the athletic teams from the University of New Mexico in Albuquerque, and she often listened with friends as the Lobos' football and basketball games were broadcast on the radio. They would share in the ups and downs of the games over a beer or a glass of wine. For a long time, she felt content and was able to keep thoughts of Charlie from invading her happiness.

Eventually, however, she began to feel the need for male companionship on a more serious level. She did have a few male friends, of course, but the relationships were purely platonic. Her brief sexual encounter with Helen's nephew had been a refreshing interruption to her celibacy, but she was human. Obviously, Charlie had no moral compunction regarding sex with another woman while still married to Anna. Why should she not enjoy some of the same? She had always enjoyed sex with Charlie, and she missed the intimacy of a romantic relationship. Yes, she was married, but that was only a formality at this point. She hadn't yet decided what to do about that, and she had several options to consider.

First of all, she knew that Charlie and That Woman must have told the Chinese government that they were married. She knew, however, that they hadn't mentioned that Charlie already had a wife and, therefore, their marriage was illegal. She could turn them in and they would be deported at best, or jailed at worst, for lying in order for That Woman to get into the country with Charlie. That might give Anna some satisfaction, but she would be shooting herself in the foot if she had any hope of eventually getting money

187

from Charlie. If he lost his job again, he probably wouldn't be able to get another…especially if he were in a Chinese jail.

Her second option was to sue Charlie for divorce. That would free her up to see and possibly even marry someone else, and she might even get a lucrative divorce settlement. But that would come from a court in the U.S. Would Charlie pay attention to her demands? Would he even sign the divorce papers? Most important of all, how could she possibly afford a lawyer to file for divorce on her behalf?

In his most recent e-mails, Charlie had subtly hinted that he had some regrets about what he had done. His health was suffering in the polluted air of China. He even said at one point that he was "sorry" he couldn't send her the money she needed. She realized, of course, that he hadn't said he was sorry for what he had done to Anna and his family, but to Anna, it sounded as if his hard shell was cracking just a tiny bit. As she looked at her options, Anna decided that filing for divorce was the best chance she had of ever getting some money from Charlie and being free to move on with her life.

She contacted the Legal Aid Society and told her story to one of the lawyers. The lawyer, whose name was Carolyn, listened attentively, shook her head, and said, "I've never heard anything like this. I would have to talk to someone and get some advice about the best way to proceed. I understand that you have no money, but are you sure your husband does?"

"Oh yes, he has money. He has made a fortune over the years that we've been married. What I don't know is how much of it he can get That Woman to let him have. It seems that she has total control of his finances."

"I guess we'll have to see if he'll pay attention to a court order from New Mexico," Carolyn said. "I will get back to you as soon as I consult with one of my colleagues who might have some insight as to how best to proceed."

Anna's hopes rose a bit. She wouldn't allow herself to think that this might be the solution to her problems, but she thought that, perhaps, there might be a reason to allow herself a spark of hope. When a week went by and she hadn't heard back from Carolyn, Anna's hopes died once again. She assumed that whomever Carolyn had consulted had told her that the case was hopeless and not to even waste her time.

Chapter Thirty-Five: The Gallery

Anna knew she had to make some money in addition to what she earned at the souvenir shop, or perhaps find something entirely different that would pay more. She looked at herself long and hard in an attempt to figure out what assets she had to offer. She was athletic and physically strong, she was a hard worker, she was artistic, she was good with people, and she was smart. Most of all, she decided, she was a survivor. *No!* she thought. *I'm a thriver!* But what good did all of those qualities do her? She didn't need credits on her resume; she needed a job—one that would pay her a living wage. She began asking her friends and acquaintances if they knew of anyone looking for an employee. She searched the newspaper and the internet job postings. Finally, she found the perfect position. It was a gallery in town, and this time the position was titled "manager". The ad stated that experience was required, but she had experience, didn't she? Perhaps she hadn't worked at the other gallery for very long, but she had worked there and was sure that the owner would give her a good reference. She called the number listed in the ad and set up an appointment for the very next afternoon. She would have to take time off from her job, but this was more important.

She printed a fresh copy of her resume, dressed carefully, and drove to the gallery. It was a well-known gallery just south of the plaza and, when she entered, she could see that there were quite a few people milling around as they looked at the art on display. She was pleased to note that, in addition to paintings and sculptures, the gallery featured several beautiful woven pieces. Anna asked for Carlos, the name in the ad, and a pleasant, gray-haired woman took her to the back of the gallery and up a steep flight of stairs. The woman gestured to a closed door at the top of the stairs and began descending the staircase. Anna took a deep breath and knocked firmly on the door.

"Enter," said a strong, male voice from within.

Anna opened the door and, trying not to appear nervous, extended her hand as she said, "Carlos, I assume? I am Anna. I am here about the position you posted."

"Yes, of course," he said, shuffling some papers together and laying them to the side of his desk. "I am Carlos and I own this gallery. You are familiar with it, yes?"

"Of course," Anna replied. "Your gallery has a wonderful reputation here in town. You are known for displaying only the best work by local artists and charging fair prices." Then she added, "Although I could never afford to buy anything here."

"And why is that?" he asked. "You look like a very successful woman."

At that point, Anna explained her situation, leaving out most of the details. She said that her experience was somewhat limited, but she was an artist herself and had a good eye for quality. She also emphasized the time she had spent in retail sales, as well as an office manager. Carlos listened attentively and nodded occasionally as she spoke. Afraid that she had said too much, Anna quickly brought her thoughts to a close, handed Carlos her resume, and waited for him to speak.

Carlos took some reading glasses out of the top drawer of his desk and put them on. He briefly glanced at the paper she had given him, nodded, and said, "Well, then, let's give it a try. I like you, Anna. You seem intelligent and, although you say you have no money, you appear to be able to present the kind of image I want my employees to have. I will give you a chance to prove yourself. You can start by working two days a week. After two weeks, you and I will sit down and evaluate your work. At that time, if things are going well, I will increase your hours and your pay. Eventually, you may be in the manager's position and make her salary. She has given me a 60-day notice, so, if you work out, you will be taking her place in two months' time."

Anna couldn't believe her good fortune. He was giving her a chance, despite her lack of experience. Thank goodness she had worn her best clothes for this interview. Before she could respond, Carlos continued, "I am only offering you part-time work, Anna. Can you get by on that until we see if you will be working here full time?"

"Yes, I believe so. I will have to ask, but I'm quite sure that my boss at the souvenir shop will allow me to stay on until you make your decision. I will ask him to schedule my days off on the days you want me to work. That way, I can work for you without taking any time away from him. It will also give him time to find a replacement for me."

"Very well. You can start day after tomorrow, if that works for you. I assume your present job is busiest on the weekends, so I'll plan on your being here mid-week. That should work for your boss, I would think."

"Oh, yes. That's very thoughtful of you. Thank you so much!" With that, she extended her hand and she and Carlos shook firmly.

"You can report to Madelaine. You will be taking her place, so she will be the one to train you. I believe she showed you up here when you came in."

"Wonderful!" exclaimed Anna. "I will see you in two days."

Afterward, Anna didn't even remember rushing down the stairs and leaving the gallery. She knew that she had stopped to introduce herself briefly to Madelaine. She had only paused a moment, however, because Madelaine was busy talking with a customer about a large, abstract painting that was hanging near the front door. Anna ran up the sidewalk and around the corner, crossing the plaza quickly, despite the rush of tourists milling about. She opened the door of the souvenir shop so hard that it slipped from her hand and banged against the wall, the bell above the door gaily announcing her arrival. Her boss looked up in surprise and saw Anna grinning from ear to ear. She quickly told him about her visit to the gallery and her conversation with Carlos. At first he didn't say anything, and Anna thought that perhaps she had overestimated his concern for her welfare. Then he broke into a huge grin and gave her a big hug.

"You'll be great!" he said. "This is just what you should be doing. I've felt bad that I can't afford to pay you more. You certainly have earned it. I hate to lose you, but I'm happy for you at the same time."

Anna was so relieved that she didn't know what to say, so she just hugged him back. What a blessing he had been. He had hired her...twice, in fact...when she needed it the most. If it weren't for him, she wasn't sure what would have become of her. She would be forever grateful to the man.
As she walked home, she knew she had to tell Helen the good news. Then it dawned on Anna that she would have no days off for the next month. She hoped she was up to the challenge.

When Anna got to Helen's and excitedly told her about the interview and the offer Carlos had made, Helen gave Anna a big, congratulatory hug. Helen offered to walk Bella and look in on Simba, since Anna was about to have such a grueling schedule. Anna also realized that her new job would require a more sophisticated wardrobe than she had worn to the souvenir shop. At least she had some time to get that together. She could wear the same two outfits each week for the first month if she had to. Helen laughed as Anna fired off all the details she was thinking.

"Sit down and have a glass of wine, Anna. You need to calm down and decide how to celebrate your good fortune."

In her next e-mail to Charlie, Anna did not mention that she might have a new job. She wanted Charlie to understand how badly she needed money. She pled her case, saying only that she was forced to work seven days a week to make ends meet, and she was barely able to do that. What about her future? She was not young and couldn't work this kind of schedule forever. Charlie had a responsibility to provide for her now and in the future.

Her plea fell on deaf ears as far as she could tell. Charlie's response was the same as ever. He would send money when he was able.

Anna began her month of working every day with a positive attitude. In light of what she was learning to do at the gallery, though, her work at the souvenir shop became drudgery. At the gallery, she was learning basic bookkeeping, as well as the duties of office manager. She had to learn the computer system on which the inventory was kept, order office supplies, fix the printer when it broke down, and greet customers. In the evenings, she would study whatever information she could find on the artists whose work was on display, so that she could converse intelligently with the customers. By the end of the second week, she was exhausted, but she tried not to show it when she went in to meet with Carlos. He and Madelaine had both been encouraging and kind, but she didn't know if she had met their expectations. Two weeks wasn't very long to try to learn all that she needed to know if she were to become the manager of the gallery.

To her great relief, both Carlos and Madelaine agreed that she had been dong a wonderful job. Madelaine assured Anna that she was going to be relieved to turn the gallery over to Anna's capable hands, and Carlos agreed that Anna would do a stellar job. Anna left the meeting feeling that, at last, things were going her way. She had two more weeks of part-time at the gallery. After that, she would be done at the souvenir shop and would work with Madelaine full time prior to Madelaine's retirement. Anna knew that she still had a lot to learn, and she was looking forward to showing both Madelaine and Carlos just how capable she was.

Chapter Thirty-Six: Gray

The next day, Anna was working at the souvenir shop when she heard the bell over the door ring. She was in the back of the store unloading a new shipment, and she was dusty and disheveled as she walked briskly to the front of the store. Her boss was at lunch, and she was the only one there to wait on customers. Standing by the door was a man a few years older than Anna. He looked at her with vivid blue eyes, and she felt her stomach do a summersault.

"Hello. My name is Gray," he stated simply. "I was told to drop by this afternoon to see about some shelving that the owner would like me to build."

"He's not here right now, but he should be back shortly. Would you like to wait? There's really nowhere to sit in the store, but there is a bench just outside. You could wait there," Anna added helpfully. She hoped he would wait around. Something about him seemed intriguing, although she wasn't sure why she found him so interesting. She decided that she wanted to get to know him better.

Gray did wait, but he and Anna didn't speak to each other any more that day. He came in the next day to do the measurements for the shelves, but he didn't talk to her at all. The following day, all he said was "Hello" and then he was on his way. She was disappointed, because she found him very attractive. Her heart told her that she should get to know this man better, but how could she do that if he wouldn't even speak to her? After a week of this, her boss said that he thought Gray might be interested in Anna, but was too shy to ask her out. This was news to Anna, who thought Gray was totally oblivious to her. She decided that time was running out. She had only one more week at the souvenir shop and then she would be working full time at the gallery.

The next time Gray came in, she walked right up to him, and said, "Hello, Gray. It's my lunch hour. Would you like to join me for lunch?" Anna was shocked at her own words. She had never been this forward with anyone, much less a man.

To her relief, Gray broke into a huge grin and told her that he'd love to go to lunch with her. As her boss watched, smiling in the background, Anna grabbed her purse and she and Gray walked out of the store.

They went to lunch together for the next several days and quickly got to know each other. They had many interests in common. They both loved reading mysteries, riding bicycles, hiking, and gardening. Anna, of course, had little time to do any of these things, but she was looking forward to a more sane work schedule in another week. Gray listened closely as she told him just the basics of her financial and marital situation. He told her that he was divorced and had a grown daughter who was in college in California. His ex-wife lived in Albuquerque, but he seldom saw her. He couldn't say their divorce had been amicable, but they weren't bitter enemies either. He no longer had to pay child support, but he paid for his daughter's tuition and books anyway, because he loved her and was proud of her. He had lived in Taos since his divorce ten years ago and loved the area. He was the owner of a small but successful remodeling company, stayed busy and was comfortable financially, if not wealthy.

Gradually, Gray coaxed Anna into telling him the details of her life story over several weeks' time. First she told him all about Charlie, how happy they had been, how foolish she had been not to listen to her misgivings about his fidelity, and about his unwillingness to send her any money despite the fact that he had abandoned her with no resources. She also told Gray about her first marriage, about Bradley and his family, and about David, Valerie, and her worries about Jordan's welfare. She spoke of her concern for Grace, and how it hadn't seemed to bother Charlie in the least to know that his own mother had been made homeless by his bad decisions.

Gray listened sympathetically to Anna's tale. He had never heard such a story and he became incensed with Charlie and his actions.

One evening over dinner, Gray looked into Anna's eyes and said, "I care deeply about you, Anna. I want to explore our relationship to see if we want to take it to the next level. But I am a moral man. I grew up with certain values that I can't break. How can I act on my feelings when I know that you are married and are, therefore, unavailable," he said with despair in his voice.

"I feel the same way," Anna declared. "But I don't know what to do. The lawyer never called me back about filing for divorce, so I think she must have decided it was hopeless. I'm stuck and can't see a way out."

"Call the lawyer back," Gray urged. "If she can't do the divorce, find another lawyer who will!"

"I can't afford another lawyer," Anna stated flatly.

"I'll pay for the lawyer for you," Gray offered.

"I couldn't let you do that," Anna countered, "but I will call Carolyn back tomorrow and see what she found out. Maybe she's just been busy."

Chapter Thirty-Seven: New Hope

The next day during her afternoon break, Anna called Carolyn "I'm so sorry I haven't gotten back to you!" Carolyn apologized. "My mother had a heart attack and I had to fly back to Atlanta to make arrangements for her care. I just got back to my office this morning. You were on my list of people to call, I promise."

"I understand. I'm very sorry about your mother. I hope she will be all right." Then, after a brief pause she continued. "Were you able to figure out if there is anything we can do about my situation?"

"From what you said about Charlie's recent e-mails, it sounds as if he might be having some second thoughts. Instead of saying that he won't send the money, he's blaming it on this other woman. I'm wondering if, perhaps, he would welcome the opportunity to get out of his marriage to you in order to make his marriage to her legitimate. What do you think?" asked Carolyn.

"At this point, I have no idea. I guess it's worth a try. But I can't afford an expensive divorce. I can't afford anything extra at all," said Anna.

"Let's make an appointment for you to come in and we'll talk about your options. I won't charge you. In fact, I'm hopeful that Charlie will end up paying for that appointment and any others that we need, in addition to coming up with a great deal of money for you!"

Encouraged by Carolyn's words, Anna agreed. She scheduled an appointment for her first day off, just a few days away.

When she got off the phone with Carolyn, she called Gray and told him what Carolyn had said. Anna found it irritating when Gray gloated, "See? I told you that you should call her!"

Anna walked into Carolyn's office the next morning feeling exhausted and nervous. She had not slept, but, rather, she had tossed in her bed until she was tangled in the sheets. She went to the kitchen and fixed some chamomile tea in hopes that the hot beverage would soothe her nerves. She wasn't even sure why she was nervous. Perhaps she was just anxious to see if there was any hope, and she was too impatient to sleep calmly while waiting to find out. She lit the fire, and she and Bella watched the flames until Bella fell asleep and snored gently at her feet. At dawn, she rose from her chair and went to her room to get ready. She dressed carefully, choosing clothes that were appropriate for a visit to a lawyer's office, but she did not wear her best outfit. She wanted Carolyn to see that she had no money and was telling the truth about her situation.

This was Anna's first time ever seeing a lawyer and she didn't know what to expect. When she opened the door to the legal firm, she was pleased to see that it wasn't opulent and snooty as were some of the firms she had seen on television. Instead, the rooms were decorated simply with the tasteful, rustic furniture found everywhere in northern New Mexico. The receptionist nodded when Anna introduced herself and said that Carolyn was expecting her. She was immediately ushered into Carolyn's office and offered coffee or tea. She declined both and took a seat across from Carolyn, who was seated at a desk cluttered with piles of file folders.

Carolyn explained that she had consulted a colleague and they had agreed that obtaining a divorce with Charlie in China might be tricky but that it could be done. The easiest thing to try first, she said, was to get Charlie to agree to the divorce before any official paperwork would be filed. Once he agreed, they would ask him to send enough money to retain the firm and begin the proceedings. Since it was Charlie who left Anna without a source of income, and since he was now employed, he should agree to those terms. After they received Charlie's retainer, they would meet with Anna again to decide exactly what they would ask for in terms of a settlement. She told Anna to be thinking about what she would need to see her through for the rest of her life.

"Think in the long term," she said, "and don't think about being kind to Charlie. He has not been kind to you!"

Carolyn explained that the next step would be to send Charlie the official documents for him to sign and have notarized. After the firm received the documents and registered them with the court, the divorce decree would be issued. Charlie would then be required to pay the remaining legal fees as well as the agreed-upon settlement.

"You make it all sound so simple," Anna said, "but what if Charlie doesn't follow through with all those steps? He's never been one to do what he's asked. Maybe he won't even agree to the divorce. I can't tell how he feels about that."

"He should be eager to get the divorce," Carolyn replied. "That will get him off the hook, legally, and he could even come back to the U.S. without having to worry about being charged with bigamy. He's a fool if he doesn't jump at the chance to be free of his marriage to you." She hesitated and then added, "I assume you do want to be free of Charlie also."

"Yes...yes I do," Anna said haltingly. "It just all sounds so complicated, and most of it rests on Charlie. If he doesn't follow through, then what can I do?"

"We can file for a divorce through the local court if we have to. That means that we would go ahead with all the same paperwork and terms of settlement, and you and Charlie would be required to appear in court before a judge, who would make a ruling. If Charlie doesn't appear (and we know he probably will not), then the judge will almost automatically rule in your favor and issue the divorce, along with granting the terms of settlement that we present. The only problem is that then you would be divorced, but you would have no real leverage to ever collect the settlement money. I'm not sure that really accomplishes your goal. You would be free of

Charlie, of course, but you would be no better off financially than you are now."

"You're right," Anna agreed. "But being divorced from Charlie would be a big step. I've managed to survive without his money up until now, and I can do it in the future if I have to." Then, after a deep breath and a pause to think, she said, "Okay, what do I need to do to get this process started?"

Carolyn outlined what she expected from Anna, they shook hands, and Anna left the office with her mind buzzing. She liked Carolyn, and the lawyer certainly seemed to understand her predicament. Anna went home with a resolve to do her best to make the divorce plan work.

She e-mailed Charlie, telling him that she had seen a lawyer about a divorce. She explained all the reasons why a divorce would be to his benefit. All he had to do, she said, was to wire a retainer to the law firm and they could get the process started. She had no idea what Charlie's reply would be, so she tried to put the whole matter aside until she heard back from him.

Chapter Thirty-Eight: Moving On

The rest of her life was going well. She enjoyed her job at the gallery immensely. Carlos had turned out to be the perfect boss. He occupied himself with courting artists and clients and left the running of the gallery up to Anna. She enjoyed the independence and the feeling that she was capable of handling a complex job without someone watching over her shoulder. Additionally, she enjoyed being surrounded by beautiful works of art each day. Now that she was making substantially more money, she splurged on a few new items of clothing so that she could dress appropriately for her work. But the money that remained after she paid her rent, utilities and bought food and other necessities, she put into a savings account. She really wanted a larger place to live, one that would allow her to bring in at least one loom, and where she could invite friends over if she wanted.

Once she started weaving again, she would have another source of income. Granted, it might be sporadic and she couldn't count on that money to pay her bills, but she could use it to supplement her savings. Besides, she thought of weaving as a sort of lifeline. It was something she could do that was unique and soothing. She felt a thrill when her mind began filling with patterns and visions of exotic yarns. Weaving was her passion, and, thanks to Charlie, she had been forced to give it up. She added that thought to the long list of wrongs that Charlie had committed. Carolyn had told her not to be kind to Charlie. That would not be a problem.

Her relationship with Gray was also a bright spot in her life. They enjoyed each other's company and spent many hours together doing all the things they enjoyed. He still kept after her about taking action where Charlie was concerned. He wanted her to be available to him without reservation. Anna wasn't sure she felt quite the same as he did. Yes, she definitely wanted to be free of Charlie. Yes, she wanted to be secure financially. But was she ready to be committed to another long-term relationship or even marriage? She didn't know. So far, marriage had not worked out too well for her. She decided that was another issue that she couldn't do anything about for the time being. Her back burner was getting quite full, she thought with a smile.

Charlie had not responded to her e-mail about a divorce. *Perhaps he's in the field again,* she thought. Then she gave herself a mental shake. *That was always the excuse, wasn't it? Charlie was always out in the field when something needed attention and he was unavailable.*

Over the next several weeks, Anna made a point of staying in touch with her family. She couldn't afford to go visit them, nor could she get time off from work yet, so she e-mailed and phoned them regularly. She talked to Grace, who was quite happy with her new living arrangements. She considered it a blessing, Grace said, that things had turned out the way they had. She loved living with Rick. She felt useful and wanted. Her grandchildren loved her and, even though they were getting older, they still seemed to enjoy Grace's company. Rick and his wife seemed quite happy with the arrangement also, despite the fact that their house was crowded. In order for Grace to have her own room, two of their children had to share a bedroom, an arrangement that often caused sibling strife. But they were more relaxed in general without the former financial worries they had dealt with, and Rick's wife enjoyed working outside of her home. Anna was happy for them. At least Charlie's irresponsibility had worked out well for someone.

Bradley and Julie were also doing well. Their boys were growing up and involved in all kinds of activities, which kept Bradley and Julie hopping from one event or practice to another. They seemed content with their lives and were obnoxiously proud of their children. They would e-mail Anna detailed descriptions of the latest sporting event or play rehearsal, along with pictures of the boys in every situation imaginable. Anna had to laugh. She felt almost as if she were there for all of this chaos instead of many hundreds of miles across the country. She very much appreciated being included in their lives.

Clare was planning on getting married to her former professor and business partner the next summer. Their gallery venture was quite successful and they were madly in love. Anna told Clare that she would do her best to attend the wedding and was pleasantly surprised when Clare asked her to be her matron of honor. Anna accepted the invitation immediately and thanked Clare profusely for including her as a part of such an important event.

Anna was happy for Clare, but she was a little envious at the same time. Clare's life seemed to be on track with love, success and a bright future, while Anna's life was a struggle on all three counts. Anna began to wonder if she had brought all of her problems on herself. She couldn't imagine life without having married Charlie. They had been happy for so many years before things started falling apart. But Anna began to analyze all the conversations they had, all the e-mails sent during Charlie's absences, all of the actions and decisions she had made over the years. She couldn't place the blame on any one event, but she certainly could identify many instances where she could have made different decisions or responded to Charlie in different ways.

When she called David, her flagging mood dropped even further. Their conversation was brief. Clearly David did not want to speak with her. In clipped responses to her questions, he said they were fine and that both he and Valerie had jobs, but he didn't say what they were doing or if their finances had improved. When she asked about Jordan, David said he was fine also. He was doing well in preschool and had lots of friends. David painted a picture of Jordan as a happy, well-adjusted little boy, but Anna had her doubts. She remembered his little face staring up at her during those story hours. He wasn't one to smile much, and she wondered what lay behind that serious look on such a young child. Anna asked David to send pictures, and he said he would, but she doubted it. She didn't dare bring up the money that David owed her, nor did David ask her how she was doing. The conversation was a dead end, and Anna ended the call feeling quite sad.

Depression began to settle over her like a thick blanket. She struggled to get out of bed each morning and had to force herself to get ready for work. Once she arrived at the gallery, her mood lifted somewhat and she was able to get through the days without anyone noticing that something was amiss; but when she got home, she found herself anxiously going to the wine cabinet and getting down a glass for her first of many glasses. She often skipped meals. The combination of the alcohol with her empty stomach and her anti-anxiety medication played havoc with her system. When Gray called, she made excuses so that she didn't have to see him or join him for any outings. She stopped calling Helen and her other friends and, except for work, became a recluse in her apartment.

It didn't take long for Helen and Gray to become alarmed. Helen let herself into Anna's apartment one evening and found her asleep on the couch. Anna struggled toward consciousness as Helen shook her shoulder and repeated her name with urgency. Finally, Anna sat up and asked what was going on. Helen recounted for Anna how her behavior had changed and told Anna that both she and Gray were worried about her. Anna listened to Helen and began to weep great, silent tears. Helen held Anna tightly in her arms and just let her cry. It had been a long time since Anna had let her emotions out, and Helen knew that a good cry would be therapeutic. When Anna calmed down, the two of them sat at the kitchen table and, over several cups of coffee, talked about what Anna needed to do in order to escape from the depression she was suffering. It would be hard, but Helen would be there to walk beside her every step of the way, she said.

Helen told Anna that she didn't think Anna was an alcoholic, but she needed to stop drinking until she was back on an even keel. Anna agreed. She went to the wine cabinet and took out four bottles of wine, along with a fifth bottle that sat open on the kitchen counter. She put them all in a paper sack and then dropped the sack into the trashcan. Helen knew that Anna could easily retrieve the bottles once Helen left, but she had to show Anna that she trusted her to leave them in the trash. She simply nodded her head in approval and they moved on to discuss other things that Anna could do to help herself. By the time Helen left and Anna fell exhausted into bed, Anna had developed a new resolve. She was going to get her life back together and she was not going to let Charlie ruin what she had managed to accomplish without his help. None of this was her fault…well, maybe a few things…and she was a strong person capable of overcoming even the most devastating situation.

She continued seeing Helen frequently for pep talks and encouragement. She also called Gray and told him that she had been through a rough patch but was better now and hoped to see him again soon. She explained that she needed to slow things down a bit. She loved his company and was probably falling in love with him, but she wasn't ready for a long-term, serious relationship. Gray said he could live with that, and, once again, they started to enjoy going places and spending time together.

A few days later, she saw a notice that there was an e-mail from Charlie in her mailbox. She opened it, feeling both dread and excitement.

> Anna,
> Sorry I didn't get back to you sooner. Been very busy at work. I'll think about the divorce. Not sure that's what I want. Will let you know later.
> Yours,
> Charlie

Anna was flabbergasted. *Charlie isn't sure that's what he wants? How dare he? What about what I want? What about what I need? How selfish he is!* Her anger grew from an ember to a bonfire, and she immediately called Carolyn, leaving her a message that she had finally heard back from Charlie and needed to see her as soon as possible.

Chapter Thirty-Nine: The Decision

Charlie read the e-mail from Anna regarding the divorce. She had asked him for money in the past. She and David had asked him for money many times, as a matter of fact. She had never mentioned divorce before. He didn't know what to think of that. He had agreed with Anna to stop giving money to David, but Charlie found it difficult to resist David's pleas, especially when he based his need on something for Jordan. When David asked for money, Charlie would send him several hundred dollars or, at times, even a thousand. It was a small enough sum that Fariha would never miss it and David was, after all, Charlie's son. He had decided long ago that it was his job as David's father to lend him a hand from time to time.

But Anna's pleas for money had gone unanswered. First of all, a few hundred dollars would do little to help Anna's financial problems if she was as broke as she claimed, and Charlie had no reason to doubt the truth of what she had told him. If he sent Anna a substantial amount of money, Fariha would throw a screaming fit. Charlie couldn't stand it when Fariha was angry with him. She would shout and carry on, sometimes even throwing things at him. He felt helpless to stop her, and all he could do was wait it out. When she had calmed down enough, he would always give in to whatever it was that she wanted. She wasn't like that often, but when she was, her temper tantrums usually had something to do with money.

At first, when Charlie told Anna that he couldn't send any money, it was the truth. He wasn't working and had gone through the money that he had taken with him from India. Money had never mattered that much to him, perhaps because he had made so much and wanted for nothing for so long. Once he started working again, he found it simpler to give control of their finances over to Fariha. She was the one living in the city, she was the one who had things to buy. Why not let her have access to it all? From time to time,

Charlie wondered if it had been a mistake to set up their finances that way, but Fariha always managed to convince him that this was the sensible thing to do. Now, however, he found that Fariha's control over his money was inconvenient. When he wanted something, he had to go to her like a child asking for an allowance. It was humiliating; but, whenever Charlie broached the subject of his taking over the finances, Fariha would become incensed and Charlie would back away, not wanting to deal with her rage.

Now Anna wanted a divorce. All the reasons for granting her request made perfect sense. The one thing Anna hadn't mentioned, however, was money. Charlie might be able to talk Fariha into letting him send the lawyer's retainer fee as a way of buying his freedom from Anna, but he knew it wouldn't stop there. Anna was sure to ask for a huge settlement, and Charlie didn't see how he would manage that. Fariha would never allow it. The money from his retirement account was still locked up in India and he had little hope of ever gaining access to it. One thing was certain: Fariha would never allow him to pay Anna what she would be granted in a divorce. Technically, he supposed, one-half of everything he had earned during their marriage was hers. During the months since he had left India alone, the amount of money he owed her would be staggering.

Beyond that, Charlie wasn't sure he wanted to be divorced from Anna anyway. He couldn't explain why, but he felt some sense of security knowing that Anna was still his wife. Did he lover her? He didn't think so. But he did have a great deal of respect for her. She was one tough lady and had kept their family together through his absences for the entire length of their marriage. She was the mother of his children, after all. That thought brought his mind around to Bradley and David. He thought of Bradley as his own son; and David, who looked just like Charlie, was definitely a chip off of Charlie's block. He hadn't seen either of them in years now. He had never seen Jordan at all. He tried not to think about his family very often, because it always gave him a twinge of homesickness. And what about his mother? How was she doing? He did feel a bit of guilt about her losing her house; but then he reasoned that, had it not been for him, she would not have had a house to begin with. After all that he had done for her over the years, he really didn't owe her anything.

So Charlie fired off a brief e-mail to Anna denying her request. That would be the end of it. She had no other choice than to go along with his decision, and he had no other choice than to decide the way he had.

Chapter Forty: Backfire

At the same time that Charlie was thinking about his family and deciding against a divorce from Anna, Fariha was reassessing her life and the goal she was working so hard to achieve. She was getting tired of sitting around waiting for Charlie's retirement account to materialize. In fact, she began to wonder if the account even existed. She had plenty of money in the bank and was able to live comfortably for the rest of her life if need be. Charlie's paychecks poured money into their account every few weeks, but did she really need more money? Was it worth it to sit here in this shabby apartment waiting for Charlie to come home week after week? She had seen and done everything Shenyang had to offer, and she was bored. Even shopping didn't excite her any more. Besides, the couture clothing lines had changed their sizes. She had to buy a larger size than she used to, and she hated that. She wondered why the clothiers had made such a change.

Suddenly she jumped up and went to the mirror. She examined her features closely and found, to her relief, that her face was still beautiful. Then she noticed a bit of puffiness around her eyes. Her cheeks seemed fuller also. As she scanned down the rest of her body, she saw curves where there used to be none. Her breasts were as full as they had been when she discovered that she was pregnant. She finally faced the truth: she had gained weight. Not a little weight, but a lot of weight. Her scheming mind went right to work and she thought of a way to use this to her advantage. She would convince Charlie that she was so unhappy that he needed to quit his job and move back to Bangladesh. Once in Bangladesh, she would figure out a way to eliminate Charlie from her life. As long as they were in China, too many people knew Charlie and his whereabouts. But no one need know that they had gone back to Bangladesh. Charlie could disappear there and no one would even care. The same plan hadn't worked before, but she had the money to make it work this time. She hadn't worked out all the details, but she knew that was where this was headed.

When Charlie came home the next time, he sensed a change in Fariha and in their relationship. She was there to greet him as always, but she seemed less excited than usual. Normally, she cooked him his favorite meal and had on one of his favorite outfits. He always looked forward to being seduced by her after dinner and spending the night making love to her for hours. This time, however, after their meal, Fariha claimed that she wanted to finish the book she had been reading and that Charlie should go on to bed without her. Charlie couldn't account for her change in behavior, but he didn't question it either. He quietly went into the bedroom, got undressed, and slipped into bed alone.

The next morning when he awoke, Fariha was behaving as if nothing untoward had taken place the night before. Charlie breathed a sigh of relief and they made plans for how they were going to spend the time together while he was home. They had a great time each day as they explored more parts of Shenyang that were new to Charlie. But, at night, Fariha still would not come to bed with him. Frustrated and curious, Charlie finally sat Fariha down and made her tell him what was wrong.

"I am getting fat," she wailed. Tears were starting to build in her eyes, and Charlie knew that she would soon be crying in earnest.

"What do you mean? You look fine to me," Charlie assured her.

"My clothes don't fit any more. I had to go out and buy new ones, because I am becoming a fat, old woman."

"No, you're not," he said calmly. "Perhaps you've put on a few pounds, but you still look good to me."

Charlie realized he had made a blunder when Fariha suddenly became angry instead of upset. "See? You just admitted it. You think I'm fat!" With that, she ran into their bedroom and slammed the door shut.

Charlie was amazed. How had this happened? He obviously had said the wrong thing, and now he had to figure out how to fix it. He got a cold beer out of the tiny refrigerator and sat down to think things over. Maybe he needed to just get all the women out of his life. If he had his retirement money, he could escape to Fiji or somewhere and not have to deal with all of this drama. But that was not practical. He had to figure out a way to make Fariha feel better so that things would return to normal. If only there were a way to do that and get Anna off his back at the same time. Then his life would be peaceful once again. He longed for the days when all he did was go to work and come home to rest up for his next shift.

After some time, Charlie came up with a plan. He hadn't completely thought it out, but it was a start. It was also a bit risky, but he was desperate to try something, so he got up, walked to the bedroom door, and knocked gently. Fariha had been sleeping, so he sat on the edge of the bed, helped her sit up, and explained his thoughts. She listened carefully, clearly analyzing every word he said.

"I think that you are unhappy being here alone while I'm at work. You have nothing to do all day, except to go out to eat and shop. I think you're bored and we need to do something different for a change."

"Perhaps you are right," Fariha admitted, craftily. She could already picture the Bangladeshi landscape in her mind. "I have been unhappy. I'm sorry for taking it out on you, but I didn't know what to do. You think I'm beautiful, right?" Charlie nodded and Fariha continued. "I couldn't stand for you to stop loving me because I am getting old and ugly. I want to be your wife forever, Charlie."

It occurred to Charlie then that Fariha was afraid he would leave her for someone else, just as he had left Anna for her. In fact, Fariha was afraid that she would lose Charlie's money if he no longer found her desirable enough to stay. It was a rare show of emotion for Fariha, even if Charlie misread her true concern.

"I have decided that we need to get away. I have vacation time coming, and I have decided that we are going to take a trip. How would you like to see the U.S.?"

Fariha's eyes got very wide as she quickly thought about her hopes of returning to Bangladesh. She asked, "You would go back there? I thought you could never return. Why would you want to do that?" Fariha was starting to get very afraid. Had her plan backfired? The farther away from Anna and the U.S. Charlie stayed, the better it was for her. Now she regretted what she had started.

"My breathing problems are getting worse lately, and I'm hoping that my asthma will go away in the cleaner air of America. Besides, I have been thinking that I would like to see my sons and my grandchildren. I have never even seen my youngest grandson, you know. I could also visit my daughter and her family, and my mother and brother. We could travel all around visiting, and you would have a chance to see lots of places you've never even dreamed about. It would be a great experience for you and we would be together. It would be like a honeymoon. We never really had a honeymoon, remember?"

Fariha didn't know what to say. The last thing she wanted was for Charlie to be close to his family again. What if he decided to go back to his old life? He hadn't mentioned Anna, but Fariha knew that he would want to talk to her again, too. As often as she had thought about getting rid of Charlie, she realized that she didn't want him with someone else, either. Especially not Anna. She didn't dare let Charlie go to the U.S. without her. He might disappear from her life just as he had disappeared from Anna's. She cuddled into Charlie's arms and took a deep breath. Charlie thought that she was happy for the opportunity he was proposing. In fact, she was thinking that, once again, she would have to use her cleverness to change a bad situation into something that would help her achieve her goal. This might be her greatest challenge yet, but she was determined to keep Charlie and his money for herself.

Chapter Forty-One: The Return

Charlie was at work on the last day before leaving for the U.S. when a registered letter came for him. It was from his old company in India. It was a form letter advising him that they were now ready to release the $2.2 million in his retirement account. All he needed to do was fill in the information called for and return the form. They would handle the transaction from there once they received the form. Charlie couldn't believe his eyes. After all these months he was going to be a rich man. But then he stopped. He already was a rich man. Fariha's handling of their money had filled their account and they could live comfortably for the rest of their lives on what was in the bank. Besides, he wasn't finished working yet. He hadn't quit his job; he was simply taking a few weeks' vacation time.

His mind went back to Anna and the plight he had left her in. He was building up savings in his new retirement account in China. Maybe if she had the retirement account money she wouldn't be insisting on a divorce. Maybe she would just leave him alone…even forget about him. Without further thought, he filled in the form, giving instructions to wire the money into Anna's bank account. He put the form in the enclosed envelope, sealed it, and gave it to the office clerk with instructions to mail it back to India. He walked out of the office congratulating himself on doing the right thing. He hadn't intended to punish Anna, but he realized that it might feel that way to her. He hoped that this would make up for all the stress and worry he had caused her, even though he considered her much to blame for his wandering eye.

The more Charlie thought about it, the more he decided that the wise course of action was to go to the U.S. without letting anyone know they were coming. He just told his company that he was taking the vacation time due to him, and he didn't let anyone else know their plan. Since he was still a U.S. citizen, and they had all the necessary papers to show that Fariha was his wife, the process of getting Fariha's travel visa was fairly simple and went smoothly. Soon they were packing their bags and heading for the airport. The flight to Chicago would be long and tedious, but Charlie was excited to set his feet on U.S. soil again. He hadn't been home in several years. *Home,* he thought. Where was that? When he thought the word, no clear image came to mind. He really didn't have a home, and that thought disquieted him. He hadn't intended for his life to turn out this way, but it had. He was wealthy and married to a beautiful woman who loved him. What more could a man ask for? Why was his heart not content? Then he realized that he had really lived two different lives…the one before Fariha and the one after. Now he was flying through the sky headed to a place where the two were about to collide. Apprehension gripped him. *Will my family accept Fariha and love her as I do? What about Anna? Surely she will at least talk with me after she learns about the money I sent. Will she be angry or resigned?* He couldn't be sure. Too much time had passed and too many things had transpired for him to predict how she would behave toward him. Finally Charlie drifted off to sleep with all of these questions swirling in his head.

They landed in Chicago on a blustery spring day. They deplaned and were swept with the crowd to the customs area. Charlie held his breath. He wasn't stupid. He knew that his marital status would be questionable by U.S. standards, even though the Chinese government had no problem in allowing Fariha to enter their country. In the U.S., bigamy was illegal, but he had never really though of himself as a bigamist. He dismissed the idea from his mind, smiled briefly at the customs officials, and they were sent on their way without any extraordinary inquiry.

Having passed that hurdle, Charlie relaxed and held tight to Fariha as they navigated the terminal and caught a cab into the city. As they exited the building, Charlie inhaled deeply. Even with the steaming exhaust from the taxis, the air here seemed pure and clear. His asthma had been almost life threatening while in China. He was hopeful that his lungs would recover now that they were back in the U.S.

They had reservations at an upscale hotel close to downtown Chicago. He had been promised a room with a view of Navy Pier. It should be spectacular at night to see the lights of boats moving on Lake Michigan and the glowing Ferris wheel shining in the distance. Surely Fariha had never seen anything like this. She was going to love the U.S. Perhaps he could even convince her to stay here. He would give Anna the divorce, he decided, so he and Fariha could live out the rest of their lives in America. Suddenly, Charlie felt tired of his life. He was tired of moving and tired of unfamiliar languages, faces and food. It would be good to find a small town somewhere and settle down with Fariha for the rest of their lives.

The hotel lived up to its promise. They had a lovely room on a high floor that afforded them amazing views of the Pier and Lake Michigan beyond. They were exhausted from their long journey, so they ordered room service and planned to enjoy their first night in America in private. But Charlie was unable to perform when Fariha came to him in bed. It had been several weeks since they had made love. Apparently, Charlie reasoned, he was just too tired from the long trip. Fariha, on the other hand, was mystified. She had always been able to arouse any man she was with. She wondered if something was wrong with her, or perhaps something was wrong with Charlie. Maybe he was getting old. If he was too old to have sex any more, would she consider that a good thing or a bad thing? She had her fill of men during her lifetime. More than enough. She decided that she would not miss having sex with Charlie. It had been good while it lasted, but she was ready for a break.

The next morning, Charlie was in a foul mood, so Fariha left to go shopping. She had heard that the stores on Michigan Avenue were famous the world over, and she wanted to check them out. Charlie waved her away and then took out his phone. He had come back to the U.S. to reconnect with his family, so he might as well get started.

First he called David. When he answered, David sounded as if he had been drinking, but Charlie didn't question him about that. He asked about David's family and how they were doing. David's answers were brief, but pleasant, so Charlie decided to confide in him.

"David, I'm in Chicago. Fariha and I decided to come back to the U.S. for a few weeks. Is there a possibility we could get together? I'd like to get to know my grandson."

David paused, thought it over, and then answered. "Sure, Dad. We can get together. But you'll have to come here. I don't have the money to get to Chicago, and I sure can't bring the whole family! Unless you want to send me some money so that I can come there, of course."

Charlie smiled briefly and shook his head. David would never change. He didn't care about seeing Charlie. He just saw this as an opportunity to get more money from him. "Okay, David. I'll send some money this afternoon. And I'll be looking forward to seeing you again."

"Sure, Dad. Me too." With that, David ended the call.

Well, Charlie thought, *that went about as well as I could expect, I guess.* He decided to put off contacting anyone else for the time being. He would wait until he and Anna had worked out an agreement about the divorce. He would have her meet him in Chicago. That would be neutral ground, and he had no desire to go to Taos ever again. He would tell Anna that he was finally willing to give her the divorce, he decided, and by the time she came to Chicago she should have received the money in the Indian retirement account. That should appease her anger.

Chapter Forty-Two: The Call

Back in Taos, Anna was making enough money now to afford a nicer apartment, but she hesitated on making any major changes in her life. For one thing, she didn't want to move again. For another, she was afraid that, just as before, when things seemed to be going well, the bottom would fall out and she would find herself poverty-stricken again. It had happened before; what was to prevent it from happening again? So, instead of looking for a new place to live, Anna found a small studio for rent, purchased a new loom and set up a space to weave in the rented space. Giving up the weaving studio would be easier than giving up another apartment if she found herself broke again. She carefully saved as much money as possible each month, and renting the studio was the only luxury she allowed herself. Overall, she was feeling good about things. She had a job she loved, an attentive admirer with whom she enjoyed spending time, and friends and family who cared about her. Her life at that moment felt complete.

But then she received a phone call that turned her world upside down. It was Charlie calling, and she was totally unprepared for what he had to say.

"Anna, it's Charlie. How are you?"

"What do you mean, 'How are you?' How do you think I am? I'm broke and I've just been through the worst months of my life, thanks to you!" She retorted.

"Now, Anna, Sweetheart. I'm calling because I want to meet with you. We need to work some things out. I don't want to part on such bad terms. We've been together too long for that."

"What do you mean, 'We've been together too long'? We haven't been together for months…actually, not for years! And why are you calling me 'Sweetheart'? What on earth are you talking about?"

"I'm talking about the divorce. You asked me for a divorce."

"You bet I did! What about it?"

"I've decided to let you have the divorce, but we need to talk about a few things first. I want you to come meet with me."

"Meet with you? Where on earth are you, Charlie?"

"I'm in Chicago."

"Chicago! You've got to be kidding me!"

"No, I'm not kidding. I want you to come to Chicago next week so we can talk things out. Will you do that?"

Anna's brain was in turmoil. What had prompted Charlie to return to the U.S.? Was That Woman with him? He had some nerve, asking her to come to him! But he said he was willing to give her the divorce. That meant she might get some of the money that was coming to her. After a long pause, Anna agreed to meet with Charlie. He gave her the details and she ended the call.

Chapter Forty-Three: A New Plan

When Charlie looked up from the phone, Fariha was standing in the doorway seething with anger. She shouted and raved at Charlie, accusing him of being a treacherous old man. He had wanted to see his children, she accused, not his wife. How dare he arrange to meet with Anna behind her back? She stormed from the room, went into the bedroom and slammed the door.

Fariha started throwing clothes out of the drawers and ripping the covers off the bed. She finally tired of this and sat in the chair by the window, looking out over the busy street below. She was losing Charlie. It was just as she had feared. All of her work, all of her planning, all of her sacrifices were going to be wasted unless she could come up with a plan. Another plan. It seemed to Fariha that she was constantly planning and revising the current plan for another plan. This had to end! She stilled her mind and began to think. She had to get Anna out of the way of Charlie's money, and she had to get rid of Charlie. She could no longer depend on her sexuality to keep Charlie under control. Slowly, a new plan began to form in her mind. She got up, straightened up the room, and went out the door to greet Charlie with a winsome smile and an apology.

Chapter Forty-Four: Taking Action

Curious about Charlie's call, Anna called Gray and told him about Charlie's request. At first, Gray told Anna not to go; but, on second thought, he said that he would go with her to Chicago. He wouldn't go to meet with Charlie, but he wanted to be right there for her when the meeting was over. He knew that this meeting would be very difficult for Anna, and he wanted to be there to support her. Anna was grateful that Gray wanted to go with her. Meeting with Charlie was going to be nerve racking, and she would need Gray right there with her afterward. With a start, Anna realized that her feelings for Gray had grown. She was fully and irretrievably in love with this man who had been patiently waiting for her for so many months.

That evening, Anna got a call from David. He hadn't called in several months, and she was surprised to see his name on the caller ID. She thought he had given up on asking her for money, so what could he want? She was to find out soon enough.

"Hello, David. How are you?"

"I'm okay," he said. "What's up, Mother?" Anna could hear that he was slurring his words. He was obviously drunk. And he never called her "Mother". The sarcastic way he said it put Anna on alert.

"I'm just enjoying a peaceful evening. What's going on with you?"

"I have some interesting news. Did you know that Dad is back in the good ol' U.S. of A.?"

"As a matter of fact, I do know that. He called me earlier today. Why?"

"Did you know that he brought his other wife with him? You do know that he got married, don't you?"

"Yes, I know that, David. But how do you know that?"

"Because Dad and I talk all the time. We're best buddies, see? He has no secrets from his favorite son. He sends me money all the time. Actually," David chuckled, "he's my main source of income nowadays."

Anna gripped her phone so tightly that her knuckles turned white. Clearly, David had called just to taunt her. He was cruel, just like his father. She needed to end this call as soon as possible.

"So, why did you call, David?"

"Just wanted to make sure you knew that good, ol' Daddy is back in town, that's all. Have a good night." And with those parting words, he ended the call.

Anna's feet felt frozen to the floor and she just stood in her kitchen breathing hard. Finally, she relaxed a little and went into the other room and sat down. She didn't understand why David had called, but he had told her definitely that That Woman was with Charlie. Would she be there when she met with him? Anna wasn't sure she wanted to meet or even see That Woman, but, on the other hand, she was curious. Who was this person who had wreaked havoc on her life? After thinking about it, she decided that she actually would like to meet That Woman. She would give her a piece of her mind, that was for sure!

Then Anna decided to take more action that just talking to Fariha. She looked up the number for the U.S. Immigration Service on the internet and dialed. Eventually, she was connected to a person who took down the information she had to offer. Anna ended the call not knowing if her report would result in any action, but it was worth a try. Anything she could do to ruin Charlie's life at this point was a bonus.

The next morning, her phone rang again, this time with an unfamiliar number showing on the screen. Anna answered with a bit of hesitation. Lately, phone calls had brought nothing but bad news and conflicting emotions.

"Hello?"

"Is this Anna?" The voice was unfamiliar, but carried an accent she thought she should recognize.
"Yes. Who's calling?"

"My name is Fariha. I am married to Charlie, and I know you are going to meet him next week. Before you do that, I want to meet with you also."

"Why would you want to meet me? We have nothing to discuss."

"Oh, we have much to discuss," Fariha replied smugly.

Anna was curious. This was certainly an unexpected turn of events. She agreed to meet with Fariha the day previous to her appointment with Charlie. They would meet for lunch in a small restaurant near the hotel where Fariha and Charlie were staying. As a matter of fact, Anna and Gray would be at the same hotel, because Charlie had made arrangements for Anna to have a room there. Charlie did not know about Gray, and Anna saw no reason for that to change.

Chapter Forty-Five: The Meeting

Anna and Gray landed in Chicago and took a cab to their hotel. Gray seemed to enjoy the ride through the city from the airport, but Anna was on edge. She was leery of Fariha's motives for meeting with her. What could That Woman possibly want with Anna? She wasn't even really sure why Charlie wanted to meet. But she was here, and she would meet with both of them to see how things played out.

Gray's take on the entire situation was that this was the chance for Anna to make sure that Charlie would give her the divorce.

"I don't care if you ever get any money from Charlie," Gray said. "I love you, and I just want you to be free of the man so that you can marry me. I have plenty of money for the two of us. We could go back to Taos and live comfortably for the rest of our lives once you're free of Charlie. Let Charlie have Fariha or whatever her name is. He deserves whatever he gets."

Anna found Gray's proposal comforting. She was in love with Gray. He was certainly different from Charlie, but, at the same time, she couldn't let go of some of her feelings for Charlie. Despite everything Charlie had done, and despite how angry she was with him, Charlie had been her first real love. She still felt something for him, even if she didn't love him any more. She believed that she couldn't have been married to the man for so many years and then just lose all concern for him. That Woman had surely duped him, tricked him, taken advantage of his passivity. Had his actions not caused such upheaval in her own life, she might almost feel sorry for him. She loved Gary, and she wanted to marry him. But she didn't know if she was ready for that yet. There had been too many other things going on for her to concentrate on her relationship with Gray. Maybe with time and some peace in her life she would be able to sort that out, but right now she didn't know. After all that she had survived, did she want to commit to another relationship so soon? Or was she better off on her own? She had certainly proven that she was capable of taking care of herself.

The following morning, Anna dressed carefully for her meeting with Fariha. She wanted to look her best, because, she assumed, Fariha would be very good looking. How else could she have caught Charlie's eye? She picked out a periwinkle blue blouse, remembering that Charlie always loved her in that color. As she picked up a silken scarf to wear around her neck, she noticed that it had cat hair scattered on it. *That Simba!* She thought, and quickly brushed the hair from the scarf. Checking herself one last time in the mirror, Anna said good-bye to Gray, told him not to worry, and walked to the restaurant. She spotted Fariha right away. She was sitting in the back at a table for two. Anna paused to assess her. She was not as beautiful as Anna had expected. Perhaps once she had been, but now she looked somewhat worn out. She was quite chubby, which surprised Anna, because Charlie always preferred women who were slim and physically fit. Fariha's make-up was overdone and Anna had a hard time guessing her age. One thing was certain, though, she was many years younger than Charlie. Anna approached the table and sat down without introduction.

"Thank you for coming," Fariha said. "I felt we should meet."

"And why is that?" Anna asked coldly.

"Because of Charlie," Fariha said flatly. "He once loved you, and now he loves me."

"Does he?" Anna replied. She didn't know where this was going, but she didn't like That Woman or her tone.

"I wanted to meet the woman I stole Charlie from. It's as simple as that."

Anna could feel the tears starting to well up. This woman was every bit as heartless and cruel as she had imagined. Anna couldn't fathom why Fariha had even wanted to see her, much less have a conversation, so she hastily said, "Well, you've met her. Now you can say good-bye." With that, Anna rose quickly from the table and, in her haste, she knocked over the chair and caused her water glass to tip over. She grabbed the glass to keep it from rolling off the table and rushed from the restaurant. Their conversation lasted less than a minute.

Fariha watched Anna leave and smiled to herself. She picked up Anna's water glass with her napkin and put it in her oversized bag, rose from the table, and began to leave when she noticed that, in Anna's haste, her scarf had fallen to the floor. Fariha pick up the scarf and put it in the bag along with the water glass. *Perfect!* She thought.

Anna was upset when she returned to the room, and Gray did his best to calm her down. She was mystified as to why Fariha had wanted to meet with her. Gray said it was just to taunt her with the fact that she was married to Charlie, but Anna felt that there was more to it. Gray, however, just passed the whole incident off as a cruel move on Fariha's part and told Anna to forget it. She would meet with Charlie tomorrow, agree to get divorced, and then she and Gray would return to Taos and live happily ever after. After having met Fariha, Anna wasn't too sure it was going to go as smoothly as Gray thought.

Chapter Forty-Six: Framing Anna

After she met with Anna, Fariha returned to the room where Charlie was waiting for her.

"How did it go?" Charlie asked.

"Fine," Fariha replied. "Anna was very interesting. She was polite to me, although I could tell that she doesn't care for me very much. I can see why you used to be attracted to her."

"Well, you needn't worry about Anna. After I meet with her tomorrow, she will be out of our lives. We can go back to China and forget about Anna and the U.S. I talked to both Bradley and my mother while you were gone. It seems that they aren't willing to see my actions from my point of view, so I am finished with them. Neither of them wants to see me while I'm here. In fact, they each said that they don't want me to be a part of their lives. They will go their ways and I will go mine."

"Does that upset you, Charlie?"

"Of course it does! How could it not? But it's their choice and their loss. I did my best to reconcile with them and they turned away," Charlie added with a note of sadness in his voice. "Besides, my asthma has been acting up. I'm using the new steroid the doctor gave me in China, but it isn't helping. I thought it would be better here, but the stress of all this is making me sicker. I just want to get back to the life I know and am used to. We can be back in China by the end of the week, and that's not too soon for me!"

"Poor Charlie," Fariha cooed. Her plan couldn't be working any better. Everyone was following the script she had worked out in her head as if they were actors in a play and she was the director.

The next morning, Anna was due to meet with Charlie at 10:00 that morning, and Fariha told Charlie that she wanted to be there for their meeting. Charlie started to object, but when he saw Fariha's face, he decided not to say anything. He was too tired to argue with her. His asthma had kept him up most of the night, and he was exhausted. Coming to the U.S. had not helped his health as he had hoped. In fact, he was feeling worse than ever! He was tired and felt almost weak, so he sat down in one of the chairs in the sitting room where he drifted off to sleep.

Fariha peeked out of the bedroom and saw that he was sleeping. She crept out of the room and came up silently behind Charlie with Anna's scarf in her hand. She carefully lifted the scarf over Charlie's head so as not to wake him and wrapped it quickly around his neck, pulling as hard as she could. Charlie woke and began to struggle, but Fariha was strong and held tight. Charlie's breathing became labored, and Fariha could hear his wheezing. She was surprised at how weak Charlie seemed. It was not as difficult as she thought it would be to keep the scarf firmly around his neck. Finally, Charlie went still. Fariha continued to hold the scarf tightly for what seemed like many minutes. Finally, she came around to face Charlie and could see that his eyes were open but unseeing. He wasn't wheezing any more; he wasn't breathing at all.

Fariha studied Charlie's face impassively for a moment. She had thought that she might feel something for him, but she didn't. Charlie was simply an obstacle to her achieving her goal: being wealthy and living independently as a rich woman for the rest of her life. Soon she would return to China and withdraw all the money from their joint account as well as from her private account. She would also make sure to collect the $500,000 life insurance policy. She guessed that those three things alone would total well over $2 million. She doubted if she could get her hands on the retirement account, but, she decided, she could do fine without that. She planned to leave China once she had the money and go somewhere else to live. Perhaps she would go to Thailand. She had heard that it was lovely and inexpensive. She thought she could do very well there.

She quickly went back into the bedroom and, using a tissue, retrieved the water glass she had taken from the restaurant. She put it on the table across from Charlie and poured a second glass of water to put beside Charlie's chair, being careful not to leave any fingerprints on either glass. She tipped each glass over, watching the water puddle on the table and spill over the side onto the carpet. Then she swept the magazines off the coffee table onto the floor and tipped the small table next to the hotel room door onto its side. Looking over the room, she decided that it looked very much as if a heated argument had taken place. She glanced at Charlie's body once more and briefly thought about taking the scarf away, but decided to leave it where it had fallen onto his lap. Surely the police would put together the clues she had left to incriminate Anna in Charlie's death.

Chapter Forty-Seven: Unexpected Visit

Fariha went to the bedroom to get her purse. Her plan was to leave, anonymously call 911 to report Charlie's death and come back later, only to find the police there investigating Charlie's murder. She would tell them about his appointment with Anna, and it wouldn't take them long to accuse Anna. Fariha was putting on her jacket when there was a knock on the door. She hesitated and then decided she had better answer it in case it was the maid coming in to service the room.

When she opened the door, Fariha was surprised to see two men standing there. They were dressed in drab green uniforms and the one in front was holding a piece of paper in his hand. She moved squarely into the doorway so that they couldn't see into the room, and her heart was pounding. They asked her name, and she was so startled that it didn't occur to her to lie to them. Then they told her that they were from the U.S. Immigration Service and she needed to come with them.

"What does this mean?" Fariha gasped.

"You can read this, m'am," said the first man politely as he handed her the paper. "We will be taking you to a detention center where your case will be heard. After that you will be deported back to Bangladesh unless it's determined that you are a political refugee, in which case you might be allowed to stay. Until then, you are considered to be in this country illegally and will be held until the disposition of your case."

Fariha was aghast. How could this have happened? And then she knew. Anna! Anna had called Immigration and reported her. She took a deep breath and put on her jacket. Leaving the door slightly ajar behind her, she walked down the corridor toward the elevators with the men. She tried to act calm and composed, but her mind was racing. Somehow she had to work her way out of this situation, but she couldn't think of any clever schemes. For the first time in many years, she was frightened and unsure what to do. And Charlie wasn't going to be able to help her out of this. The men helped her into the back of a large SUV. One of them drove while the other sat in back with Fariha. As they drove away, Fariha looked back toward the hotel and wondered what was happening inside.

Chapter Forty-Eight: Finding Charlie

Anna knocked on the door of Charlie's room. Her emotions were in a jumble. She hoped Fariha wouldn't be there while she talked with Charlie. Her anger over her encounter with Fariha hadn't subsided. She was angry with Charlie, too, and she didn't even understand what Charlie wanted to say to her, but it didn't matter. She felt a bit nervous in anticipation of the difficult conversation that was about to take place. She was done with Charlie now that he had agreed to the divorce. There was nothing more to talk about. Money was no longer the issue, although she still felt that Charlie owed her for all the misery he had caused. She knocked again, and the door opened a crack. She stuck her head in and called Charlie's name, but there was no answer. She took a few steps into the entry and saw that the table was overturned. Curious, she went into the sitting room and saw Charlie slumped over in the easy chair. She ran to him, lifted his wrist and felt for a pulse. Finding none, she raised his head and looked at his face. His skin was waxy and his lips were blue. His eyes were open and rolled back in his head. Realizing that he was dead, she stifled a scream, turned, and ran from the room. She had to call the police, but she couldn't stand to be in that room for another second. She was so hysterical that she didn't even notice the overturned glasses or her scarf lying in Charlie's lap

.

Anna rushed into their room and saw Gray sitting on the bed talking on his cell phone. He looked up and saw how upset she was and told the person on the other end that he had to go. Anna was crying hard and ran to the room phone and dialed 911, but she had a difficult time telling the operator what was wrong. Finally, she choked out the word "dead" and the name of the hotel and room number. The operator asked her to stay on the line, but Anna hung up when Gray came over to her. He held her tight and smoothed her hair, running his hands up and down her back to calm her. Finally, she was able to tell him about the horror she had found when she went to Charlie's room.

Gray convinced her that they should go back to Charlie's room to wait for the police. The police would be able to tell where the 911 call had come from, he said, and they would want to question her. So she and Gray went back up to Charlie's room. Gray wanted to look at Charlie, but Anna refused to go inside. They waited in the hallway for the police to arrive.

When the police came, they were polite and efficient. Anna explained why she had gone to Charlie's room and what she had found. She also told them about Fariha being in the U.S. illegally with Charlie and that she suspected Fariha of murdering Charlie. The detective in charge, whose name was Ben Davis, finally told her that she was free to go but not to leave Chicago until he gave her permission. She was not a suspect *at this time*, he said, but he might have more questions for her.

Clearly shaken, Anna went back to her room with Gray. She didn't say anything. She just sat in a chair and stared out the window. She tried to identify her feelings. She didn't love Charlie any more, but he didn't deserve to be murdered, did he? Then she remembered that she had wished him dead more than once over the past several months. Could she have caused his death by wishing it so? Of course not. That was ridiculous, she decided. Then her mind drifted back over the many years that she and Charlie had shared as a married couple. Despite the unhappiness of the past, there were many good times, too. As she thought about those times, she realized that she needed to make some calls to let their children and Charlie's mother know what had happened.

When she called Bradley and Christina, they each told her about their calls from Charlie and how they had told him to stay out of their lives. Bradley even admitted that he had told Charlie that Charlie could "drop dead for all I care". Anna was shocked at the harshness of Bradley's words, but she assured him that neither he nor she had caused Charlie to die. Grace cried and was unable to speak any longer, so Rick came on the phone and listened as Anna relayed the day's events one more time. By the time she finished talking to them, she was exhausted, but she had one more call to make.

"David, it's your mother. I need to tell you something important," Anna began.

"Yeah, what is it?" David snarled.

"It's your father, David. He's dead," Anna reported as calmly as possible.

"So...did you finally kill him? That's what you wanted, isn't it?" He shot back. Then, after a pause, he added, "Now you can have all his money. You only wanted his money anyway, right? Oh, I forgot. He has another wife. I suppose she'll get his money now instead of you. I guess neither of us will get any more money from dear, old Dad."

"David, I can't believe you're saying all that. What's the matter with you?" Anna demanded.

"What's the matter with me is you and Dad. You never loved me as much as wonderful, perfect Bradley. Isn't the saying, 'You reap what you sow?' Well, you sowed me as the bad seed and here I am to prove you were right."

"Oh, David. That's not true! None of it is true! When this is all over we need to talk. I just want you know that I love you. I have always loved you."

"Sure, Mom. We'll talk." And with that, he ended the call.

Anna stared at her phone as if she could conjure David up so she could talk to him some more. She began crying again, and Gray came over to comfort her.

"Once we are free to leave Chicago, we are going away for a while. You need to get away...far away...from David and the rest of your family. You're in shock and hurting. I don't know what

David said to you, but it obviously wasn't helpful. I want to help you, Anna. I want to be here for you. Will you let me?"

Wearily, Anna replied, "Yes, Gray. You've been a big help already. I don't know what I'd have done without you!"

Detective Davis came to Anna's room late that afternoon. He questioned her for almost two hours before leaving. Anna divulged the entire ugly truth of Charlie's desertion and her desperation when she didn't know where he was. She even admitted how she had become almost homeless and lost everything because of Charlie's disappearance. The detective listened without commenting, took a few notes, and told her that he would call her in the morning.

When he came by the next day, Detective Davis told Anna that she was free to leave Chicago and return to Taos. He gave strict instructions that she was not to leave the country, and, if she chose to travel anywhere within the U.S., she needed to let him know where she could be contacted. When she asked about Charlie's body, the detective told her that, because Charlie died under mysterious circumstances, there would be an autopsy. Because of a backlog in the Coroner's Office, however, it would be at least a week before they could get to Charlie. Anna asked him to call her when they released Charlie's body so that she could make burial arrangements. As Detective Davis was leaving, she asked him if he had talked to Fariha.

"No, we haven't," he said. "She never came back to the hotel as far as we know. She is certainly a person of interest and we will do our best to find her."

"Please let me know what you find out," Anna added. "Charlie and I were not on good terms, but he was my husband for many years and I want to know how he died."

With that, the detective left, and Anna and Gray called the airline and packed their things.

Chapter Forty-Nine: Fariha in Holding

While Anna was being questioned by the police, Fariha was working on a plan to get herself out of the immigration holding facility. Being sent back to Bangladesh wasn't necessarily a bad thing, she reasoned. If the United States of America wanted to pay her way back to her homeland, that was just fine with her. After all, she had planned to escape from China to Bangladesh anyway. But she had learned that it would be more than a week before she would actually be deported, and she didn't think that she could stand being in that horrible place for even one more day. The building was clean, she supposed, but it was painted a putrid shade of green and she was forced to sleep in a common area with twenty-two other women who were also being deported. She hated that. They were far beneath Fariha's status. She was a wealthy woman, while these other women were common laborers, hardened by who knew what circumstances. Besides, she had killed Charlie; and, even though she had framed Anna, she was afraid that the police would track her to the immigration facility. She needed to get out of the country before someone discovered where she was. So, Fariha came up with another scheme.

She had overheard one of the guards telling another that he thought Fariha was sexy. *Good!* She thought. *I have power over men just as I always have.* With that, she began to flirt with the man, hoping that she might at least get some special privileges while she waited for deportation, and, if all went well, she could convince him to help her get out of there. She could feel the hostile looks from the other women as they watched her play with the guard's emotions.

Slowly approaching him, she smiled and looked him directly in the eyes, quietly saying, "You seem like a gentle and caring man. I am getting depressed from being inside this building all day. Would you allow me to go outside for a little while? You can escort me yourself, if you think I'm going to escape."

He answered back, "That's against the rules. I couldn't possibly do that." And then he quietly added, "at least not so that anyone knows."

Then he closed is eyes and thought for a minute. "I'll tell you what," he whispered. "When you have finished dinner, ask to use the restroom in the cafeteria. Don't wait until you come back here. I'll make sure the matron is distracted and signal you from down the hall which way to go."

Fariha did as she was told and, when they were outside of the building, she let the guard kiss her and feel her breasts. Stopping him before he went any farther, she asked him, " Would you help me get out of this horrible place?" She smiled seductively and continued, " I promise that there is much more I can do for you to repay you for your trouble."

"I can't do that," he stated flatly. "I'd lose my job, and, besides, my wife would kill me if she found out!" And then he looked at her and grinned.

Fariha was furious. Men never turned down an offer from her. Vowing to get even, she turned around and marched back into the facility without a backward glance.

Later that night she was approached by one of the other female detainees. She was younger than Fariha and had a hardness around her eyes. "So, I hear you tried to get out of here by selling yourself. Don't you know you're an old hag? The men here want someone young and sexy, not some used-up whore like you!"

Fariha heard the woman's words and felt the fury growing inside her heart. *I have murdered before, and I could do it again*, she told herself. She grabbed the woman's hair and wrestled her down to the floor. She was about to punch the woman, when she saw the woman's hand coming toward her face. She was holding a long nail file, and she sneered as she shoved the sharp weapon into Fariha's eye. Fariha's hand flew to her eye and she felt searing pain. She could feel blood and gore spilling from her eye socket, and she could hear the other women shouting and clapping their hands, chanting, "Fight, fight, fight…"

Then the woman came at her with the file again, this time shoving it into the side of Fariha's neck. Fariha cried out in pain once again, and then she felt herself being pulled away from the other woman. All of a sudden she felt her knees give way and she was being lowered to the floor. Someone grabbed her neck, and Fariha struggled weakly, thinking that it was the other woman trying to strangle her. But the person put a hand on the side of her neck and began to push hard. It was then that Fariha felt the sticky blood streaming down the front of her blouse. She could smell a coppery odor, but the pain had stopped and with her one good eye she could see blurry faces staring down at her. She was tired, so tired, and she allowed herself to be swallowed up by the darkness.

Chapter Fifty: Accusation

Relieved to be getting away from the site of Charlie's death, Anna and Gray took the next available flight to Albuquerque and drove back to Taos. Anna picked up Bella and Simba from Helen and Lee, spending a long evening telling her good friends all that had happened. She took two extra days off work to pull herself together and then went back to the gallery. From the outside, it looked as if Anna's life had returned to normal and all of this would blow over.

David called Anna three days later. After saying hello, he began to apologize. "I'm sorry for the way I talked to you the other night. I was pretty drunk and, when I heard about Dad, I just reacted without thinking. I've been sober since then and I've been doing a lot of thinking. I hope we can talk about things sometime."

"Whenever you're ready," Anna replied. "I..."

David interrupted, "But that's not the main reason I called. I saw an article in the Chicago paper that I thought you should know about. It was kind of buried on the third page, so I'm not even sure why I noticed it. The headline read, 'Bengali Woman Dies in Lockup'. I think the word 'Bengali' is what caught my attention. It didn't say her name, but I think it was Dad's wife. I guess, from what the paper said, she was being held by Immigration waiting to be deported back to Bangladesh because she had entered the country under false pretenses. I assume that was because her marriage to Dad wasn't legal? Anyway, she was bragging to the other detainees about how rich she was and how she was going to bribe everyone to get out of detention. The article said she had worked as a prostitute and had even propositioned some of the male staff at the Detention Facility. Apparently she pissed the other detainees off, and one of them stabbed her. She was already dead by the time the immigration staff got to her. I mean, this has to be Fariha, right? How many women from Bangladesh could be waiting for deportation? Did you call Immigration on her? If so, I'm glad you did. She got what she deserved."

Anna didn't speak. She just ended the call. *David is right,* she thought. *This has to be about Fariha. I called Immigration about her and now she's dead. Fariha is dead because of my actions. Up until now, I was the victim. I survived the worst and came out all right. But when I finally took some action against the person who caused all of my grief, I became something else. I am no longer just a victim. I wished Fariha dead and set into motion the events that would eventually kill her.* She felt a keen stab of guilt. *Am I somehow responsible for Charlie's death, too? Had he come back to the U.S. to reconcile with me, even though he said he would give me a divorce? Was Fariha threatened by Charlie's desire to reconnect with his family? Had my pleading and all of my e-mails somehow softened Charlie's heart?* She would never know the answers to these questions and she knew the guilt they instilled in her would haunt her for the rest of her life.

As she was thinking all this, David called back. "Mom? I guess we were disconnected. I have to tell you something else even more important. A friend of mine works in the motor pool for the Chicago Police. He overheard a detective…Davis maybe?…saying that he was going to issue a warrant for your arrest as soon as the autopsy report came through. He thinks you killed Dad! Did you?"

"No, of course not! I didn't kill your father; I would never do such a thing!" Anna cried.

"Well, I thought you should know. I don't know when it's going to happen, but you'd better hire a good lawyer. I'll let you know if I hear anything else. What a mess! We'll talk soon."

A warrant for my arrest? Thought Anna. *That man can't possibly think that I murdered Charlie! What am I going to do now?*

Chapter Fifty-One: Flight

Anna immediately called Gray and he hurried over to her apartment. She was in a panic.

"Maybe I should do what David said and hire a lawyer. I don't know why they would think that I killed Charlie, but apparently they do. What kind of evidence is there to implicate me? I wasn't even in his hotel room for more than a minute."

And then she thought of Fariha. "Could Fariha have framed me for Charlie's murder and then murdered him herself? I knew Fariha was an evil person, but was she *that* evil? If so, how did she convince the police that I was the murderer?"

When she posed all these questions to Gray, he agreed that Fariha's framing Anna seemed to make the most sense. Gray pointed out, "Fariha had to have been a very clever and ruthless woman, or she never would have been able to take over Charlie's life and finances as she did."

Then, after a pause he added, "I wouldn't put anything past her. Without knowing the details of what she's done, it would be very hard to convince the police that you're innocent. They would have to charge you with murder and reveal all the evidence before you would even have a chance of defending yourself. It might be too late by then."

"Oh, my God!" wailed Anna. "What am I going to do?"

"We could run away," Gray stated plainly. "I'd already been planning a get-away vacation for us. We'll go someplace where no one can find us."

"I can't afford to just quit my job and run away. What about Bella and Simba? What about my family?"

"What about your life?" Gray retorted. "Can you risk being found guilty of murder?"

"No, of course not."

"Look, Anna. I love you, and I believe you love me, too. If not, I intend to take care of you and treat you so well that you can't help but fall in love with me eventually. I want to protect you and have you for my own. Now that Charlie is dead, there is nothing holding us back from being together. We can get married. We can go somewhere totally unexpected and no one will ever find us. Please, Anna. Please let me do this for you! I have plenty of money to get us someplace safe. We will figure it out from there. What do you say?"

Anna was silent for a long time as she thought over her options. "You're right, Gray. I can't defend myself when I don't know what Fariha has done. I was the one to find Charlie's body. Who is there to say that I wasn't the one who killed him?"

She saw no other option than to follow Gray's lead. This man clearly loved her, and she loved him, too, even if she hadn't really let him know that. She trusted him. He was willing to give up his home and his career for her. He was offering to give up his whole life for her. How could she refuse him?

"All right," she finally said. "I think I'd better do what you say. It makes me sad and it makes me angry. Even though she's dead, That Woman is still screwing with my life!"

And with that, Anna and Gray began to make preparations to run. They knew they had to move quickly and get away before Detective Davis issued the arrest warrant. Surely, Charlie's autopsy would be completed any day now. They sat down and made a list of things they needed to do and decided that they could be on their way out of the country in two days. Fortunately, both of them had valid passports, and Gray's assets were liquid enough for him to get plenty of cash to take with them. After researching countries without extradition to the U.S., Gray made a reservation at a luxury resort by the sea in Bali.

Anna asked Helen and Lee to watch Bella and Simba while she and Gray were gone. She needed a rest, she told them, so she and Gray were taking a vacation for a few weeks. She was careful not to tell them the real reason she was leaving, nor did she tell them where she was going. She didn't want them to know anything if they were questioned by the police. She told Carlos the same thing, and he told her that she could take two weeks away from the gallery, but no more. He needed her too much. This brought on another wave of guilt for Anna. *How could I deceive these people who have been nothing but kind to me? What kind of a person am I becoming?*

Anna and Gray packed hastily and drove to Albuquerque, where they left Gray's car in long-term parking. Their tickets would take them to Barcelona, Spain. Once there, Gray planned to figure out how to get false papers so that they could travel on to Bali under assumed identities. Neither he nor Anna had much doubt that eventually the authorities would catch up to them; but, by then, they should be safely in Bali and there would be no extradition back to the U.S. The both knew, however, that the best plan would be to prove Anna's innocence. They did not know how to do that from such a long distance, however. The unasked question was whether or not they could stand to permanently disappear. They both had strong ties to the Taos community, their families, friends and jobs. Even with each other, their exile would be very lonely.

Chapter Fifty-Two: Spain

The flight seemed endless to Anna, whose mind was filled with unanswered questions and concerns. Gray slept most of the way, and Anna tried to busy herself with reading. Since she couldn't bring knitting needles on the plane because of security concerns, she brought a project to crochet. Crocheting wasn't her area of expertise, however, and she soon became frustrated and put the yarn and hook back in her carry-on bag. When they finally landed, Anna couldn't get off the plane, through customs, and out of the airport quickly enough. The taxi ride to the hotel was uneventful, although Anna expected to hear sirens and see flashing lights at any moment. She and Gray had decided on Spain because, even though it was often overlooked, officially the policy in Spain was not to extradite to the U.S. Their hotel was mediocre, away from the upscale tourist area of the city. They wanted to remain as inconspicuous as possible while they were here. Giving the hotelier a story about a belated honeymoon, they went directly to their room, where Anna stayed while Gray went to see about new papers.

It seemed to Anna that Gray was gone far too long and she began to become worried. The only way to procure false papers was to deal with some unsavory people, and she didn't know how Gray would do that. He was one of the most forthright and honest men she had ever met. It was a mystery to her that he even thought he would be able to find someone to do this for them. Despite her doubts, however, Gray came back four hours later and said that he had made arrangements for the papers. They would pick them up the next afternoon and leave for Bali the following morning. *Two days!* Thought Anna. In two days she would be a fugitive living under an assumed name. That was if they managed to get out of Barcelona without being arrested. She was frightened. Gray suggested that they get some rest and then find a quiet restaurant. After that, they could enjoy seeing some of Barcelona since they were there anyway.

Anna was bewildered by Gray's nonchalant attitude about the entire situation. She thought he was acting more like an international spy than a quiet man with a remodeling business in a remote area of New Mexico. She wondered if there were things about Gray that she didn't know, but she was in no position to question him at that point. Her life was literally in his hands and she had to trust him implicitly.

After a restless night in the hotel, they found a quiet restaurant and ordered breakfast. Anna simply pushed the food around her plate, but Gray ate heartily and declared the meal delicious. Next, they walked several blocks and caught an open-air tour bus that took them around the city. Once again, Anna found herself just counting the minutes until the tour was over, while Gray seemed to enjoy the dialogue of the guide and asked several questions as the bus meandered through the city. When they got off the bus, Anna practically ran back to the hotel. Gray saw her safely to their room and then left to get their new papers. He was gone for a little more than an hour and came back with a satisfied look on his face. He had brought dinner with him and began to lay it out on the small table by the window in their room.

"Did it go okay?" Anna asked anxiously.

"Yes, everything is fine, Anna. You need to try to relax," he replied.

"I can't relax. I can't even believe that we're doing this! I feel as if I've been thrown into someone else's life, for Heaven's sake! How can you be so calm?" She asked, her voice rising.

"I'm calm because it doesn't help to be upset. Getting new papers was easier than I expected, but it did cost more than I had hoped. We're probably not going to be able to afford Bali for more than a month. But let's not worry about that now. For the time being, we just need to get there. We'll figure out the next step once we're there," he said calmly, sensing Anna's rising hysteria. He took her into his arms and just held her until he felt her begin to relax. "Let's eat and get a decent night's sleep. Then we'll be on the plane again before you know it."

Anna was famished and ate everything Gray had brought for her. She was also exhausted and fell into a restless sleep, awaking with a start the next morning when she heard Gray running the shower in the bathroom. She got up and stretched, sore and tired but more rested than she had been when she arrived. *I can do this*, she told herself. *But I have to be calm. If I'm nervous going through security or customs, we're both in trouble. I deserve the trouble, but Gray doesn't. He doesn't deserve any of this. This is my problem and I should have taken care of it myself. Why did I drag him into it?*

But her doubts faded when Gray came out of the bathroom and hugged her tight, saying, "Good morning, sleepyhead. Did you rest at all?"

"Yes, some," Anna said, forcing a smile on her face. "I'm all right. I just want to get this next part over with."

"It will be fine," Gray reassured her. "You just need to stay calm and keep a cool head. Follow my lead. Everything is going to be all right."

Anna sighed and got ready to leave for the airport. She did her best to disguise her nervousness by holding tight to her handbag and keeping a big smile on her face. When she offered her passport and ticket to the woman at the security gate, she smiled and told the woman how excited she was to be going on vacation in Bali. *Maybe she'll think I'm hyper because of the excitement of the trip, not because I'm running away with false papers,* Anna thought. The woman looked the papers over without expression, stamped them, and told Anna to move on to the x-ray section of the security area. Anna let out a lung full of air and realized that she had stopped breathing while going through the last part of the security screening. But she had made it through, and she could see Gray moving through the security station right behind her.

When the plane's wheels left the ground, Anna began to relax for the first time in days. She went over the events of the past week in her mind and couldn't believe all that had happened. For the first time, she had a few moments to think clearly about Charlie's death. *What did the police find that made them think that I killed him?* She replayed her meeting with Fariha, and suddenly it came to her. *My scarf! I left my scarf in the restaurant. Did Fariha pick it up and somehow use it to frame me for killing Charlie? Or did Fariha just leave the scarf in her hotel room for the police to find? Surely that isn't enough to make them suspect me of murder, is it?*

Chapter Fifty-Three: Exile

Anna slept fitfully and ate little on the plane to Singapore. From there, they boarded a plane for Denpasar where Bali's international airport was located. Anna was surprised by the size of the aircraft going to Bali. She had expected a smaller plane, but they boarded a 737 filled with people headed for the tropical island. Once they arrived in Bali, they moved on to Candidasa, a small village noted for surfing, scuba diving, and beachside resorts. By staying in a less populated area, Gray reasoned, they were less likely to be found.

The resort was everything they had expected. It was luxurious and filled with beautiful young people from all around the world. There were many Europeans and Asians, but very few Americans. At first, they found that a bit disconcerting, because all of a sudden they stood out from the crowd instead of blending in. They soon realized, however, that everyone was so wrapped up in their own activities that they didn't have the time or the inclination to pay attention to Anna and Gray.

When Anna first opened the door to their room, she gasped in appreciation. The first thing that caught her eye was an elaborately carved screen that shielded the bed from the door to the hallway. The bed itself was a huge four-poster beautifully draped with soft fabric. It was so high off the floor that small stools were stationed on each side of the bed so that they could climb into bed without having to jump up from the floor. Their room was on the first floor, and they could walk right out the door directly to the beach. There were palm trees everywhere, and the resort featured two different swimming pools. One pool had a full-service bar right in the middle, which amazed Anna, who had never seen such a thing before. They had three different restaurants to choose from and, because it was an all-inclusive resort, the concierge was happy to direct them to the many activities the hotel had to offer.

Slowly Anna began to relax and enjoy herself. Her situation and all the questions associated with it were never far from the front of her mind, but she was able to enjoy walking on the beach and lying in the sun by the sparkling pool. While strolling on the beach, she found some perfect seashells and put them in her bag. She planned to give them to Jordan when she got home. *Will he ever have a chance to see the ocean and pick up shells for himself as his father did as a boy?* Then her thoughts turned to David. *He sounded as if he were ready to make amends and begin a new relationship with me. Will I ever have the chance to follow up on that?*

Anna and Gray gradually got into a routine. For the next two weeks, they slept in and enjoyed leisurely breakfasts in their room or by the pool. After a swim, they walked the beach or rented scooters and rode around the town. Anna quickly discovered that the traffic in Bali was even crazier than in India. There seemed to be no rules and chaos reigned on the roads. The village was at the base of a volcano, which made a beautiful backdrop to the picturesque area. Sometimes they hiked the low hills behind the town, and they often stopped to talk to the locals and made friends with some of the shopkeepers. They were amazed that almost everyone in Bali was given one of four names that designated their birth order. It all seemed very confusing to Anna, who decided that at least it was easy to remember people's names when there were only four for men and four for women to choose from. But most memorable were the monkeys. Anna had always found monkeys somewhat frightening, with their screeching and constant movement. Here there were monkeys everywhere, and Anna swore that she would never visit the primate section of a zoo again.

By evening, they changed and went to dinner at either the resort or a local restaurant. The food was enjoyable, and they especially liked Nasi Goreng, a dish of Indonesian fried rice served vegetarian or with chicken. Gray liked it so much that he ordered it everywhere they went and declared, "I could live off this stuff!" They tried Durian, which was also called "stinky fruit", with its creamy-textured, pungent flavor, and decided that they would remember that smell and taste for the rest of their lives.

They occupied the rest of the evenings by reading or playing card games in their room, trying to walk a fine line between appearing to be tourists and not calling attention to themselves.

Both of them were beginning to feel somewhat relaxed when Gray brought up the topic of what was going to be their next move.

"My money is going to run out before too long," Gray said matter of factly. "I have enough to stay another two weeks and buy plane fare back to the U.S. That," he said, "is option one. The other option is to find somewhere less expensive to live outside the U.S. We would have to find work to support ourselves in a place without extradition. Continuing to move around with our assumed identities could eventually pose problems."

As they brainstormed their options, it became clear to both of them that eventually they would need to go back home. Gray missed talking to his daughter and was wondering how his business was faring in his absence. He had worked hard to build the successful company for many years, and he wasn't anxious to just throw all of that away. Anna, too, was missing her family, and the guilt she felt over Fariha's and Charlie's deaths was haunting her
.

"I didn't have to kill them with my own hands to be responsible for what happened to them," she sobbed one night.

"What happened to them was their own doing, Anna. Can't you see that?" Gray reminded her.

"I just don't think I can go on unless I can clear my name. I will always feel somehow responsible for what happened, but I can't have my family thinking that I'm a murderer. I can't keep living like this, on the run from the police. I need to go back and get some of this resolved one way or another, no matter what consequences I have to face."

"I understand," comforted Gray, "but there's no guarantee that you will be cleared of Charlie's murder."

"I know. I've been thinking about that. I just have to believe in the justice system. I know innocent people are found guilty all the time, but surely that won't happen to me. They just can't have enough evidence to convict me of something I didn't do, no matter how carefully Fariha tried to frame me. They just can't!"

"Okay," Gray conceded. "I'll give them a checkout date a week from now here at the hotel. I'll also make return reservations for us."

What he didn't say was his concern about his role in Anna's flight. *Will they prosecute me for harboring a criminal? Will I end up in jail? Lose my business, family and friends?* He knew he appeared calm to Anna, but that was for her sake. Inside, he was churning with stress. As much as he loved Anna and wanted to keep her from the authorities, he, too, was ready to return home and face the consequences of his own actions. He said nothing and just held Anna in his arms. This was a turning point from which there was no return for either of them.

Chapter Fifty-Four: Revelation

That evening, they were at dinner in the resort's upscale restaurant when a man walked up to the table and asked if he could join them. Shocked and apprehensive, they reluctantly agreed. He appeared to be an American, tall and broad shouldered, about sixty years old with greying hair and a neatly trimmed goatee.

"My name is Joshua Davis," he said.

His last name caused a frisson of fear to slide down Anna's spine.

"I believe you've met my brother, Detective Ben Davis, from Chicago." With that, he paused to see what their reaction would be. Both of them remained outwardly calm, but he could see fear in Anna's eyes and Gray's hand shook as he set his wine glass on the table.

"I want you to know that you have nothing to fear from me," he reassured them. "In fact, I'm here with good news, the best of news, in fact." Then he paused. Perhaps it was a bit sadistic on his part, but he wanted to watch them as they processed what he had said.

"What news?" Anna asked impatiently. "What could you possibly have to say to us?"

"Let me start at the beginning, okay? Just listen for now, and then you can ask me all the questions you want when I'm done. That will save us all some time and energy."

Just then Anna and Gray's meals came, the waiter set the plates in front of them and then quickly left the area. He could sense the friction in the atmosphere at this table.

"First of all, my brother is a good guy and an excellent detective. I am also a good investigator, by the way. That's how I found you. It was actually Ben who asked me to try to find you and convince you to go home."

At those words, Anna and Gray just looked at each other. Was this as hopeful as it sounded? They sat quietly and listened carefully to what Joshua Davis had to say.

"Let me start again. When the Crime Scene team gathered up the evidence in the hotel room where your husband died, Anna, Ben noticed some anomalies. First of all, it was clear that what you said about Charlie's other wife was true. Her things were all over the room, but she never appeared. Ben attempted to find her, but was unable to locate her for several days. Finally, the U.S Immigration Service informed him that she had been detained for deportation for entering the country illegally, since her marriage to your husband was not valid in this country. Immigration told Ben that she had died in detention and her body was transported back to Bangladesh at the request of her family. So, Ben never questioned her about the events of that day."

"When he looked at the other evidence, he had more questions. The water glass next to the body had been tipped over but had no fingerprints on it. That was very unusual in itself, but the other glass raised even more questions. It contained two prints— both yours, Anna."

Anna gasped and looked at Joshua. "How could that be? I never even sat down in that room. I found Charlie's body and ran right back out to call 911!"

"Just let me finish, Okay? The unusual thing about your prints was that it was a thumb and forefinger. The thumbprint was on the outside, facing downward, and the index fingerprint was on the inside of the rim of the glass, also facing downward. Someone drinking from the glass would not have made those prints. You just couldn't hold it that way and drink from it. Instead, Ben theorized that the prints were put on the glass when someone—you, Anna—picked the glass up, perhaps after it had tipped over. Another thing that caught Ben's attention about the glasses was that they were not the same. The one by Charlie's body was from the hotel room. The other glass, it turned out, was from a nearby restaurant. When Ben checked, the hostess at that restaurant remembered seating you in the back with a lady she described as, 'very pretty and exotic looking'. You told Ben yourself that you had met Fariha there and had left in a hurry. When Ben questioned the busboy, he recalled that the tablecloth was all wet. He remembered, because he was told to change it quickly, because another party was waiting to be seated. He also remembered that only one glass was on the table when he cleared it. The glass that would have caused the spill was not there."

"I see," said Anna tentatively. "So that would mean that Fariha had taken the glass and put it in the hotel room. Was that enough to convince Ben of my innocence?"

"No, not then. But there is more. When you and Gray disappeared, Ben called Taos and talked to a lot of people there to find out more about you. The Taos police's desk sergeant remembered your outburst from the time you asked them to file a missing person's report." Joshua smiled a bit and continued, "He told Ben that you acted pretty angry and crazy that day. He said you had a real temper on you."

"Yes, I was very upset that day," Anna recalled. "I'm sure he remembered me well. But that couldn't have helped my cause any."

"No, it didn't. But Ben went farther than that. First he talked to your boss, Carlos. Carlos had nothing but good things to say about you. But, then, you hadn't ever been angry with him. The same went for your former boss at the souvenir shop. He thinks the world of you, by the way. Then Ben talked to your lawyer, Carolyn. She couldn't divulge much because of client privilege, but she also assured Ben that you just wanted to find a solution to all of this, not murder your husband. Ben also talked to your friends, Helen and Lee. After giving Ben the entire story of how Charlie disappeared and deserted you, they told Ben that there was no way you would have killed Charlie no matter how angry you were with him. They told him about how carefully you provided for your animals, even when Charlie had deserted you and you were flat broke. They convinced Ben that you were not a murderer and just wanted the entire situation to be resolved. That, they said, was why you had agreed to meet Charlie in Chicago, in hopes of his agreeing to a divorce. While Ben was at their house, he met Bella and Simba, by the way. Ben is not a cat person, but Simba jumped right onto his lap and rubbed up against his jacket. Ben had quite a time getting the cat hair off."

Anna and Gray both smiled at that, and Anna realized how much she had missed her pets the past weeks.

"Then Ben remembered that the scarf they found in Charlie's lap had cat hair all over it."

"Yes!" Anna cried. "I was in such a hurry to leave the restaurant that I forgot about my scarf. Fariha must have picked it up and put it in the hotel room." Then, after a pause, "But that doesn't help my case at all!"

"No, it didn't. But wait. I'm not through yet. The scarf was in Charlie's lap and there were clear bruises on his neck, so the obvious connected to make was that the scarf had been used to strangle Charlie. When the lab tested the scarf for DNA, however, they found something interesting. There was lots of cat hair belonging to Simba, of course, and a lot of your DNA, too, which was understandable. But, on both ends of the scarf they found DNA from an unknown female. A lot of it. There were also flakes of skin, as if the scarf had abraded the person who was holding the ends. Ben, of course, began to realize that perhaps someone else had killed Charlie using the scarf. Fariha's body was already on its way to Bangladesh, but they had her hairbrush and other items from the hotel room. She was a match to the DNA on your scarf, so that led Ben to believe that Fariha was the one who had strangled Charlie."

"Oh, my God," Anna cried, "Does that mean that I'm not wanted for murder?" When heads turned toward them, Anna picked up her napkin and stifled a joyous outburst before she called too much attention to herself.

"Yes and no," Joshua continued. "Ben was convinced that you had been framed, but he was still waiting for the autopsy results. They were quite surprising."

"What do you mean?" Gray asked. "It seems pretty obvious that Fariha strangled Charlie," he stated firmly in Anna's defense.

"Fariha tried to strangle Charlie, yes. But the autopsy showed that Charlie died from asthma, not from strangulation. The bruises on Charlie's neck were only superficial. The Medical Examiner declared the cause of death to be a fatal asthma attack brought on by close exposure to cat hair and other possible stressors. So, technically, Charlie died of natural causes."

"Oh, poor Charlie," Anna whispered. "What a horrible way to die. The woman you think you love is trying to kill you and you find yourself gasping for air. I've seen Charlie having an asthma attack, and it was frightening. He told me then that it was like drowning without any water involved. You just can't get any air into your lungs no matter how hard you try."

Anna just sat still and stared out the window, thinking over what Joshua had just told her. Gray and Joshua waited until she turned back to them before Joshua continued speaking.

"If Fariha had lived, Ben would have prosecuted her for Charlie's murder, since he died because of her actions. That, of course, was no longer an option, so Ben closed the case. You are officially no longer wanted for murdering Charlie," Joshua reassured Anna. "But Ben was intrigued by your story. How Charlie left you penniless and how you struggled to survive. He asked me to search for you and bring you home. Neither he nor I believe that you deserve to spend your life on the run."

Chapter Fifty-Five: Windfall

Anna jumped up from the table and ran around to Joshua, giving him such a big hug that he almost tipped over backward in his chair. When the other diners turned and stared, Anna composed herself and calmly sat back down. "How can I ever thank you for coming all this way to tell me about this? You are an angel!"

"Oh, I'm no angel, Anna. I had my own reasons for finding you. Please, let me continue."

Anna and Gray both leaned forward in order to hear what Joshua was saying. The dining room had become more crowded, and the muffled sounds of conversations and dinnerware made it difficult to hear him.

"I am not here just because Ben asked me to find you. In fact, I contacted Ben, because I was looking for you at the same time he was. You see, I retired from the Evanston Police Force about eight years ago. Since then, I have been working as an insurance investigator for a major life insurance company. That is why I was looking for you. It seems that Charlie took out a substantial life insurance policy, and a claim was made on that policy even before Charlie died."

"You mean someone tried to collect his life insurance, even though he was still alive?"

"Yes, that's what I'm saying. We assume it was Fariha who called in the claim. Apparently she had planned to kill Charlie and didn't want any delay in collecting the insurance money, since she was the benefactor. Because she was unable to furnish my company with a death certificate, and because we could find no record of Charlie's death, the company asked me to try to figure out what was going on. I was working on the case and discovered that Charlie had been killed after the claim was made. Again, Fariha was the prime suspect by then, but you had vanished and there was no way for Ben to let you know your name had been cleared."

"But why come all the way to find me?" Anna asked. "You didn't have to do that. Fariha was dead and there was no need. There was no one for the insurance money to go to."

"Ah, but there was…is," Joshua corrected. "Apparently, when Charlie purchased the life insurance policy, he listed you as a second beneficiary in case Fariha was unable to collect the money."

"You're kidding! Why would he do that? I don't understand!"

"I'm not sure either," Joshua continued. "But I was intrigued with your story by then and decided to try to locate you. Both Ben and I had talked to all those people, and we had a pretty clear picture of what had transpired between you and Charlie over the past few years. I couldn't help but think that, after all you'd been through, you deserved that insurance money. The policy is for five-hundred thousand dollars."

Anna was speechless. She looked at Joshua with wide eyes and then turned to Gray and stifled a joyous scream.

"All I know is this. You and Gray need to go home. There will be some formalities and paperwork to be done so that you can collect the money, but all that shouldn't take more than a few weeks. I wouldn't say that you're now a wealthy woman, Anna, but you're certainly much more comfortable financially than you've been for a very long time. It looks like Charlie tried to make up for his mistakes, at least as far as you're concerned."

Anna and Gray thanked Joshua profusely for making the effort to find them. They were also extremely grateful to realize that, had Joshua's news been different, they could easily be heading back to the U.S. to face prosecution. They boarded a plane two days later with light hearts and high hopes for the future.

Chapter Fifty-Six: Redemption

Anna and Gray arrived back in Taos both exhausted and exhilarated. The past month had taken its toll on both of them, but they were so grateful for the way things had turned out that they ignored their fatigue. The first thing Anna did when she got home was go to Helen and Lee's to retrieve Bella and Simba. She hugged Bella fiercely and was rewarded with the usual barrage of doggie kisses. Simba, as aloof as ever, simply brushed by Anna's legs and leapt onto Helen's couch to lie in a patch of sunlight that was coming through the window. Anna had to laugh. That cat had no idea of the role he had played in her life. In fact, it was Simba who was indirectly responsible for Charlie's death. And there he was, blissfully unaware of all that had happened. When Anna told Helen and Lee what had gone on, they were incredulous. It was a miracle, they thought, that someone of Joshua's character had been assigned to that case. Surely, no one else would have bothered to find Anna.

After taking Anna back to her apartment, Gray told Anna that he needed to get home. He had to check on his business to see what had happened in his absence, and he needed some time to process everything that had occurred. Anna didn't say so, but she was glad to see Gray drive away. He had been wonderful, no doubt. And she could guess that it wouldn't be long before he would ask her to marry him. She wasn't sure how she felt about that and needed time to herself to think things through. Besides, she also had some catching up to do and other decisions to make. She needed to call Carlos, but she didn't know if she was going to tell him she was quitting or tell him she would be back at work in a couple of days. She also needed to call everyone in the family and tell them what had happened.

Those calls alone would take hours, and she decided that she was too tired to tackle that so soon after her return. Instead, she ran a tub of hot water with lots of bubble bath and soaked until the water was cold. *Sometimes, the best thing to do is to do nothing,* she thought. Then she sighed. *I guess that's sort of the way Charlie lived his life. He was so passive that he let the circumstances around him make his decisions for him.*

The thought made her sad, so she went to the kitchen and poured a glass of wine. She saw her computer sitting on the desk in the corner and realized that, despite her forthcoming windfall, she had better see what her finances looked like at the present time. She didn't have the insurance money yet. In fact, from what Joshua had told her, several weeks would pass before the money would be hers. In the meantime, she had to live, buy food, put gas in her truck, and pay her bills. In fact, she realized, some of her bills were probably overdue by now. She would probably have to pay late fees on top of the regular charges. She opened her bank's home page and went to her account. Anna studied the screen for a long moment. Surely there must be some kind of mistake. Her account showed a balance of over two million dollars! How could that be? Her first errand in the morning would be to go to the bank and correct that error.

After a dreamless night's sleep, Anna rose to a brilliant sunrise over the mountains to the east. She had missed Taos while she was gone, and it felt good to be back home. She lingered over a second cup of coffee while she waited for the bank to open and then, still trying to save on gas money, walked the twelve blocks to the bank. When she entered, the vice president of the bank, Mr. Bennett, strode over and greeted her personally, inviting her into his office and offering her another cup of coffee. Anna was puzzled. The balance on her account was obviously a mistake. Perhaps Mr. Bennett was afraid she'd be angry about the error and was trying to get on her good side before he explained what happened. Instead, the man pulled up a chair beside Anna's and asked about her welfare and her travels overseas. He tactfully didn't mention Charlie's death, but Anna could tell that he was thinking about that, too. Perhaps he was going to tell her that a suspect in a murder was not welcome to have an account in his bank. Anna didn't know what to think.

Finally, Anna broached the subject of her account balance. "I'm afraid there's been an error on my account, Mr. Bennett. When

I checked last night, the balance was far too large. I don't know what happened, but I need you to calculate my actual balance so I know how much money I have. I have bills to pay and don't want to be overdrawn."

"Oh, Anna," Mr. Bennett protested, "that balance is correct. Just after you left Taos on your vacation, a large money transfer came in from a company in India. The money in your account is yours indeed!" With that, he broke into a huge grin, rose, and shook Anna's hand vigorously.

Anna was dumbfounded. Then it occurred to her. The elusive retirement account. Charlie had given her the money from the retirement account! Maybe that was why he wanted to meet with her in Chicago. Was he going to tell her that he had given her all that money? That there was no need for her to sue him for a divorce settlement? *Oh, Charlie!* She thought. *Was Fariha so angry that you gave me the money that she killed you?*

Anna left the bank with her mind in a muddle. As she walked home, she tried to think about what all this meant for her, for her future, for her family. She was a wealthy woman. Was she prepared to deal with this? She didn't know, but she was certain that she needed to act slowly and carefully. She vowed that she wouldn't tell anyone about this latest development until she had worked out a plan. She wouldn't even tell Gray.

Chapter Fifty-Seven: The Proposal

That evening, Gray came over. As soon as he came in the door of her apartment, he got down on one knee, grinning from ear to ear, and asked Anna to marry him. "We've been through the worst together, Anna. We are a good team and I love you more than words can say. I want to spend the rest of my life with you...not because of the life insurance money...but because I love you so much I can't stand to think about life without you. When we were in Bali, I was so afraid I might lose you if you came back here. I prayed that everything would work out so that we could be together forever and God answered my prayer. Please say 'yes'!"

Anna just stood there. She had thought all of this through over the past few days, so Gray's proposal wasn't a surprise. But she wanted to make sure that she was giving the right answer. Gray had put his entire life and future on the line for her. He wasn't unafraid, as she had thought; instead, he was brave enough to do what had to be done despite his fear. He was courageous. They enjoyed each other's company and respected each other. And, most important, she knew that she was in love with him. She got down on her knees in front of Gray, took his hands in hers and said, "Yes, Gray. Of course I will marry you."

Helen and Lee witnessed the simple ceremony in a small chapel just off the plaza. The newlyweds decided that a honeymoon was unnecessary, since they had just spent a month in Bali. Instead, Anna moved her animals and other belongings into Gray's old adobé home on the outskirts of Taos and they settled into their new life. Anna quit her job at the gallery, but she made Carlos promise to display her weavings once she was able to get her loom up and working again. Shortly after they moved into Gray's house, the couple had a talk about finances. It was only then that Anna revealed the extent of her wealth to Gray. He was amazed and happy for Anna, but he wanted nothing to do with how she spent her money. They decided that each of them would contribute an equal amount toward their monthly expenses and put another equal amount aside for other things they might want or need. But Gray insisted that Anna do what she would with the remainder of her money. He wanted no part in her long-term financial plan.

Anna met alone with a financial planner. The bulk of her money was to be invested, but she had several specific requests that she wanted the financial planner to carry out on her behalf. Her family was aware of the insurance money she had received, so they knew she could help them out. She had told no one except Gray about the retirement fund, however.

With Clare's wedding approaching, Anna sent money to cover the expense of a honeymoon anywhere in the world Clare chose. Anna even suggested to Clare that Bali was a lovely place to spend some time. She also told Clare that, as the matron of honor, Anna would throw her the best bridal shower ever.

Next, she made arrangements to pay off Rick's house and gave him a substantial amount of cash to do some remodeling to accommodate Grace's living arrangements with them. She also set up college funds for each of Rick's children and Bradley's boys with the stipulation that they had to maintain their grades and be accepted into the school of their choice when they graduated from high school. She did the same for Christine's children, but she had other plans for David and his family.

She called David and they had several long conversations. In the course of their talks, Anna realized that David had felt for years that she and Charlie loved Bradley more than they loved him. Bradley was the super star in David's eyes. He was a good student and an athlete. It seemed to David that Bradley could do no wrong where Anna and Charlie were concerned, and David held no hope of being as successful as his brother. David's reaction was to act out in whatever ways he could in an attempt to get their attention. When Charlie refused to help David get a job after graduation, as he had for Bradley, David lost the final remaining shred of his self-esteem. He turned to alcohol and drugs and sabotaged every chance for success that came his way. David continually hounded Charlie for money in an attempt to find proof that Charlie loved him and to even the score with Bradley. Anna grieved for David and the years he had thrown away in self-pity and alcohol. She also felt guilty for not realizing what was going on in David's mind. But she wasn't going to rescue David from the self-destructive path he had chosen.

When Charlie died, David had been shocked into sobriety. He mourned the relationship he might have had with his father, and he vowed that he would not squander the opportunity he had to be a good father to Jordan. David also realized that he was frightened for Anna when he found out that she might be prosecuted for Charlie's murder. It shook him to the core to think that his own mother might have murdered his father, but he found it hard to believe. Anna had assured him of her innocence, but it wasn't until she was officially exonerated that he breathed a huge sigh of relief. He realized how quickly life could turn into the unexpected, and he vowed to get control over those things that he was able to control. He attended AA meetings regularly, and he and Valerie found steady jobs. David was even taking classes at the community college.

David's relationship with Anna was improving, but they still had a lot of processing to do. David's abrupt change had taken place only two months before, and Anna wasn't ready to believe that the change was permanent, despite how much she hoped it was. Anna decided that the best way to help David was to offer to pay for his education, but only if he kept his grades up. He would pay the tuition to begin with, and then, if he did well, she would reimburse him for the cost of his classes. If he failed, he was out the money. In addition, she gave David and Valerie money for a down payment on a decent starter home in a nice neighborhood, away from the seedy environment in which they had been raising Jordan. Finally, she set up a college fund for Jordan with the same guidelines that she had set for her other grandchildren.

In the course of her talks with David, Anna realized that she had some soul-searching of her own to do. She had been a good and faithful wife to Charlie, despite his indiscretions over the years. His abandonment of her and his family seemed unforgiveable, but as she listened to David talk about his feelings, she began to realize that there must have been reasons why Charlie was willing to give up everything to be with Fariha. Anna knew that she would never completely understand Charlie's actions, but she was willing to take responsibility for her part in the failure of their marriage. She began to see a counselor in an attempt to better understand what had happened. In the end, she realized that she had been selfish. In Charlie's absence she had created a life for herself. It was her way of surviving the loneliness of his being gone. In the process, however, she had excluded him almost entirely. When the children were young, they were a family and did things together as such. Once the boys were grown, however, Anna set off on her own course and, as the counselor pointed out, she had actually left Charlie long before he left her.

That truth was hard to absorb, and Anna was upset for many days once the realization of the consequences of her actions hit her. She felt the fingers of depression reaching out for her once again, but she was determined not to let her past mistakes ruin her present or her future. She had long talks with Gray about the revelations she had discovered, and he was compassionate and understanding. He tried to tell her that the responsibility was on Charlie's shoulders, not hers; but Anna owned her own culpability for what had happened. The result was that she vowed to live her future with and for Gray and her family as well as herself. She would be the best wife and mother she could be, and those roles would be the greatest part of who Anna was as a person. She could be herself and pursue her interests in weaving and relationships with her friends, but her husband and family would come first and foremost.

Chapter Fifty-Eight: The Present

Anna looked out the kitchen window and smiled as she saw Jordan trailing behind Gray, his miniature tool belt swinging on his hip. The two of them were quite a pair, and Gray accepted Jordan's company as easily as if Jordan were his own grandson. They were walking toward the barn to do some repairs to the siding where their alpacas had chewed on the wood. Soon it would be time to shear the alpacas, and Anna would be busy cleaning, carding, and spinning the wool. She had several patterns in mind for the weavings she wanted to work on over the coming winter months, and she was excited that, at last, her dreams seemed to be coming true. She watched her two favorite men as they turned the corner and Bella came running across the field. Her dog was getting older, and Anna was not sure how she would handle watching her ever-faithful friend come to the end of her life. But for now, Bella was still active and beautiful as she streaked toward Jordan and Gray.

It had taken a great deal of convincing, but Anna had finally persuaded Gray to spend some of her money on a new home for the two of them. She and Gray had found a beautiful piece of land in the mountains just east of Taos. Gray built the home that they had designed together. It not only included a wonderful studio in which Anna could do her weaving; it also was home to Gray's business, with a huge workshop and storage area, as well as a fully-equipped home office. They had been careful to include two extra bedrooms to accommodate their children and grandchildren when they came to visit, and they were looking forward to having great grandchildren staying with them in the years to come.

But right now, Jordan was spending the summer with them. David and Valerie had brought him to Taos a few weeks after school was dismissed. Their visit had been good, with late-night discussions and self-examination on the part of everyone. Anna was thankful that she once again had her son in her life in a positive way. When David and Valerie left for home, Jordan was so excited to be spending the summer with Anna and Gray that he barely told them good-bye. As their car disappeared down the dirt road, Jordan grabbed Gray's hand and led him into the workshop where Gray and he were building some secret project for Anna.

It was hard for Anna to grasp how her life had turned around. The greatest blessing was her relationship with Gray, of course, but there were other relationships for which she was thankful. She had never hoped to mend the hard feelings between her and David, and yet the long process of talking things over had resulted in a new level of love. She and Bradley were on the same good terms as always, but somehow the resolution of years of friction with David made that relationship the more rewarding of the two. She would always treasure Helen and Lee and the support they had been when her life was at its lowest point. And her former bosses were still her friends, along with so many other people she had interacted with in Taos over the years. It was hard for her to recall the feelings of desperation and despair that she had endured, but she knew in her heart how difficult her life had been for a while. She had been all but without a home. She had no resources left except her own will to survive. She was proud of herself for overcoming impossible odds, and she was grateful that she had endured everything that had been thrown at her.

She glanced up again and saw Jordan running toward the house with a large, wooden object in his hand. He burst in the back door and tried unsuccessfully to hide the treasure behind his back. Gray followed him in and smiled warmly as he watched Jordan present the birdhouse to Anna.

"Oh, it's lovely!" Anna exclaimed. "Did you make this all by yourself?"

"Yep! Well, Gray helped me some, but I did all the work myself. I even painted it, see?"

Anna looked closely at the colorful wooden object that Jordan was holding out to her. She took it carefully into her hands and read the words he had written in his childish script above the door: "Anna's Home".

Yes, thought Anna, *I am home.*

Questions for Discussion

1. The book is titled, *Deadly Circumstances*. What are the circumstances that influence the basic personalities of the main characters (Anna, Charlie, Fariha)?

2. Who do you consider to be most at fault for the failure of Anna and Charlie's marriage?

3. Anna, Charlie and Fariha each have their own goals in life. How do their circumstances affect their achieving these goals?

4. Much of the book hinges on Charlie's wavering feelings about the women in his life and about his job. How do his circumstances affect these feelings?

5. What do the following reveal about Anna?
Her relationship with Clare?
Her love of animals?
Her relationship with her friends and employers in Taos?
Her ability to survive the hardships she faces?

6. Anna's concern for Jordan is woven throughout the story. Why doesn't the author say more about Anna's other grandchildren? Does she love Jordan more than her other grandchildren?

7. On first reading, Grace appears to change drastically between the time Charlie first describes her and when Anna meets with her. What do you think accounts for the change?

8. Anna's animals play a continuous role in the book. What purposes do they serve in developing the story?

9. What do Anna's travels tell you about her?

10. How might the story have ended differently if the author hadn't introduced Gray into Anna's life?

11. Why didn't Fariha just let Immigration send her back to Bangladesh instead of trying to get free?

12. Clearly Fariha was obsessed with money? What were her other obsessions?

13. With what was Charlie obsessed?

14. How might the story end if David had reacted differently to his circumstances?

15. Psychologists have identified four basic personality types:
Passive Aggressive (the indirect expression of hostility, such as through procrastination, stubbornness, sullenness, or deliberate or repeated failure to accomplish requested tasks for which one is responsible);
Passive Resistive (nonviolent opposition, especially a refusal to cooperate or obey through non-action);
Active Aggressive (behavior that causes physical or emotional harm to others, or threatens to. It can range from verbal abuse to the destruction of a victim's personal property)
Active Resistive (behavior that is physically or purposefully disruptive).

Which personality types would you attribute to Charlie, Fariha, Anna and David at various times   in the book?

16. Anna is a strong woman, but she has her faults. What are her main strengths and weaknesses?

Acknowledgements

Writing a novel has been an education. The initial writing came quickly. The ideas flowed and the characters came to life in my head and on my computer almost without any thought from me. What an amazing process that was! Then came the rewriting and revising.

There are many people whom I need to thank for giving me their opinions and advice, as well as encouragement, about this story. First of all, I have to thank Tracy for giving me permission to take some of the actual events of her life and turn them into what I would call a "fictional biography". Only a dear friend would be so trusting as to let someone fictionalize her life.

Researching the settings was a challenge, since this is a book that takes the reader all over the world. The following friends and family contributed personal experiences and anecdotes that, I hope, help take the reader's imagination to the various settings in the book: Tracy Hogle (Taos, Peru, Greece, India), Bill & Sandy Young (Taos, Peru), Mark & Misti Ruthven (Bali), and Aaron Ruthven (China). Thank you for sharing your stories!

My fellow counselor, Shirley Brown, was the first person to read the beginning chapters, and, without her encouragement, I might not have finished the manuscript. Before it was over, I think she read this story at least three times! Will Young, my good friend and fellow writer, gave me invaluable suggestions on how to improve the story and make it more appealing to readers. Janine Reed and Becky Whitmore also read the early manuscript and contributed helpful suggestions, many of which I have incorporated.

Most of all, I want to thank my husband, Gary, for tolerating my frequent disappearances into the office for hours at a time. He is, as always, my greatest encourager.

May each of you who read this story find yourselves inspired by the courage, passion, and humanity of these characters. I pray that you will never find yourselves in such dire circumstances; but, rather, that your circumstances will lead you to lives of happiness and fulfillment.

Made in the USA
San Bernardino, CA
18 January 2017